# Books by

## *Historical Western Romance Series*

### MacLarens of Fire Mountain

Tougher than the Rest, Book One
Faster than the Rest, Book Two
Harder than the Rest, Book Three
Stronger than the Rest, Book Four
Deadlier than the Rest, Book Five
Wilder than the Rest, Book Six

### Redemption Mountain

Redemption's Edge, Book One
Wildfire Creek, Book Two
Sunrise Ridge, Book Three
Dixie Moon, Book Four
Survivor Pass, Book Five
Promise Trail, Book Six
Deep River, Book Seven

### MacLarens of Boundary Mountain

Colin's Quest, Book One,
Brodie's Gamble, Book Two
Quinn's Honor, Book Three

# *Contemporary Romance Series*

## MacLarens of Fire Mountain

Second Summer, Book One
Hard Landing, Book Two
One More Day, Book Three
All Your Nights, Book Four
Always Love You, Book Five
Hearts Don't Lie, Book Six
No Getting Over You, Book Seven
'Til the Sun Comes Up, Book Eight

## Peregrine Bay

Reclaiming Love, Book One
Our Kind of Love, Book Two

**The best way to stay in touch is to subscribe to my newsletter.** Go to *www.shirleendavies.com* and subscribe in the box at the top of the right column that asks for your email. You'll be notified of new books before they are released, have chances to win great prizes, and receive other subscriber-only specials.

# Deep River

## Redemption Mountain
## Historical Western Romance Series

## SHIRLEEN DAVIES

**Book Seven in the Redemption Mountain**
**Historical Western Romance Series**

For permission requests, contact the publisher.

Avalanche Ranch Press, LLC
PO Box 12618
Prescott, AZ 86304

Deep River is a work of fiction. Names, characters, places, and incidents are either products of the author's imagination or used fictitiously. Any resemblance to actual events, locales, or persons, living or dead, is wholly coincidental.

Book design and conversions by Joseph Murray at 3rdplanetpublishing.com

Cover design by Kim Killion, The Killion Group

ISBN: 978-1-941786-44-4

I care about quality, so if you find something in error, please contact me via email at shirleen@shirleendavies.com

# Description

**Deep River, Book Seven, Redemption Mountain Historical Western Romance Series**

**Beauregard Davis,** ex-Confederate Captain and bounty hunter, has put his past behind him to focus on his future. He's a lawman with a purpose and a dream—do his job to the best of his abilities, and build a life with the woman he loves. Beau believes his life couldn't be better...until the day she boards a stagecoach, leaving him behind.

**Caroline Iverson** has a dream she won't deny. Traveling west, she expects to experience adventure. Instead, Caro finds a good man and unanticipated love. She never imagines the difficult decision to leave him behind would come back to haunt her.

After months of burying his pain in alcohol, Beau emerges stronger, determined to concentrate on a future without Caro. Doing his best to forget the past, he focuses his energy on work and preparing to build a home.

He never expected her to return, looking to recapture the love the two once shared.

Adding to Beau's concerns, two threats hang over him—outlaws have targeted his town, and he's being tracked by unidentified foes.

Keeping the town, Caro, and himself safe are his main priorities. He'll do whatever it takes to protect them. Guarding his heart is another matter.

How does a man ignore an all-consuming love without exposing himself to a threat worse than the physical dangers he already faces?

Deep River, book seven in the Redemption Mountain historical western romance series, is a full-length novel with an HEA and no cliffhanger.

**Visit my website for a list of characters for each series.**
http://www.shirleendavies.com/character-list.html

# Acknowledgements

Many thanks to my husband, Richard, for always being by my side during this wonderful adventure. Your support, insights, and suggestions are greatly appreciated.

As always, many thanks to my editor, Kim Young, proofreader, Alicia Carmical, cover designer, Kim Killion, and Joseph Murray who is superb at formatting my books for print and electronic versions.

# Deep River

# Prologue

*Atlanta Campaign*
*July 1864*

"You're late, Captain Davis." Confederate Lieutenant General William Hardee glanced up from the map spread out on the table before him. Studying the position of his troops, he tapped a finger on a location not far from where the men Beauregard Davis commanded waited for his instructions.

Removing his hat, Beau stepped up to the table. "My apologies, sir. Bullets fired in my direction held me up." His face remained impassive.

Hardee's eyes met his, the corners of his mouth quirking up before his lips drew into a thin line once again. "I won't lie to you, Captain. We're in a serious situation."

Beau nodded. The Army of Tennessee was bleeding men. Desertions had increased as the soldiers sensed the end might be near, most heading home to the northern hill country.

"This is where I want you." Hardee touched a spot on the map. "Captain Coulter's men are moving to intercept Union General McPherson's

1

left flank." He straightened, his gaze boring into Beau's. "You must hold the line, Captain. Do you have questions?"

"No, sir."

Hardee sucked in a slow breath, nodding. "Thank you, Captain, and good luck."

Riding back to the encampment, doing his best to dodge the increasing number of Union troops, Beau thought over Hardee's instructions, an unsettled ball of dread building in his chest at the deep concern in his commander's voice. He knew this would be no ordinary battle.

Riding low in the saddle, winding through the trees, his thoughts turned to his friend and fellow captain, Cash Coulter. They met after each joined the Army of Tennessee, soon becoming close friends. They planned to start a business after the war, either in Savannah, Cash's hometown, or Augusta, where Beau grew up. They never discussed the dangers of war or their own mortality. Meeting with Hardee made him wonder if either of them would survive this campaign.

Shouting and a single gunshot drew him away from his thoughts and toward a clearing not far from where his men waited for their orders. Reining his horse toward the noise, he slowed, his gaze narrowing as he took in the sight.

"Lieutenant Eldridge. What in the hell is going on here?" Sliding to the ground, Beau dashed to a prone body, blood pooling on the ground underneath it. Kneeling, he checked the man's pulse. Nothing. Cursing, he stood, glaring at the officer, his voice unyielding. "Who did this?" He focused on three other men, all on their knees, hands behind their heads.

"I did, sir. He was trying to desert."

"That's a lie, Captain." A muscular man with a scraggly beard and tattered uniform sneered at the lieutenant. "He weren't no quitter."

"Shut your mouth, Private." Eldridge lifted his gun, pointing it at the man.

"Put your weapon—" Before Beau could finish, Eldridge fired, hitting the private in the chest. Drawing his own gun, he trained it on the lieutenant. "Lower your gun." When Eldridge hesitated, Beau took a step toward him, his voice lowering to a deadly growl. "Now."

Waving his gun in the air, Eldridge paced in a circle, then walked toward the man he'd shot, showing no emotion as the private clutched his chest. "He's a slacker who planned to desert. I've been watching." He looked at the last two, still kneeling, their faces full of fear. "They're cowards, every last one of them." Starting to raise the gun again, he stopped when Beau stepped in front of the two men.

3

A muscle in Beau's jaw twitched as he worked to control his revulsion. "You will put your weapon down *now*, Lieutenant Eldridge, or I will be forced to shoot."

He threw his head back and laughed. "You aren't going to shoot me."

"Don't test me. If you don't lower your gun, I'll have no choice." Beau glanced down at the wounded man, letting out a relieved breath when he saw the wound was near the right shoulder. "You've exceeded your authority, Lieutenant. Drop the gun before I'm forced to do something we'll both regret."

Ignoring the warning, Eldridge stared straight at Beau, pointing the barrel of his gun toward one of the other men. "Sorry, Captain. We can't have men like—"

Beau's eyes narrowed, his instincts taking over as the lieutenant's finger began to squeeze the trigger. A shot rang out, Eldridge's eyes going wide, then blank as he fell backward, a hole in the center of his forehead.

"Damn, Captain. What happened?" One of Beau's sergeants ran up, his rifle pointed at the men still on their knees.

Beau's mind barely registered the words as he lowered his gun, his heart racing, stomach churning.

"Captain?"

Shaking his head, Beau looked at the sergeant. "Lower your weapon and see to the two men Eldridge shot. I believe one is dead. Take all four back to camp and hold the two uninjured ones for questioning."

"What about the lieutenant?"

"Take Eldridge's body back with you. Leave him in the bushes for now. We move out within the hour."

# Chapter One

"Sarah Murton is riding with us to the celebration for Bull and Lydia. Cash went to fetch her. You don't mind, do you?" Alison Coulter tossed an extra blanket onto the back seat of the wagon they'd borrowed from Noah and Abby. Even though the sun perched high in the sky, bathing the day in a warm glow, the cooling late fall temperatures could drop without warning.

Beau helped her step up onto the front bench seat. He'd planned to ride to the Pelletier ranch alone, wanting to be able to leave whenever he chose. Cash had talked him into riding in the wagon with him and his wife, Allie. He groaned, wishing he'd gone with his original plan.

Beau didn't look forward to riding next to the local schoolteacher, a woman who hadn't been subtle about expressing an interest in him ever since Caro had moved to San Francisco. Caroline Iverson might be hundreds of miles away, yet she still held a strong hold on his heart.

6

"I don't mind at all, Allie. The more the merrier." He winced at the lie, then stilled his features at the sound of footsteps behind him.

"Evening, Beau." Cash Coulter walked up, Sarah Murton's arm laced through his. "You know Miss Murton."

"Of course. How are you this evening, Miss Murton?" Beau helped her onto the wagon's back seat, then climbed up beside her.

"I'm good, Mr. Davis, and so pleased Allie invited me to ride along. I only had a glimpse of Bull and Lydia's baby boy, so I'm looking forward to spending time with them."

Beau settled into the hard wooden seat as Sarah droned on about the party, then talked with Allie about her students and the planned expansion of the schoolhouse.

"What do you think, Mr. Davis?"

He blinked, then turned toward Sarah. "I'm sorry. What was the question?"

"Do you support the schoolhouse expansion? Some of those in town don't, although for the life of me, I can't figure out why." Sarah moved closer to him so their thighs touched.

"If those on the town council believe it's necessary, I'm certain it is." Easing away, he created a couple inches of distance.

"Excellent. The more town leaders who support it, the better."

Seeing Cash's shoulders shake in amusement, Beau curbed the impulse to reach out and smack his friend on the head. "I'm not really a leader in town, Miss Murton."

"Oh, I don't think you give yourself enough credit, Deputy. In the opinion of many, you definitely are."

Stifling a groan, he offered her a weak smile, wishing he could jump off the wagon and walk back to town for his horse. Forcing himself to focus on the celebration for his friends, he ignored the continuing conversation between Sarah and Allie.

"Look at all the wagons and horses. Seems a lot of people want to celebrate Bull and Lydia returning to Splendor with their son." Cash reined the horses to a stop, then jumped down to help Allie out of the wagon.

Beau did the same, offering his hands to Sarah, who took them in a tight grip as he set her on the ground.

"Thank you, Mr. Davis." She smiled up at him, not releasing her hands from his.

Tugging enough to loosen her grip, he dropped his arms and stepped away. They followed Cash and Allie to the front door, Beau careful to keep several feet between him and Sarah. He had no intention of giving his friends the impression he held an interest in her. As much as he respected her, Beau wouldn't be courting another woman for a long time, if ever. Caro had been the only woman to capture his interest since the war ended. With her gone, he spent his days working as one of Gabe Evans' deputies and planning the house he thought would be his and Caro's.

The noise from inside spilled onto the porch when Rachel Pelletier opened the door, her brow lifting in question when she spotted Sarah and Beau. Waiting until Sarah stepped out of earshot, Rachel held her hand out for Beau's coat.

"Seems you had a chance to get to know Miss Murton."

Beau shrugged. "She's a nice lady who didn't have anyone to escort her." Rachel's brow arched. "What?"

She chuckled. "Nothing. You've been so busy working and planning your house, I didn't think you had time to court."

Beau shook his head. "I am *not* courting Sarah Murton, Rachel. Working for Gabe and getting ready to build in the spring takes all my time." He didn't say how much time he still spent thinking of Caro, hoping she'd found happiness in her decision to leave. Over the months she'd been gone, he'd accepted love wasn't for him— especially with a woman who saw social status as an important part of her life. Stifling a bitter laugh, he shifted from one foot to the other. "Believe me, I've learned my limitations."

Rachel's eyes narrowed, but she didn't respond. Hanging up his coat, she gestured toward Bull and Lydia. "Why don't you go on in and greet the guests of honor." Lowering her voice, she leaned toward him. "I'm sure Dax can find you some whiskey."

He picked up her hand, made a slight bow, then kissed it. "Thank you, Rachel."

Laughing, she nudged him away. "Go on with you."

Beau scanned the room. The first people he wanted to talk with were Bull and Lydia. Unfortunately, Sarah stood next to them, holding out her arms for baby Joshua. He would've changed directions, but Bull called him over, giving him no choice.

After exchanging small talk with Lydia and Sarah, Bull nodded for Beau to take a couple steps away with him, turning their backs to the women as they talked.

A commotion at the door had everyone in the house shifting their attention to the newest guests. Several of the women gasped and backed away. The men straightened, waiting to see what happened next.

"Will you look at that?" Bull moved forward, a broad smile on his face.

"Running Bear. You are welcome in our home." Dax motioned the two Blackfoot inside.

"We are pleased to be here." Running Bear turned toward the young man accompanying him. "This is Swift Bear. He is my grandson."

"You are both welcome."

"Excuse me, Beau. I need to speak with Running Bear." Bull set his drink down, making his way toward the Blackfoot chief.

Bull, Running Bear, and Swift Bear walked into Dax's study and closed the door, making Beau wonder what their sudden appearance meant.

"Interesting." Cash stood next to him, holding out a fresh drink. "You look like you could use this."

Taking the glass, Beau took a swallow, a grin spreading across his face at the taste of whiskey.

"Dax gave me a bottle to pass around. After all, it *is* a celebration." Cash took a sip, glancing behind him at Allie and Sarah. "Sorry about Miss Murton. I know she's been trying to get your attention since Caro left town."

"She's relentless. Shows up at the jail with pie or fresh bread, usually when I'm the only one there. I don't know how she knows when you and Gabe are gone."

"I hope you have the good sense to take the food," Cash quipped.

Beau chuckled. "If the woman wants to spend her time baking for me, I'm not going to turn it down. I also don't encourage her. I have no interest in any woman right now, except occasionally one of the girls at the Dixie or Wild Rose."

"If Sarah knows you're frequenting the saloons, she might not be so inclined to spend her time pursuing you. If you want, I'll put the word out."

Beau choked on his drink. "Hell no. I can handle the schoolteacher."

"Doesn't seem as if you're doing a very good job of it." Cash shrugged and finished his drink, shifting his gaze to Allie, then back to Beau. "My wife's pretty fond of Sarah. Whatever you do, let her down easy."

"I've no intention of courting her, so letting her down won't be a problem." Beau needed to move the conversation away from Sarah. "Has Gabe heard back from his friend about coming to Splendor to be a deputy?"

"He hasn't said and I haven't asked. The way the town is growing, we could sure use the help."

"Would either of you gentlemen be willing to get Sarah and me another glass of punch?" Allie slipped her arm through Cash's, smiling up at him.

"I'll get it." Taking the empty glasses from the women, Beau walked over to the table, dipping a ladle into the yellow-colored liquid.

"You doing all right?"

Beau set down one of the glasses to shake Luke's hand. "Fine. Getting the ladies some more punch."

"So, you and Sarah Murt—"

"Don't even think it." The words came out harsher than intended. "We rode in the wagon together, nothing more." His humor improved at the sight of Noah Brandt walking up to join them. "Noah." He held out his hand, which his friend grasped.

"Are you courting Sarah Murton?"

"Ah, hell." Beau shook his head, stepping around Noah to head back to the women.

Glancing at Luke in surprise, Noah shook his head. "What did I say?"

Luke grinned, taking a sip of his drink. "It may be best not to mention Sarah around Beau. He's a little touchy where she's concerned."

Noah's brows lifted. "Guess he's not courting her."

"You'd be right." Luke noticed Beau hand Sarah her drink, then attempt to step away, stopping when she placed a hand on his arm. "Looks like she won't give up easily."

Noah chuckled, turning his attention to the entry. "Appears Gabe and Lena finally made it."

Cash stood a few feet away from Noah and Luke, watching Gabe and Dax disappear down the hall. He turned toward Beau. "Something's going on. It wouldn't surprise me if you and I have to head back to town early."

"Why's that?"

Before Cash could answer, Rachel walked into the room. "Hey, everyone. Caro just arrived from San Francisco."

Beau's head snapped toward Rachel, his gaze locking on Caro. Beside him, Sarah linked her arm through his. Without thinking, he settled a hand over hers.

His chest seized the instant Caro's gaze locked on his. She was even more beautiful than he remembered—blonde hair pulled into a loose bun, her violet eyes searching his. She offered a hesitant smile as she walked forward, her gaze shifting to the woman beside him, then down to their joined hands.

Stopping abruptly, Caro's smile faded before she turned away.

Beau's feet wouldn't move, his body locked in place next to Sarah. Caro's sudden appearance knocked the wind from his lungs. It had been close to a year without any contact.

"Aren't you going to say hello to Caro?"

He looked at Cash, the pain in his chest becoming a ball of ice in his stomach. Months had passed since she'd boarded the stage for San Francisco, leaving without a backward glance. Beau had gone from being committed to making her his wife to pushing her from his thoughts. It took him weeks to stop pouring a bottle of whiskey down his throat each night, months to pull himself together enough to face a future without her. Losing himself in work and planning the house he'd designed with Caro in mind had filled the crushing loneliness.

If it weren't for Cash, Gabe, and his other friends, he might still be wallowing in self-pity, wondering if he should have gone after her. Once rational thought returned, Beau accepted the fact if she'd wanted him, truly loved him, she would've stayed. Nothing good could come from pursuing her.

Beau shrugged. "No reason to. She's here to see her friends, not me. Excuse me." Aware of where she stood talking to Noah's wife, Abby, across the room, he walked to the dining table, Cash stepping up beside him.

Reaching into a pocket, Cash pulled out a flask, offering it to Beau. "Drink it all. I'm sure you need it more than me."

"Thanks." Beau turned his back to the crowd, twisting off the top, taking a long swallow. Taking a deep breath, he handed it back to Cash. "I'd better stop or I'll never make it back to Splendor."

"I wonder why she's here. From what Lydia said, she has a pretty comfortable life in San Francisco."

Beau shrugged. "I don't know, and don't care."

Cash didn't agree, but it was Beau's decision. "Looks like Gabe is headed our way."

"Evening, Cash, Beau. I hate to end this evening so soon, but I need the two of you to ride back to Splendor with me."

"Trouble?" Cash asked.

Gabe nodded. "Could be. Boyden Trask and his men were spotted heading our way."

Cash cursed under his breath. "I'd hoped that lowlife would be hundreds of miles from here by now."

Beau and Gabe nodded in agreement. Trask had been responsible for blackmailing a group of orphans into rustling cattle from the Pelletiers. When the orphans were caught and confessed, Gabe sent a telegram to the sheriff in Big Pine,

16

where Trask owned several businesses. Overnight, the man had disappeared. Few believed he'd truly left the Montana Territory, most expecting him to reappear, taking revenge on the orphans who'd exposed his crimes.

"I spoke to Dax. He's saddling horses for you two. His men will take Allie and Sarah back to town after the party. Lena will drive Caro back in the wagon."

"Thanks, Gabe. I guess I'd better let Allie know what's going on." Cash shot a look at Beau. "I'll make sure Sarah knows."

Beau nodded, his mind traveling to the beautiful blonde across the room. Talking with Isabella and Travis, Caro had glanced at him a couple times, then looked away when she saw him watching her. He'd given her plenty of time to come to him, start up a conversation. After all these months, her lack of interest hurt more than it should.

"I'm ready to leave when you are, Gabe."

"Go ahead to the barn. Cash and I will meet you out there."

Beau grabbed his hat and gunbelt, stopping long enough to say goodbye to Bull and Lydia. Pushing Caro from his mind, he walked out the door and bounded down the porch steps. He couldn't wait to leave. Facing a band of dangerous outlaws was preferable to staying in a room with a woman who owned his heart but didn't want it.

# Chapter Two

Caro let out a slow, painful breath, feeling her shoulders slump as Beau disappeared outside. The brave front she'd erected in San Francisco by attending parties, shopping, and eating at the best restaurants hadn't changed her love for Beau. The first sight of him after almost a year had taken her breath away—until she'd seen him holding Sarah's hand.

"Would you excuse us, Travis? I'd like to speak with Caro for a few minutes."

Isabella Boucher, a longtime friend of Lena Evans', had moved to Splendor from her home back east after her husband died. Although he had been over twenty years her senior, she loved him with all her heart. She didn't believe love would come her way twice, and certainly not in the form of Travis Dixon, a quiet southerner and ex-Confederate soldier who still dealt with the loss of his wife and daughter while he was away fighting the war. His friendship, steadfast loyalty to the Pelletiers, and gentle way with horses worked on her heart. Over time, they'd come to mean much more to each other than ordinary friends.

Travis nodded, his mouth curving into a smile. "May I get you ladies more refreshments while you talk?"

Isabella squeezed his arm. "I believe I'll wait."

"Nothing for me right now, Travis. Thank you." Caro had a hard time focusing. After traveling hundreds of miles, thinking of Beau every minute, her shock at seeing him with another woman hadn't quite settled in, even as pain continued to ripple through her.

"Shall we go out back, Caro? I believe you'd find Rachel's garden quite interesting."

Caro blinked, her gaze rising to meet Isabella's. "Garden?"

Isabella slipped her arm through Caro's. "Why, yes. She has quite a knack for growing vegetables and flowers."

As they stepped outside, Caro followed Isabella down the steps, sucking in a deep breath of cool afternoon air. Shivering, she wrapped her arms around her as they walked to a small fenced area on the side of the house.

"Are you cold?"

Caro shook her head, forcing herself to concentrate on Rachel's garden. When they were well away from the house, Isabella turned toward her.

"Why didn't you send me a telegram about coming home?" Isabella had accompanied Caro to San Francisco, planning to stay long enough to see the Pacific Ocean before returning to Splendor and the life she hoped to build with Travis.

Crossing her arms, Caro glanced back at the house before answering. "I'm sorry, Isabella. It was a sudden decision. I just arrived yesterday and am staying at the St. James Hotel."

Isabella studied her friend. Always cheerful and full of energy, she'd never heard such sadness in Caro's voice before. "Did you come back to marry Beau?"

Few people knew Beau had asked her to marry him days before she left for San Francisco. Telling him no and leaving had been the hardest decisions of her life, ones she regretted every day.

Blinking back the moisture building in her eyes, she nodded. "Silly, I know. It appears he's already found someone else."

Isabella's eyes widened as she tilted her head to the side. "What are you talking about? Beau isn't courting anyone."

Caro shot her a look. "Didn't you see him with Sarah Murton? From what I saw, they are more than mere acquaintances."

Shaking her head, Isabella touched Caro's arm. "I don't know what you think you saw, but word would be all over town if he was courting Sarah. Not that she wouldn't be interested. She's made her interest in him perfectly clear."

"What do you mean?"

"You know how the women talk after church. Appears Sarah has mentioned more than once she'd very much like Beau to notice her." Isabella saw Caro's face still. "Of course, that doesn't mean he shares her interest."

Pacing a few feet away, Caro felt a gentle breeze caress her face, a sudden gust of wind stirring the leaves in the garden. She'd never planted anything, always having people who tended the family garden, cooked their meals, and cleaned the house. From the day she was born, she'd looked to others to supply her needs, never imagining she'd crave something else. Looking at the ground, Caro had the sudden urge to drop to her knees and dig her hands into the soil.

"Caro, did you hear me?"

Glancing up, she nodded. "I heard you. Still, they touched in a way he never did with me in public."

Isabella smiled. "That's because you were adamant people not learn about the two of you, and Beau respected your wishes. You met in secret, traveled to Big Pine to get away, and wouldn't allow him to show you any affection in public. I wondered if…" Her lips drew into a thin line.

"Wondered what?"

"Please don't hate me for saying this, but I often wondered if you were embarrassed to be seen with Beau."

Caro's jaw dropped, her eyes growing wide. "I was never embarrassed to be with him." Pushing aside the doubt Isabella's comment caused, she shook her head. "I didn't want people to think poorly of him when I left for San Francisco."

"I don't understand."

Caro paced away, then turned back to Isabella. "When it started, I never dreamed I'd fall in love with him. My plan had always been to travel to San Francisco, perhaps meet a suitable, wealthy gentleman, and start a new life. Unfortunately, no matter how hard I tried, I could never rid Beau from my thoughts, nor push him out of my heart."

"I know, Caro. You put up a brave front. If someone didn't know you well, they would've thought you were a young widow trying to get on with her life, attending soirees, dining at the best restaurants with the most eligible men."

"You knew differently, Isabella."

"Yes, I did. Each time Beau's name came up, the sadness in your eyes broke my heart."

A sad smile crossed Caro's face. "It took me a while to realize how much Beau meant to me, understanding the grave mistake I made when I turned down his offer to marry." She drew in an unsteady breath. "It now appears I came to my senses too late."

"I'm certain it isn't my place to give you advice."

A bitter laugh escaped Caro's lips. "Please. Any advice is welcome right now."

Isabella walked up to Caro. "Are you certain you want to stay in Splendor, even if it's without Beau?"

"I'm not sure. All the way back here, the miles on the train and stagecoach, I never imagined him with someone else. I don't know that I could stay in Splendor if he marries another woman."

"Caro, if Beau believes you're back in Splendor for good, if he's confident you aren't going to run back to San Francisco, he won't marry anyone else. Trust me."

"You truly believe that, Isabella?"

"Absolutely."

She glanced around, trying to come to terms with what her friend proposed. "I'm not sure how to start."

Smiling, Isabella slipped her arm through Caro's, then started walking back to the house.

"Don't worry. I have some ideas. Do you have plans for supper tomorrow?"

Caro's eyes sparked with the first signs of enthusiasm since she'd arrived at the ranch. "It appears I do now."

"I don't know what kind of businessman Boyden Trask is, but he's not much of an outlaw." From his seat outside the sheriff's office in Splendor, Cash focused on one of the upstairs windows of Suzanne's boardinghouse.

"Nick isn't too happy about Suzanne allowing Trask and his two men to stay there." Beau sat next to him, rubbing his chin.

Cash smirked. "Nick won't be happy until she agrees to marry him and live in the same house."

Beau looked at Cash, lifting a brow. "I didn't know he'd asked her."

"That's because you don't pay attention."

"Suzanne must have said something to Allie."

Cash pulled out his gun and checked the cylinder. "Yep."

Beau grinned before his features stilled. "Trask is walking outside."

Straightening, Cash slid the gun back into its holster. "Gabe, Bull, Dirk, and Doc McCord are covering Rosemary at the clinic, and the boys are safe at the Pelletier ranch. We just have to wait until Trask makes his move, then arrest him."

Rosemary, her brother, and two other orphans had been swept into Trask's plan to steal cattle from Dax and Luke. Bull and the Pelletier's other foreman, Dirk Masters, had captured the four, taken them to the ranch, and listened to their confession. They'd been given a second chance, Rosemary learning to be a nurse, and the three boys attending school and working off their debt at Redemption's Edge, the Pelletier's ranch.

"You make it sound easy."

Cash nodded. "I believe Mr. Boyden Trask is about to spend a good deal of time behind bars."

Trask didn't glance toward the jail as he and his two men walked down the boardwalk toward the clinic. It seemed none of them realized what they were walking into.

Gabe had spoken to Suzanne and Nick the night the three men rode into town and took rooms at the boardinghouse. He explained the plan. If Trask asked about Rosemary, Suzanne was to tell him she worked at the clinic. By the confident stride and the arrogance on the man's face, it appeared Trask would be walking into their trap.

"The place we're looking for is just ahead." Trask moved easily, paying little attention to those around him. Stopping, he turned toward his men. "Stick with our plan. You two keep an eye on anyone else in the clinic while I escort Rosemary out the back. Meet me where we left the horses."

Nodding, the three moved on, stopping outside the clinic. For the first time, Trask looked around, noting a few people on the boardwalk, a few wagons, and several riders traveling down the main street. Nothing caught his attention. Settling his hand on the latch, he opened the door and strolled inside, his men right behind him.

"Doc? Are you in here?"

A door opened to what Trask assumed to be an examination room, the doctor stepping into the front waiting area.

"You the doctor?"

"I'm Doctor McCord." Clay glanced at the three men, seeing nothing warranting medical treatment. "What can I do for you?"

"We're looking for my niece, Rosemary. I was told she's working with you."

Clay glanced over his shoulder at the partially open door. "She's with a patient right now. Why don't you have a seat and I'll have her come out when she's finished." He turned, stopping when Trask grabbed his arm.

"If you don't mind, I believe I'd like to surprise her. Keep an eye on the good doctor, boys." Pushing Clay aside, he brushed past him. Shoving the door open, Trask stepped inside, seeing a woman bent over a patient on the table. Closing the door, he leaned his back against it. "Well, if it isn't my little niece, Rosemary."

Straightening, she turned toward him, glancing at the man on the table and nodding. "Hello, Uncle Boyden. How are you?"

Before Trask could utter another word, Dirk Masters sat up from the table, pointing his gun at the man's chest. "So you're Boyden Trask."

"Who the hell are you?" Trask reached for his gun.

"I wouldn't do that."

Trask turned to see a man with a badge emerge from a back room, his gun drawn. An instant later, the exam room door crashed open, his men walking in, followed by Bull and Clay.

"That's the way, men. Nice and easy." Bull shoved one in the back. "Everything good in here, Gabe?"

Gabe looked at Rosemary. "Is this Boyden Trask?"

"Yes, Sheriff, it is."

Gabe nodded toward the other two. "Do you recognize either of these men?"

"They always rode with Trask when they came for the cattle."

The back door opened, Beau and Cash strolling in, their guns drawn.

"I'm disappointed, Gabe. I thought Trask would put up more of a fight." Beau moved behind him and secured him with handcuffs, Cash doing the same with the other two men.

Gabe walked up to Trask. "You're being arrested for stealing cattle."

Trask threw his head back and laughed. "You've got the wrong men, Sheriff. It's that little girl right there who did the stealing."

"Blackmailing children to rustle cattle is also a crime. Guess you've got two charges to deal with."

Trask's eyes widened marginally. "You have nothing except the word of a few children."

"Believe me. Their testimony will be enough to either hang you and your men or put you in jail for a long time." Gabe glanced around the room. "Dirk, take Rosemary back to the ranch for now."

"But—"

"No arguing with the sheriff." Dirk placed his hand on Rosemary's shoulder, escorting her toward the door. "I'll let Dax and Luke know you have Trask and his men."

Gabe nodded. "Thanks, Dirk. Doc, I appreciate your help."

Clay smiled. "It was my pleasure, Sheriff."

"All right. Let's get these men to the jail."

"Are you certain you're all right watching those three by yourself?" Cash leaned against the door, watching Beau clean his gun. Gabe had already left for the night, giving Beau instructions to get him if he needed anything.

"They're locked in separate cells, been fed, and took care of business out back. Nothing to do except wait for morning. Go on home to Allie. I'm sure she's missing that pitiful face of yours." Beau chuckled, although Cash noticed the humor didn't reach his eyes.

"You know where to find me."

Beau glanced up as Cash closed the door, thankful for the silence. With Trask and his men in town, he had little time to think about Caro.

It had been several days since the party, and even though Lena said Caro had a room at the hotel, there'd been no sign of her. He had no idea why she came back, and didn't want to waste time guessing the reason for her return.

Sarah had stopped by each day, bringing a loaf of bread, a pie, and a huge bowl of pudding.

Each time, he'd taken the food, thanked her, then sent the schoolteacher on her way. Beau knew he should tell her the truth—he had no interest in courting her or anyone.

Pushing up from his chair, Beau checked on the prisoners. Two snored, while Trask leaned against the back wall of his cell.

"You aren't going to hold us, Deputy. There's no real proof, just the word of a few children who already confessed to rustling."

"I don't agree, Trask, but it's not up to me to decide."

"Guess we'll be taking up a lot of time in your jail until the judge arrives."

Beau leaned his shoulder against the wall, crossing his arms. "Didn't the sheriff tell you? You're going to Big Pine for trial. Seems the Pelletiers aren't the only ones who want to see you behind bars."

The arrogant smirk disappeared from Trask's face.

"Nothing more to say?" Beau asked as he pushed away from the wall. "Guess I'll leave you to think on the error of your ways."

Grabbing his hat and coat, Beau walked outside, taking a seat on one of the wooden chairs. Thanksgiving approached, and Rachel had already informed him he'd be expected. She'd embraced the day ever since President

Lincoln declared it a holiday in 1863 in celebration of the Union Army victory at Gettysburg. As an ex-Confederate captain, he held no adoration for the Union Army, but he sure loved Rachel's cooking. She and her sister-in-law, Ginny, sure knew how to prepare a feast.

"Hey, Beau. You hear the old Miller place sold?" Noah walked up, taking a seat next to him.

He glanced at his friend, wondering why he wasn't home with his pretty wife, Abby, and young son, Gabriel. "Haven't heard anything about it." His gaze scanned the street, appreciating the growing quiet.

"I had business with Horace Clausen at the bank today. He told me the house and land sold yesterday—to a lady."

"That a fact." Beau didn't care who bought it as long it was someone respectable. "She bring men with her to work it?"

"I can't say and didn't think to ask." Noah leaned back, resting his arms behind his head.

"Well, whoever it is, it's going to be better to have someone living there, working the land, rather than having it sit vacant. No sense wasting such a fine piece of property."

"Doesn't it butt up against your place?" Both the Miller property and Beau's were southwest of town, easily accessed by well-worn wagon trails.

Beau thought about it, then nodded. "A little bit on one side where the river runs through both properties. The house is too far away to bother me, though." He guessed at least a mile separated the old Miller house and the one he planned. At one point, he'd hoped to buy it, adding it to his existing property.

Noah chuckled. "I hear she's starting repairs to the house next week. You might want to go over and pay your respects."

Beau settled his hat lower on his forehead as the sun began its descent behind the western mountains. "I suppose I should."

"You should probably know her name then."

Nodding, Beau glanced at Noah. "Guess it would be best."

"Caroline Iverson."

# Chapter Three

Beau sprang out of the chair, causing Noah to rear his head back and laugh. "I didn't mean to startle you."

Staring down at him, Beau fisted his hands on his hips. "How the hell did you think I'd respond to Caro moving in right next door?"

Noah's laughter turned into a grin. "Pretty much the way you did."

Pacing a few feet away, Beau ripped off his hat, running fingers through his hair before letting out a string of muffled curses.

"I got the impression you didn't care one way or another about her. Guess I figured her buying the Miller place wouldn't bother you." Standing, Noah walked to the edge of the boardwalk. "Well, it's done, and according to Horace, she's real excited about it."

Beau snorted, settling his hat back on his head. "The woman's never done a lick of work in her life. She'll be sitting on the porch, drinking tea, issuing orders to the men she hires."

"You're being pretty hard on Caro. She's just like the rest of us, trying to find her place after the war. You may not want to admit it, but I know you're not over her leaving." Noah scratched his chin, a sure sign he was thinking about his next words.

"Just say it," Beau prompted in a frustrated voice.

"Well, she came all the way back here and bought a place. Maybe you ought to consider going a little easy on her."

Crossing his arms, Beau's eyes narrowed. "You know, as well as any of us in Splendor, Caro can afford to buy a dozen houses and hire people to run them. She came back here to visit her friends. It doesn't mean this will become her home. She'll stay for a spell, then move back to San Francisco or Denver or someplace else until the desire to wander passes and she meets someone who means enough for her to settle down."

Resting a hand on the rail, Noah studied his friend, then shook his head. "I suppose I can't blame you for being cynical when it comes to Caro. And, by rights, maybe you should be. All I'm saying is she's going to be your neighbor. It would be best to understand she'll be crossing your path from time to time." Glancing up at the fading light, Noah took the steps down to the street. "I'd better get home before Abby sets out to find me."

Beau moved to rest his hip against the boardwalk railing. "Noah?"

"Yes?"

"Thanks."

A sad smile tugged at the corners of Noah's mouth as he nodded and walked away.

Beau strode back into the jail, took a quick glance at the cells, then settled in a chair. Reaching into a pocket, he pulled out the tattered paper showing his first attempts at sketching a plan for his house. It wasn't fancy, certainly not up to the standards Caro was used to, but he believed they would've added on bedrooms and enlarged the porch over time.

Smoothing it out on top of the desk, he noted the date in the corner. Over a year had passed since he'd bought the property and, for the first time in his life, started to dream about a wife and family. A few months later, Caro was gone.

He'd almost shredded the paper, the same way she'd shredded his heart. Instead, he stowed it away in a corner of the small house he lived in behind the jail. After several months and gallons of whiskey, he'd pulled it out, vowing to make a fresh start.

Materials had been ordered from Silas Jenks at the lumber mill, with plans to start building in the spring. Several of Beau's friends had offered to help. With luck and good weather, he figured it would be finished enough to move in by the end of summer.

"Hey, Deputy. How about something to drink back here?"

Beau recognized Trask's voice and sighed. Folding the paper, he slid it back into his pocket, careful not to tear it. Bull had helped him prepare a regular set of plans, which he kept at his house. He didn't want to think about why this first sketch meant so much to him. Ignoring the dull ache in his chest, he stood.

"I hear you, Trask."

*Big Pine, Montana Territory*

"Anything else, Miss Caroline?"

Caro cocked her head. "Travis, I've asked you to call me Caro or Caroline numerous times."

He gave her a wry grin. "I know, ma'am. But where I come from, I'm doing what my mama taught me."

She placed her hands on her hips. "I've heard you call Isabella Izzy more than once."

Color traveled up Travis's face, his eyes crinkling at the corners. "Well, ma'am, I guess that's different."

Caro knew it was, wondering why Travis hadn't asked Isabella to marry him yet. Her friend didn't seem concerned about it, content to have him in her life, allowing him time to make a decision. After all, the same as Caro, Isabella was a widow with a certain amount of financial security who could afford to wait.

Then why did waiting seem so hard now that Caro had decided she wanted nothing more than to marry Beau?

Looking at the almost full wagon they would drive back to Splendor, she glanced across the street at the second wagon. Luke had instructed both Travis and Tat to drive the wagons. They'd been in the territorial capital for two days and would head home within the hour. If all went well, they'd pull into Splendor early tomorrow, leaving the wagons locked in Noah's livery. Afterward, Tat and Travis would ride back to Redemption's Edge.

Luke and Dax had refused to take her money, but they did graciously accept a donation toward the building of the new clinic. She'd learned Bull had been placed in charge of the design and construction, the same as he had been in charge of the Pelletier shipping business in San Francisco.

"Is this dresser the last of it, Miss Caroline?"

Caro walked up the steps and peered into the general store. It held three times as much as the one in Splendor, which eliminated most of the orders she expected to make from back east.

"That's the last of it. I'm ready to leave when you are."

Ten minutes later, Travis had the dresser secure. With Caro next to him, he lifted his chin at Tat. When he nodded, Travis slapped the lines and started for Splendor.

"Shouldn't be too bad a trip if the weather stays with us."

Caro shifted on the uncomfortable bench seat, straightening her skirt. "I'm so happy to have the help. Everyone has been so generous."

"It's the way people are in Splendor. Besides, Isabella would have my hide if I didn't offer to help."

"So tell me something, Travis. When are you going to make an honest woman of her?"

He choked out a laugh, slapping the lines again. "Well, ma'am, I haven't made a *dishonest* woman of her yet."

Her eyes wide, Caro shot him a quick glance, seeing his lips twitch. Laughing, she placed a hand over her mouth.

"I do believe that's the first time I've heard you jest, Mr. Dixon."

An uncharacteristic grin formed on Travis's face. "Isabella says she has to listen real close so she doesn't miss them."

"I suppose so."

They settled into a comfortable silence, Caro's thoughts turning to Beau. She wondered if he'd heard about her buying the Miller place. Isabella had been the one to let her know about the abandoned farmhouse, setting up a meeting with Horace Clausen at the bank. He'd been willing to sell it at an excellent price, leaving her with enough money to hire men to make repairs and furnish the house before the snows began to blanket the ground.

She knew many in Splendor, including Beau, thought she had endless wealth. Although Caro knew Cornelius Vanderbilt and his wife, Sophia, no one would ever confuse her financial status with theirs. Growing up with money and privilege didn't mean she was careless with what she'd been given. Caro had set aside a monthly amount to live on and an allowance to purchase the house in Splendor. She had placed the remainder of her money safely in investment accounts back east and in San Francisco.

The Miller place needed a good amount of repairs. Surprisingly, she relished the challenge and planned to work alongside the men. She chuckled at what Beau would say if he saw her, hammer in hand, securing one of the broken windows.

"Did you say something, Miss Caroline?"

Shaking her head, she pushed away the amusing thought and focused her gaze ahead. "No, Travis. I was just thinking of all the work needed at the new place."

"Luke said he could provide some help."

"I couldn't accept that, Travis. He and Dax have done enough. Horace Clausen says he knows of some men who would be happy to work for me."

"You want to be careful who you hire. Might be best to have Gabe check them out before you make a decision."

Straightening in her seat, she glared at him. "I am perfectly capable of hiring men to make repairs to the house."

"I'm not questioning your ability, ma'am. There are a good number of men making their way across the country who haven't found work and may not care what they do to put food in their stomachs. And I'm not speaking of hammering nails. These are men like Boyden Trask."

More than three years after the war, vast numbers of men still couldn't find work, farms lay in ruin, and widows with children found it hard to survive. Groups of men roamed the land, robbing banks and trains, ravaging farms, and killing innocent families. They arrived disguised as hardworking men looking for a chance. Instead, they brought death and devastation.

Caro had heard of Trask and his men, knowing Beau had been involved in the arrest. "I realize there are bad people out there."

"All I'm saying is it's sometimes hard to separate the bad from the good. Especially now with so many unsavory men moving our way. If it were me, I'd want someone else to give me an opinion."

Her mind shifted to Beau. Caro wondered if he'd be willing to help her select men, provide advice on how to work with them. Sucking in a trembling breath, she shook her head. Asking him would only cause problems between him and Sarah. Even though Isabella remained convinced Beau held no interest in the schoolteacher, Caro wasn't so certain. The way Sarah looked at him, his hand resting over hers, was more of a public statement than he'd ever made with her. Most people still didn't know Beau had courted her, asking her to marry. And it was her own fault.

"You may be right, Travis. I'll speak with Gabe. Maybe he and Nick would be willing to give me some guidance."

Holding the lines loosely in his hands, Travis leaned back, stretching his muscles. "I'm not the smartest man around, Miss Caroline. Lord knows I've made some unforgiveable mistakes. But I do believe you're making a real wise decision."

At the sound of spurs hitting the wooden floor, Nick Barnett lifted his eyes from his spot at the bar in the Dixie Saloon where he stood reading the newspaper. Keeping his gaze hooded, he noticed a stranger make his way to the bar.

"What'll you have?" The bartender, Paul, shot Nick a quick glance before settling his gaze on the man wearing a tattered hat, indicating a Union Army officer.

"Whiskey."

Grabbing the bottle and a glass, Paul filled it to the rim. "Don't believe I've seen you in here before."

Picking up the glass, the man seemed to study it before tossing it back. "Nope."

Nick's mouth twitched. Pushing away from the bar, he moved next to the man, holding out his hand. "I'm Nick Barnett, one of the owners of the Dixie."

Hesitating an instant, the man grasped the outstretched hand. "Caleb Covington."

"What brings you to Splendor?"

"I believe Major Covington is looking for me." Gabe pushed through the swinging doors, making a path straight for Caleb. "It's good to see you."

A smile transformed Caleb's face as he held out his hand. "Colonel."

Turning to Nick, Gabe nodded when Paul held up a glass. "Caleb served under me during the war. He's the man I mentioned contacting about becoming a deputy."

Nick's suspicions eased, his features relaxing. "I'd say that's good news. Hope you're serious about taking up Gabe's offer."

Caleb didn't take his gaze off Gabe as he answered. "The colonel and I have a lot to talk about, but I'd say I'm interested."

"Caleb's been with the Texas Rangers the last few years, Nick."

"You ever hear of Dax and Luke Pelletier?" Nick asked, leaning back against the bar.

"Knew *of* them. They left the Rangers before I ever met them. Why?"

Gabe swallowed his whiskey, setting the empty glass aside. "It's something we'll talk about, but Dax and Luke own Redemption's Edge, just north of here. They have the biggest spread in western Montana."

Caleb's brows lifted. "Heard rumors of them inheriting a ranch from another Ranger. Guess they were true."

Gabe clasped him on the back. "Finish your drink, then we'll talk."

Taking one last swallow, Caleb grinned. "I'm ready."

"Good to meet you, Caleb. I'm sure we'll be seeing a lot of each other."

"Thanks, Nick." Nodding at Paul, Caleb followed Gabe outside.

"Thought you'd look me up when you first arrived." Gabe headed toward the jail, knowing Beau was inside, keeping watch on the prisoners.

"Whiskey, women, and work, in that order, Colonel. It hasn't failed me yet."

Gabe laughed, knowing it wasn't true. Caleb had always been focused on his job, doing whatever had to be done. Nothing competed with it, including whiskey and women.

"That a new motto for you? I never knew you to put *anything* ahead of your work."

Caleb's features stilled as they took the steps up to the jail. "War changes a man's priorities and view of humanity, including mine. I let work control my life once too often. I'll never make that mistake again."

Opening the door, Gabe glanced over his shoulder, vowing to learn more about what happened to his friend after the war. "Beau, you in the back?"

"Right here, Gabe." Beau stepped around the corner, stopping when he saw another man.

"Beau, this is Caleb Covington. He served under me during the war, but don't hold that against the man." Gabe looked at Caleb. "This is ex-Confederate Captain Beau Davis."

Beau walked forward, extending his hand. "I can put it aside if you can, Covington."

He didn't waste any time grasping Beau's hand.

"You'll find we have a lot of people from both sides living in Splendor, Caleb. My other deputy, Cash Coulter, was also a captain for the Confederacy."

"No issues with me, Colonel."

"Caleb, we've been friends a long time. I'd appreciate it if you started calling me Gabe or Sheriff. Either is good. I'm no longer a colonel."

"Is he the man you sent for, Gabe?" Beau asked.

"He is, Beau." Gabe looked at Caleb. "I'm hoping he'll be joining us."

Beau studied Caleb, then grabbed his hat. "Good to meet you, Covington. Since you're here, Gabe, I'll head over to Suzanne's for dinner and pick up food for the prisoners."

"Take your time. I'll take Caleb over when you get back."

Stepping out into the noonday sun, Beau pushed the hat down on his head, his thoughts already moving from Caleb to Caro. Bull told him she'd gone to Big Pine with Travis and Tat. From what he knew, she hadn't returned. Not that he cared.

"You heading to Suzanne's?" Cash joined Beau as he crossed the street, dodging wagons and horses.

"Didn't have time for breakfast. I've been surviving on your bad coffee all day." Lifting his hand to the latch on the front door, his movement stilled as a wagon approached with Caro sitting next to Travis. It took seconds for her to spot him, their gazes locking. Without breaking eye contact, he dropped his grip on the handle, taking a few steps to the edge of the boardwalk as Travis pulled the wagon to a stop.

"Beau, Cash." Travis set the brake, then jumped down as Tat pulled up behind him.

"Travis. You and Tat just getting back from Big Pine?" Cash asked, feeling Beau stiffen beside him.

"We are. I need to find Noah. He's going to store the wagons holding Miss Caroline's belongings in the livery until she's ready for them." Helping Caro down, he turned back to Cash and Beau. "Do you mind taking Miss Caroline inside with you? She hasn't eaten since this morning."

Caro's eyes darted between Beau and Travis. "Oh, that's not necessary. I'll go on up to the hotel, Travis."

Cash took a few steps toward her, taking her arm. "Come on inside with us, Caro. I want to hear about what you plan to do with the Miller place."

Catching her lower lip between her teeth, she sent a worried look at Beau.

"I'd also like to hear your plans, Caroline." Beau's use of her full name didn't feel right, yet she found herself moving forward.

"I'll come inside once Tat and I get the wagons secure." Travis waved as he walked toward the livery.

Caro couldn't stop her heart from pounding as Cash escorted her past Beau and into the restaurant. She hadn't expected him to be the first person she saw on their return to Splendor, hadn't wanted to see him until after moving into her new home.

"You're back." Suzanne Briar walked up, giving Caro a hug. "Did you get everything accomplished?" She looked between her and Beau, feeling the tension.

Caro let out a breath, doing her best to relax. "Why, yes, I did. Travis and Tat were wonderful."

"I'm so glad. You must be starved. Let's find you a table." Suzanne looked around, settling on one near the window. "Follow me."

Caro spotted four chairs and looked at Suzanne. "I believe Tat and Travis may join us."

"I can fix that." She pulled up one more chair. "There. Now, I'll get you all some coffee."

An uneasy silence enveloped them as they waited for Suzanne to return, which didn't take long. Setting down the cups, she took their orders, then headed back to the kitchen.

"I'm sure you're anxious to move into your new place."

Taking a sip of coffee, Caro nodded, doing her best not to look at Beau. "Yes, I am. Although I'm afraid much needs to be done before I can spend the night. Some of the windows are broken, which shouldn't take too long to replace. It needs a thorough cleaning, and the kitchen sink has rusted out. As soon as those and a few other things are fixed, I'll move in. The broken locks and front door can wait."

Beau's anger rose at her words, finding he couldn't control his thoughts. "You're not moving in until the place is safe."

Moving her gaze to his face, she saw the hard set of his jaw. "Excuse me?"

"You won't be living in a house that isn't secure." Beau didn't know what had pushed him to make demands, other than his growing desire to reach out and haul her onto his lap. Desire had slammed into him the instant he'd seen her on the wagon, forcing him to ignore what he wanted. He'd controlled the urge, but weakened when her safety became an issue.

Caro bit her lower lip to still her response. She didn't need to get into an argument with Beau or anyone. It was her house and her decision.

"Thank you, Deputy. I will certainly consider your advice." Her sarcastic remark wasn't lost on either of her tablemates.

Beau leaned toward her, ignoring what he knew to be her growing anger. "When was the last time you lived outside the boundaries of a town?"

"Well, never."

"Exactly. You have no idea what can happen living alone several miles from town."

Cash cleared his throat. "Beau's right, Caro. You shouldn't move into the place until all the windows and doors are fixed and you've got new locks installed. Noah can help with the locks, and he'll make sure they're solid."

Sitting back in the chair, she crossed her arms. "Fine. I'll talk to him today." Blowing out a breath, she looked at Beau. "Satisfied?"

He had to glance away so she wouldn't see the amusement on his face. "Yes, Caroline. I am."

"Who's doing the repairs?" Cash asked, glad one obstacle had been crossed.

"Mr. Clausen has some men in mind. I'll be speaking with them tomorrow."

"Maybe Beau or I should go with you." Cash held up a hand when she opened her mouth. "I'd recommend the same to any woman on her own. There are a lot of scoundrels out there, Caro."

She nodded. "Travis already convinced me to have Gabe or Nick speak with them."

"I'll do it." The words were out before Beau could stop them.

"I don't think—"

"It's settled, Caroline. I'll speak with Clausen about his suggestions in the morning."

"You certainly will not, Beauregard. I can speak with him myself."

Cash choked on his coffee at the use of Beau's full name. Nobody used it—ever.

A muscle in Beau's jaw twitched, his eyes dark as they bored into hers. "I'll meet you at the bank when they open. You'll not be changing my mind."

Their gazes locked, neither willing to look away. After a few moments, Caro tossed her napkin on the table and stood.

"Fine. Just don't bring Sarah Murton with you." Not waiting for a response, Caro stomped toward the front and out the door.

"What the hell?" Beau mumbled, stunned, his gaze following Caro's retreating back.

# Chapter Four

"Come inside, Beau. Mrs. Iverson is already in my office." Harold Clausen led the way, opening the door to his office. "Take a seat and I'll tell both of you about the men I'm suggesting."

Taking off his hat, Beau took the chair next to Caro. "Good morning, Caroline."

"Beauregard. It's such a pleasure to see you again so soon." Her too sweet reply almost made him laugh.

Beau had lain awake much of the night wondering why he offered to meet with her and Clausen. She'd made it clear she didn't want his involvement, yet he'd kept insisting, determined to change her mind.

Clausen sat down across his desk from them, ignoring the exchange. "There are two men who are finishing work for Ty out at the Murton ranch." He looked at Beau. "That would be Sarah Murton's cousin."

"I know who he is," Beau responded through clenched teeth.

"How convenient." Caro directed the comment to Horace, but had no doubt Beau knew it was meant for him.

"Do you have a problem with them, Mrs. Iverson?"

"None whatsoever, Mr. Clausen. Do you, Beauregard?"

He scowled at her. "None, Caroline."

"Excellent. Ty said to ride out anytime. They should be finished up for him within a few days." Seeing them nod, he rested his arms on the desk, clasping his hands together. "Is there anything else I may help you with?"

Caro stood, prompting the other two men to also stand. "No, Mr. Clausen. You've been quite helpful." Nodding at Beau, she turned to leave.

"I'll walk you out." Beau took a light grip on her elbow.

"I can make it outside by myself."

"Of course you can." Ushering her outside, he released his grip. "When do you want to ride out to Ty Murton's place?"

Blinking against the mid-morning sun, she faced him. "I've already arranged to use one of Noah's wagons. I'll be leaving right away." Starting to walk away, she stopped when he touched her shoulder.

"I'll meet you at the livery."

Placing fisted hands on her hips, she glared up at him. "I plan to go alone."

Beau almost laughed at her bravado. "When was the last time you drove a wagon, Caroline?"

Catching her bottom lip between her teeth, she closed her eyes, calming her building temper. "I'm certain I can learn."

Cocking an eyebrow, he crossed his arms. "Does that mean you've never driven a wagon?"

"Well, I...um..."

"Have you *ever* handled a wagon, Caro?"

"How hard can it be? I've ridden in them so often, I'm certain I can manage."

Shaking his head, Beau took hold of her elbow, directing her down the street toward Noah's livery. "I'll drive today. When you have time, I'll teach you how to do it yourself."

Her eyes widened. "You'd do that?"

Stopping, he turned her toward him, his brows furrowing, his hands resting lightly on her arms. "Why wouldn't I?"

Caro shook her head, working to hold his intense gaze. "I thought, after seeing you with Sarah Murton—"

"There you are, Mr. Davis." Sarah walked up, holding out a covered plate. "I know how much you like my cornbread, so I made extra." Nodding at Caro, she stood within inches of Beau.

Inwardly groaning, Beau dropped his hands from Caro's arms, seeing her features still. "Although I'm grateful, Miss Murton, you don't need to bake for me." He made no move to accept the plate.

Her face flushed, her body shifting as her gaze moved between Beau and Caro. "I made this because I wanted to, Mr. Davis. Not because I felt obligated."

The look of distress on her face tugged at Beau's heart. He had no intention of causing Sarah any pain. Reaching out, he took the plate. "Thank you. I appreciate the thoughtfulness."

"Well, I should return to the schoolhouse." She moved her gaze to Caro. "One of my older students is keeping watch on the other children."

"Of course." Caro didn't know what else to say to the woman who seemed to have caught Beau's attention.

After a quick smile at Beau, Sarah left, hurrying back down the boardwalk.

He glanced at the plate in his hand, showing no interest in the still warm bread. "I'll leave this at the jail."

Caro pushed away what felt like jealousy, a sensation she'd never experienced before returning to Splendor. "She's a very nice woman, Beau."

"I can't argue with you." As much as he wanted to clarify his lack of interest in Sarah, Beau didn't believe it would matter to Caro. She'd made it clear she had no desire to marry him, which was all that mattered, and she didn't show any sign of changing her mind. "I'll be right back."

Caro turned toward the building across the street, shoulders slumping as Beau disappeared inside the jail. He'd said nothing to change her perception he courted Sarah. Caro didn't know what she'd expected. Always the gentleman, it would've been out of character for him to say anything uncomplimentary about her. Still, he didn't act as if he had much interest in the woman.

Caro wondered if Isabella was right in saying she'd heard nothing of Beau courting the schoolteacher. Maybe what Caro saw at the party hadn't been what it seemed. So lost in her own thoughts, she didn't hear him step up beside her.

"Are you ready?"

She spun toward him, offering a distracted nod. "Don't feel you must go with me."

Beau let out a frustrated sigh. "It's already been decided, and Gabe is fine with me going." He glanced behind her toward the livery, seeing his friend standing next to the wagon. "Noah is ready for us. The sooner we leave, the sooner we can get back."

Knowing he wouldn't change his mind, Caro nodded, then waved to Noah. "I suppose you're right."

Beau almost chuckled at the lack of enthusiasm in her voice. He didn't care. Watching her wrangle a wagon for the first time held no interest, nor did worrying about her safety.

"Are you going with her, Beau?" Noah stepped forward, bending to give Caro a kiss on the cheek.

"I'll be driving her to Ty Murton's. Mind if I borrow a pair of your gloves?"

"Go on inside. You'll see some on the work table." Noah waited until Beau stepped into the building, then turned to Caro. "Does he know?"

"What do you mean?"

"Maybe it's not my place, but it seems obvious you came back to Splendor because of Beau. Have you told him that?"

Surprise flickered in her eyes before she let out a weary sigh, shaking her head. "No."

"You need to tell him, Caro."

She looked past Noah, seeing no sign of Beau. "What would I say, Noah? From what I saw, he's shifted his interest to Sarah."

Noah chuckled at the thought of Beau courting the teacher.

"What's so funny? They were together at Bull and Lydia's party, and I understand she stops by the jail several times a week, delivering pies and, well...whatever."

"Sorry, Caro, but you've gotten the wrong impression. You don't need to worry about Sarah. She brings pie to *all* the single men. Before I asked Abby to marry me, it drove her crazy when she saw Sarah come by the livery. I finally had to confront her on the matter, letting Sarah know I planned to marry Abby." Noah sighed. "As a single man, it was hard turning my back on fresh baked pie." Seeing Beau walking toward them, he lowered his voice. "Think about it."

Stopping next to them, Beau held up a pair of gloves, a question in his eyes.

"Take them. Just remember to leave them with the wagon when you come back."

"Thanks, Noah. We'll be back this afternoon."

Caro straightened her spine, searching for a comfortable position on the hard wagon seat without moving closer to Beau. They'd been on the trail over an hour, most of it in silence. He'd pointed out a few sights, including the turnoff to her new place, not mentioning it was the same trail he took to his own ranch. She didn't need him to tell her. Mr. Clausen had already mentioned Beau was the closest neighbor, a fact Isabella had failed to mention when she first told her about the property. Caro had almost backed away, reconsidering when she saw the house and land.

"Another few miles and we'll be there. How are you doing?"

"I'm doing fine."

The tone of her voice had Beau glancing at her. "You sure? I can stop the wagon, let you get out and stretch your legs."

"You wouldn't mind?"

Without answering, he pulled on the lines, bringing the wagon to a stop. "Hold on. I'll help you down." Reaching her side of the wagon, he held up his arms. "Put your hands on my shoulders."

Bending down, she did as he asked, his touch setting off a stream of memories. The feel of his hands on her, even through the dress she wore, made her shiver, remembering when they'd been intimate. How she'd missed him stroking her back and arms as he peppered kisses across her cheeks and down her neck.

Although she'd loved her husband, welcomed their time in bed, she'd never realized until Beau how heated and passionate making love could be. He'd fulfilled her in ways she never imagined possible, taking his time, giving her pleasure before taking his own. She swallowed the heat burning within her, forcing her thoughts to the present.

Taking his time setting Caro on the ground, he felt her body tremble, his own responding. He'd been a fool to believe being so near wouldn't affect him.

"Cold?" He didn't let go of her waist as he waited for her response.

Her legs shook, unsteady after being in the wagon so long. At least that was what she told herself as she tried to ignore her body's reaction to Beau. It took all her willpower to fight the urge to wrap her arms around his neck, tell him she loved him and had made a terrible mistake walking away. The assurances of Isabella and Noah raced through her mind. Still, she couldn't summon the courage to confess her true reason for coming back.

"No, I'm fine. A little stiff." She rubbed her back and moved away, breaking his hold. "I just need to walk around a few minutes, then we can continue."

Beau's gaze hooded, chest tightening at the brief contact. "Take your time." He did the same, trying to calm the desire pulsing through him. After so long, he'd been certain the passion he felt for Caro would've burned out, his constant need for her evaporating as pools of water on a hot day. Instead, the longing intensified to an almost painful level.

"I'm ready to go."

The voice at his back had him shifting to face her, forcing himself to gain control. Nodding, he walked to the wagon and helped her up. Without a word, he climbed up beside her, taking the lines.

"Thank you for stopping."

Again, he nodded, not taking a chance of looking at Caro and letting her see the desire he knew would be clear on his face. Over the years, he'd learned to control his reaction to almost any situation. The skill failed him when it came to Caro.

Continuing on the trail, he willed himself not to look at her, almost wishing he'd asked someone else to drive her to the Murton's. But this was his battle. With her being his neighbor, he had to fight it sometime. Besides, he'd been the one to push her, forcing Caro to accept his help. Now he had to see it through.

"Is that the Murton's?" Caro pointed to a house up the trail.

"It is."

Within minutes, he pulled to a stop and jumped down.

Ty strolled out of the barn, extending his hand to Beau. "Mr. Clausen said you might be coming out. Didn't think it would be this soon. I hear you're doing a good deal of work getting ready to build your house. Now it appears you'll have a new neighbor."

Gripping Ty's hand, Beau glanced over his shoulder at Caro. "I won't start until spring, but Mrs. Iverson is going to need help as soon as she can hire the men."

Ty walked over to the wagon. "I'm Ty Murton. May I help you down?"

"Yes. Thank you." Once on the ground, she turned to Ty. "I know we've never met, but I've heard so much about you and your family. I'm Caroline Iverson. Are those your children?"

"Nice to meet you, Mrs. Iverson." Turning at the sound of laughter, Ty grinned. "Yep. We have two children, but Tilly says she wants more." The glint in his eyes indicated how much he agreed with his wife. "So you're looking to hire some men?"

"Yes. Mr. Clausen said you have a couple who might be in need of more work."

"Merritt and Augustus." Ty glanced at her. "He goes by Gus. They're brothers. Moved out here when they couldn't find jobs after the war."

"Did they fight for the South?"

"No, ma'am. The Union. I have to say, they're right handy. There hasn't been a job I've given them that they couldn't finish."

"Are you sure you're ready to let them go, Mr. Murton?"

63

"Call me Ty, and yes. They've finished all I have for them. Although I would like to have them back in the spring."

Caro nodded as Beau walked up next to them. "The work I have should only last a few weeks."

Beau considered her comment. "You might want to plan for a little longer. From what I saw the last time I was on the property, my guess is it'll be at least eight weeks before you can move in, especially with the cold weather setting in."

Caro stopped, staring up at Beau. "I can't possibly wait that long. Christmas is only seven weeks away and I will *not* spend it in a hotel room."

Ty looked between them. "It's none of my business, but it might be best to have Merritt and Gus look at what you want done, Mrs. Iverson. Maybe they can finish what's needed for you to at least move in before Christmas."

"Good idea. When can I meet them?"

"They're behind the barn, finishing some repair work to the walls. Come on. I'll introduce you." Taking a path around the barn, he stopped next to the two men, who quickly removed their hats when they saw Caro. "Mrs. Iverson, this is Merritt Teal and his brother, Gus."

"Ma'am," they said in unison, drawing a smile from Caro.

"Gentlemen, it's nice to meet you. Ty says you're looking for more work."

"Yes, ma'am. We can do just about anything you want done. Right, Gus?"

"That's a fact, ma'am. We start at sunup and don't stop until after dark." They fidgeted with the brims of their hats.

She smiled. "Would it be convenient for you to follow us to the property and let me know what you think?"

Both glanced at Ty, who nodded.

"Yes, ma'am. We can do that." Merritt pushed his hat back down on his head.

"We just need to saddle our horses." Gus started to follow his brother into the barn.

"Hold up." Ty crossed his arms. "My brothers, Gil and Mark, will be riding in to eat. Tilly will skin me alive if you all don't join us. She has a big pot of stew on the stove and is baking biscuits."

"Sounds good to me, Ty." Beau wanted more time to get to know Merritt and Gus before Caro made a decision.

"Tilly will love spending some time with another woman. Besides my ma, she's the only female. My brothers aren't married. It's always good to know people who can help you out when needed."

Sitting on the hard seat of the wagon, Caro thought about the last couple hours. The meal had passed in a blur. Listening to the Murton brothers banter back and forth, Beau, Merritt, and Gus joining in, Caro couldn't recall the last time she'd laughed so much. Tilly did her best to keep them in line while watching the two children, never complaining or raising her voice. At least she allowed Caro to help with the dishes.

Caro marveled at the ease with which the young woman worked, wondering how she'd cope if she were ever blessed with two beautiful children and a man who obviously adored her. Once her house was in order, Caro vowed to have them all over for supper...although she'd have to learn to cook first.

"When you come from the Murton's, this is the fastest way to your property." Beau nodded to a turnoff on his right. "Coming from town, take the trail I pointed out before."

"Will either trail go by your ranch?"

His head whipped toward her, his eyes wide. "I didn't know you realized the properties were so close."

"Don't you remember bringing me out to your land? You showed me where you planned to build your house."

He wanted to set her straight, tell Caro it was *their* house he planned to build. "I remember."

Pursing her lips, she wondered if she should say more or stay silent. Clearing her throat, she continued. "When Mr. Clausen brought me out to the Miller place, I recognized the trail to your property. I hope you don't mind that we're neighbors."

*Hell yes, I mind,* he thought, knowing there was no use complaining over something he could do nothing about. "Your money, your decision."

It wasn't the answer she had hoped for. "Once I move in, you're welcome to come over, have supper with me." She could sense the instant the air shifted, like a cloud falling over them.

Easing back on the lines, Beau stopped the wagon, turning toward her. "I won't be coming by for supper, Caro. When you left, you made it clear I'm not the man you want to spend time with. I'm sure you'll find someone else to fill that spot." The instant the words were out, he wished he could pull them back. His response was honest, needed to be said, but the look on her face made him feel as if he'd punched her. Reaching over to touch her arm, he drew back when she flinched. "I'm sorry..."

"No, you're right. Besides, it wouldn't be right with you courting Sarah Murton."

His nostrils flared at the assumption. He knew that was what she believed at the party, still believed, yet he'd done nothing to change her mind.

He slapped the lines, his gaze focusing on the trail ahead. "I'm not courting Sarah. Fact is, I'm not courting anyone."

Caro sat silent, a thread of relief wafting through her. She had no right to feel a sense of satisfaction at his confession, but she did. Now if she could just convince him to give her a second chance.

# Chapter Five

*Montgomery, Alabama*

"It's time, Eddie." Julius Eldridge placed a hand on his older brother's shoulder. "She wouldn't want us to be late."

Edmond Eldridge let out a bitter laugh as he set aside the bookkeeping, which seemed to take less and less of his time. "Even in death, Mother still influences what we do." Standing, he took his black coat off a hook and slipped it on.

Julius shook his head, letting out a ragged breath. "It happened so fast. I still have a hard time believing she's gone."

"I know, Jules. First Father, then Perry, now Mother." Clutching his hat in one hand, he opened the door to the study and stepped into the entry. Their younger sisters, Prudence and Alma, stood by the front door, their expressions reflecting the loss. Ushering them to the waiting wagon, Eddie took a moment to stop at the edge of the large covered porch and look around.

Groups of former slaves, now sharecroppers working Eldridge land, nodded as the four settled onto the wagon. The same as their father,

Adelaide Eldridge had been loved by most everyone, including those standing around today. She'd woken earlier in the week with a high fever, chills, and a rash that spread quickly, making her skin feel as if covered with sand. Within a few days, the severe case of Scarlet Fever had ended her life, leaving an emptiness in her children, as well as the former slaves who called the Eldridge plantation home.

Slapping the lines, Edmond guided the wagon up a sloping hill to the family cemetery where their father and other brother already rested, along with a younger sister who'd died at birth. He pulled the wagon to a stop, jumped down, then helped Prudence and Alma to the ground.

Already crowded with mourners, the four siblings stopped to talk with those they knew before making their way to the freshly prepared grave. Taking off their hats, Edmond and Julius stood shoulder to shoulder, each holding the hand of one of their sisters.

The minister's remarks hit everyone hard, sealing the reality Adelaide Eldridge had truly left this world. When the service ended, the brothers draped their arms over the shoulders of their grieving sisters. No one spoke as they returned to the wagon and their eerily quiet home.

As the afternoon wore on, their former slaves brought food, insisting they take it. Moving from a system of slave labor to sharecropping hadn't been easy. After more than a year, newly freed men, croppers under the sharecropper arrangement, and struggling landowners were beginning to see improvement. Since few croppers owned equipment, animals, or the tools required to farm cotton, they made a living based on labor only. In many cases, it amounted to thirty percent of the crop. The Eldridge family hoped to pay more, depending on the market for cotton.

By evening, everyone had left, leaving the four siblings to their own private grief.

"We need to talk, Eddie." Although low, his voice carried across the room where Prudence and Alma sat huddled together.

Edmond knew what Julius wanted to discuss. The same topic concerning both of them ever since their brother, Perry, a lieutenant in the Confederate Army, had died during the Atlanta Campaign.

Edmond let out a weary sigh, sending his brother a warning look. "Not now, Jules."

Crossing his arms, he felt the frustration roll through him at being put off again. "When then?" He turned his head at the sound of footsteps behind him.

Lowering his voice, Edmond scowled at his brother. "Not in front of the girls."

"What are you whispering about, Edmond? I hope it isn't another discussion about Perry's death."

Julius cringed at the look on his sister's face. "Mother's funeral would remind us of Perry's death, Prudence."

"I hope that's all it is. Mother would not have wanted you to continue with this, Jules. She made it clear it was time to let it go and move on. He died during battle. A hero. There's nothing more to it." Prudence's voice shook, although her shoulders were square, chin jutting out. A year younger and a few inches shorter than Julius, she could still be a formidable presence when arguing a position.

Edmond shook his head. "We've heard more than one account of his death. We don't know which is true."

"Will finding out bring Perry back?" Prudence's voice cracked. "We agreed to accept what the army told us, the same as all the other families who've lost loved ones. Why do you insist on continuing to question what we were told?"

Alma jumped up, her voice rising in emotion. "I don't want to talk about Perry anymore. He's gone and isn't coming back." She swiped a tear from her cheek, her eyes puffy and red. Alma and Perry had been close. The youngest at fourteen, she'd been ten when they got the news about his death.

Standing, Edmond walked to Alma, wrapping his arms around her. "You and Pru are right. Mother's death caught us all by surprise, bringing back unwelcome memories of Perry. Why don't you take Alma upstairs, Pru? I think we all need some time to ourselves."

Taking her sister's hand, Prudence started for the stairs. "Come along, Alma. You'll feel better after a nap."

Edmond motioned for Julius to follow him into the study, then closed the door, piercing his brother with an angry glare. "We cannot discuss our plans in front of the girls. You know it only upsets them."

Running a hand through his hair, Julius nodded. "You're right. I wasn't thinking." Slumping into a chair, he rested his arms on his legs, his head hanging. "What are we going to do?"

"I've contacted the Pinkerton Agency about locating Perry's commanding officer."

Julius sat up. "Pinkerton? All we have to go on is the story of a disgruntled ex-Confederate sergeant."

"There's no reason for him to lie about seeing the officer shoot Perry. He said the man did it to protect a group of deserters. If that's true, the man is guilty, no matter what the army told us."

Julius nodded. "Do we have the funds?"

"We have enough. It's either hire someone or track the man down ourselves. With Mother's death, we're both needed here." Edmond leaned his hip against the desk, crossing his arms.

"What do you plan to do once Pinkerton locates him? It's my understanding the agency has no authority to arrest someone without a warrant."

"Right now, all I want to know is where he's hiding." Edmond thought of Perry, his bright, energetic younger brother, and his enthusiasm to fight for the South's independence. The memory brought a lump to his throat.

"And then?"

Edmond's mouth turned up into a cruel smile. "Then Captain Beauregard Davis will face the same degree of mercy he gave Perry."

*Omaha, Nebraska*

Finishing the last bite of his mediocre steak, Dutch McFarlin pushed the plate away. It was a celebration of sorts. He'd completed his current assignment for his employer, the Pinkerton Agency. As always happened, within a few hours of sending his final report to headquarters, a telegram came for him with another job. This one brought a smile to his face.

A few years before, he'd received an assignment to assist another agent, one he'd worked with during the war. He and Luke Pelletier met during their employment with the Confederate Secret Service, both ending up at the Pinkerton Agency—Luke for only a brief period after inheriting the ranch in Montana. They'd completed the job, then Luke returned to work the ranch with his brother, Dax. It looked like Dutch would now be heading to Splendor, confirming the man Pinkerton identified was the same person their client wanted to locate. A strange request, but no assignment was ever the same with the expanding detective agency. He planned to take the train as far as possible, then finish the trip on the horse he'd purchased in Omaha.

"Here's your pie, Mr. McFarlin." The server set down the plate, cocking her head, a question in her eyes. "I heard you may be leaving us."

"Taking off for Montana tomorrow morning."

"Well, that's too bad. I'll miss seeing you in here."

"Thanks, sweetheart. You never know. With my job, I may be coming back." A brief bit of melancholy hit him in the chest as she walked away. Having no real home worked well for most Pinkerton agents. It also resulted in a fair amount of lonely nights.

Finishing his pie, Dutch pushed out of his chair and strolled outside. Stopping on the boardwalk, he turned as a man hurried up to him, waving a telegram.

"Mr. McFarlin. Another message came for you. A longer one this time. I knew you'd be leaving soon and wanted to be sure you got this." The older man's breath came in gulps, his heart pounding from the brief exertion.

Pulling money from his pocket, Dutch exchanged it for the telegram. "Thank you. I appreciate you finding me."

Grinning, the man clutched the tip in his hand as he walked away. "Have a safe journey."

Opening the message, he scanned the contents, a frown crossing his face. Pinkerton had provided more details on the man, a former captain in the Confederate Army.

The company had been hired to find Beauregard Davis, a task headquarters had already accomplished. Dutch's job was to confirm the identity and report back to his boss. Brows furrowing, he folded the paper, slipping it into his pocket.

He'd never had such a bland assignment. In his mind, Allan Pinkerton could contact the sheriff in Splendor, or even his former agent, Luke Pelletier, who he was certain knew the man, and confirm. Dutch never questioned his orders and wouldn't start now. If nothing else, he'd be able to spend time with his friend, resting from running down notorious bank and train robbers, before returning to more challenging work.

*Splendor, Montana*

"Your timing is excellent, Covington." Beau finished securing Boyden Trask and his two men in the back of the wagon for the trip to Big Pine. Caleb had accepted Gabe's job offer. His first assignment would be riding with Beau to guard the prisoners, ensuring they arrived safely at the territorial capital.

"I never did care much for sitting around." Caleb checked the saddle, his guns, and rifle one last time before mounting his big buckskin gelding. Twister, a gift from an elderly neighbor who could no longer afford to keep him, had entered his life after the war. Caleb had done his best to get his friend to take payment, being rebuffed each time. Instead, he worked the man's farm for several months, doing whatever he could to help him out. Over the last few years, he and Twister had become partners.

"You two ready?" Gabe stepped out of the jail, a cup filled with tepid coffee in his hand.

"If all goes as planned, we'll be back tomorrow evening." Beau climbed onto the wagon, settling himself on the bench seat.

"I understand you'll be bringing back some more supplies for Caro." Gabe leaned against the rail, seeing Beau's eyes widen a little before narrowing.

"Her new hired men, Merritt and Gus, asked for some materials she hadn't brought back from Big Pine. It's not a problem, is it?"

Gabe shrugged. "Not by me. Glad you decided to help her out."

Beau winced, knowing his closest friends would've understood if he decided to turn his back on her, letting someone else help her out. He couldn't find it in himself to ignore her needs.

He picked up the lines. "See you tomorrow."

Gabe held up his cup, nodding at him and Caleb as they rode out. Stepping back inside the jail, he picked up the telegram from Sheriff Parker Sterling, reading it a second time. Clem and Louis Dawson, former members of the

Penderville gang, had been seen in eastern Montana. Tossing the missive on his desk, he lowered himself into his chair.

The Penderville brothers had come after Cash, planning to kill him for a perceived wrong to their family. Two of their men, Clem and Louis Dawson, had been ordered to kill Noah Brandt. Their bullets hadn't accomplished their goal, although they had gravely wounded Noah and Bull, who'd been riding beside him.

Clem and Louis had escaped to form their own gang. In the opinion of several lawmen in the territory, the Dawson gang couldn't be ignored. They rustled cattle, stole horses, and robbed banks, making it hard to figure out where they'd strike next. And, unlike the Pendervilles, they weren't driven by revenge. Greed was what motivated them and their men, not caring who got hurt or killed.

Gabe had done what he could, sharing the news with Beau and Caleb before they left, letting Cash know before he began his rounds that morning. He needed to warn Noah, his closest friend since childhood, and Bull. Gabe didn't want them taking up arms in revenge, but they had to be prepared in case the Dawsons were foolish enough to show their faces in Splendor.

"Gabe, do you have a few minutes?" Bull walked in, a roll of paper under his arm, Nick following him inside.

Gabe motioned to a couple chairs. "Now is fine. What do you have?"

"I want to get your thoughts on a few changes I'm recommending for the new clinic." Rolling out the paper, he pointed to several areas on the layout he'd eventually use as plans for construction. "If I rearrange some walls, I can fit in one more examination room. The size of the surgery room can also be enlarged." Bull looked between Gabe and Nick. Along with the Pelletiers, they were the biggest contributors to the new clinic. "It will cost a little more in materials."

"Have you talked to Doc McCord?" Nick continued to study the changes, not looking up.

Bull nodded. "I have. He thinks it's a good idea, and thinks Doc Worthington would feel the same."

Nick sat back in his chair. "Then I'd say we go ahead with your recommendations."

"Good. I'll get started." Bull rolled up the plans.

"Before you leave, I received news from Sheriff Sterling about the Dawson brothers."

Bull's features stilled. "What did Sterling say, Gabe?"

"They've been seen in eastern Montana. Sterling hasn't heard of anyone seeing them around Big Pine."

"Have you told Noah?"

"Not yet." Gabe picked up his hat, securing it on his head. "I'll be speaking to him next."

"He's working at the forge, finishing a tool order for Dax and Luke. I'll go with you."

Gabe looked at Nick. "I'd appreciate it if you'd let Horace Clausen know. After I meet with Noah, I'll be riding out to the Pelletier ranch to let them know."

"I'll go to the bank right now, Gabe. Is there anyone else I should warn?" Nick walked to the door, following Bull and Gabe outside.

"No one else, Nick. I'll talk with you at supper tonight." Gabe's wife, Nick's longtime business partner, had followed Nick to Splendor to open the Dixie Saloon, meeting and marrying Gabe. The three had formed a partnership, building the St. James Hotel, enlarging the boardinghouse, and spending supper together most nights. "Let's hope the Dawsons aren't foolish enough to come around.

Bull stepped next to him. "We'll be waiting if they do."

"Good morning, Rachel. I didn't expect you in the clinic today." Doctor Clay McCord finished putting away an order of bandages and medicines he'd received, closing the cabinet door. "What brings you in today?"

Rachel Pelletier, Dax's wife and the clinic nurse, shrugged out of her coat, placing it on a hook by the door. "I believe I'm pregnant."

Clay grinned. "That's wonderful news. I suppose you're here for me to confirm it."

She nodded. "I don't think I'm wrong, but with Ginny and Luke trying so hard to have a baby, I don't want to say anything until you've made certain."

Nodding, Clay indicated for her to get on the examination table. Ginny Pelletier's first pregnancy had ended in tragedy, losing the baby while Luke was away from the ranch. It had been hard to recover from the miscarriage, but they had, deciding to try again.

Clay looked down at her. "You know what to expect."

Rachel nodded, letting her mind clear as he went about his exam.

A few minutes later, she grabbed her coat off the hook. "Then it's official?"

"It is, although you already knew what I'd find. I'd expect the newest Pelletier to join the family in late spring."

Slowly slipping on her coat, she glanced up at him, her eyes filled with sadness. "Dax will be thrilled. I'm a little concerned about how Ginny will take the news."

"You'll have to tell her and Luke soon, Rachel. They're both adults. Do you really think they'd expect you and Dax to hold off growing your family because of their loss?" He placed a hand on her shoulder. "I won't pretend to know God's plan, but I can't believe He'd allow a couple such as Luke and Ginny to go through their life without children."

"Dax and I believe the same." Buttoning her coat, she took a few steps toward the door. "I'd appreciate it if you wouldn't say anything until we've had a chance to talk with Luke and Ginny."

"Of course. Will I see you in the clinic this week?"

"I've made plans to meet Rosemary here tomorrow. She's a quick learner and wants so much to be a nurse. It won't be long before she can take over for me."

Clay chuckled. "Don't go pushing yourself out of a job so soon. She reads everything I give her and asks great questions, but there's nothing better than actual experience. My guess is that's how you became so good so fast. Working in Union field hospitals will turn an inexperienced nurse into an expert in a short amount of time."

A slow smile spread across her face. "You have me for at least a few more months. After that..." She shrugged.

They both turned as the front door opened. Ginny walked inside, her eyes widening at the sight of Rachel. "I didn't know you would be in the clinic today."

"I hadn't planned to, but needed to speak with the doctor. Are you ill?"

Ginny's face brightened. Clasping her hands in front of her, her gaze moved between Clay and Rachel. "I feel wonderful. I think I'm pregnant."

# Chapter Six

It had been over a week since Beau took Caro, along with Merritt and Gus, by her property. The brothers had taken their time looking at every aspect of the house, telling her what they thought needed to be done, the additional supplies required, and how much time it would take.

If the weather held, they figured the most critical work could be completed before Christmas. The rest would take at least another month. Neither balked at setting up their bedrolls inside the house or cooking their meals over a campfire, and the wage they asked for seemed fair to both her and Beau.

Other than commenting about repairs, she and Beau had spoken little since he'd made it clear he wasn't courting Sarah. In fact, he'd stayed silent on the ride back to town. The only concession came when he honored his promise to teach her how to drive a wagon by asking Noah if they could borrow it again.

Lying in bed, the early morning sun beginning to lighten the room, she thought of all that needed to be done over the next few weeks.

Caro had agreed to meet Merritt and Gus at her property today so they could start work.

Beau hadn't offered to drive her back out, and knowing he'd left two days before to deliver the prisoners to Big Pine, she had to figure out a way to get there. A soft knock on the door had her rolling out of bed, grabbing her wrapper.

"Mrs. Iverson, there's a gentleman downstairs waiting for you."

She cocked her head, opening the door a crack. "A gentleman?"

"Yes, ma'am. Deputy Davis says you have an appointment at your new place."

A slow grin tipped up the corners of her mouth. *He remembered.*

"Thank you. Please let him know I'll be down in a few minutes."

"Yes, ma'am."

Scrambling to dress, she grabbed a brush, drawing it through her blonde hair before twisting it into a tight bun at the back of her neck. Slipping into her heavy coat, she picked up her reticule before heading downstairs to meet Beau. Stopping on the last step, she saw him standing at a window, his gaze fixed on something outside. Careful not to make a sound, she took advantage of his back being to her, allowing herself a few moments to study him.

He'd cut his dark brown hair since she'd left for San Francisco. Before, he'd worn it loose, falling to his shoulders, sometimes securing it at the back of his neck in a queue. Now it curled around his ears, just touching the collar of his shirt.

She sighed. It had been much too long since she had the right to run her fingers through it.

"Didn't your mother tell you it isn't nice to stare?" Turning, he fixed her with an intense look.

Caro startled, her face flushing at being caught watching him. Lifting her chin, she joined him in the hotel lobby. "I wasn't staring."

Beau chuckled. "You never could lie, Caro."

Her face softened, her mouth curving into a smile. "You're right. I don't know why I even try." She let her gaze wander outside before returning to focus on him. "I don't remember you offering to take me out to the property this morning."

"I'm not taking you. *You'll* be taking *me*."

Her jaw dropped, eyes widening when his meaning became clear.

"Today is your first lesson. Maybe the only one, if you catch on as fast as I expect." Taking her hand, he threaded her arm through his. "Noah has the wagon waiting."

Stepping outside, he sensed her hesitancy, felt a slight tremble rush through her. "You're not worried about driving the wagon, are you?"

Indignation crossed her face, her gaze narrowing. "Of course not. In fact, it's doubtful I even need your assistance."

Squeezing her hand, he nodded. "I guess we'll find out."

"Easy, Caro. You don't need to jerk the lines."

"Why can't I figure this out? It didn't seem so hard when you were doing it." She glanced at Beau, catching her bottom lip between her teeth.

He patted her thigh, then drew his hand back. For a moment, he'd forgotten he had no right to be so familiar. "I've driven a wagon since I was seven. This is your first time. Give yourself a chance to get used to the feel of the lines and how the horse responds. I know you can ride a horse."

"Only because you taught me. My late husband hated the thought of me riding, even though he'd ridden his entire life."

He leaned back against the seat, enjoying watching her, ready to help out if needed. The sound of her voice soothed him in a way he'd never appreciated until he lost her.

"I don't understand why he didn't want me on a horse. All the ladies I socialized with owned their own and rode almost every weekend. Did the women in your family ride?" She spared him a quick glance before returning her attention to controlling the horse.

A grin tilted up the corners of his mouth as memories washed over him. "They did, and all were quite accomplished."

"See. You prove my point." She nodded toward a fork up ahead. "Isn't that the trail to my place?"

He sat up. "It is. Are you comfortable making the turn?"

Nodding, she drew in a deep breath, straightening in the seat. Taking the lines in each hand as Beau instructed, she mentally went through what he'd told her, focusing on the horse and the trail ahead. As the wagon straightened, she let out a relieved breath, flashing a triumphant smile at Beau.

"I did it."

"Yes, you did, sweet...uh...Caro." He scolded himself for almost speaking out of turn. She wasn't his sweetheart or anything else.

Her smile faded when she glanced over at him. "Thank you for taking the time to bring me out here."

"You're the one driving the wagon."

"Yes, but it was you who insisted I learn the right way. Thank you for that."

Beau nodded, not knowing what else to say. She'd done well, picking it up much faster than he expected. It wouldn't be long before she'd learn what she needed to manage her property, maybe keep a cow, raise a few head of cattle. All things he'd hoped they'd do together.

"Look. There it is."

Ignoring the pain in his chest, Beau shifted his gaze toward the house where Merritt and Gus waited. The supplies he'd picked up in Big Pine filled the back of the wagon. He grinned, remembering the look on Caro's face when she'd seen it that morning.

"Morning, Mrs. Iverson." Merritt stepped up to the wagon, helping Caro down when she drew it to a stop.

"Good morning. I hope we didn't keep you waiting."

Merritt turned toward his brother, shrugging. "Waiting's no problem for us, Mrs. Iverson." He peered into the back of the wagon. "Seems you got the supplies we asked for."

"Actually, Mr. Davis traveled to Big Pine for them."

Beau rounded the wagon, placing his hand on the side of it. "Hope it's what you wanted."

Gus jumped into the wagon and started handing material to Merritt. "Seems to me we have what we need."

"Do you have time to show me around the house again? Show me what you plan to do inside?"

Beau's request surprised but pleased Caro. "I have plenty of time." She glanced at the brothers. "Gentlemen, I'll be inside with Mr. Davis if you need me."

He helped her up the dilapidated steps to what had once been a pleasant front porch. Weather, age, and neglect had reduced it to slats of wood more suitable for a bonfire.

"Is there something specific you want to see?" Caro walked around the parlor, yanking down curtains so worn they nearly deteriorated before touching the floor.

"How long since the Millers lived here?" Beau followed her, taking stock of what used to be fine wood paneling.

"Horace Clausen said close to six years. They kept making payments for a long time. One day, the money stopped coming. He's been trying to find a buyer for about two years."

"I know." There was a hint of regret in Beau's voice.

She stopped assessing the room and turned to look at him. "Were you planning to buy it?"

He thought of the many times he'd spoken to Horace, trying to find a way to finagle a purchase with the wage of a deputy. Few knew of the funds he had available in a bank back east. If he'd dipped into it, he could've bought the Miller place and several other sections of land around Splendor. Family obligations always held him back—obligations he refused to discuss with anyone, even his closest friend, Cash.

When he didn't answer, Caro stepped up next to him, resisting the urge to rest her hand on his arm. "You *were* planning to buy it, weren't you?"

"No." He moved away, needing more distance. "I think I'll head upstairs. Seems the fireplace in the main bedroom needs some work Merritt and Gus may have missed."

Standing still, she let out a breath as he walked up the stairs, perhaps the only part of the house not needing repair. She knew he'd lied about not having an interest in the place. His eyes always gave him away. At least with her owning it, he could visit or come to supper whenever he wanted. If what she hoped for didn't work out, she'd sell it to him at a price he couldn't refuse.

Following him, she stopped, almost laughing at the absurdity of her thoughts. He'd made it quite clear he had no intention of visiting, staying for supper, or being a presence in her life beyond what he'd already done. After today, his promises would be fulfilled. He'd go about his business and she about hers. The thought brought a painful knot to her heart.

"I heard the news." Rosemary Thayer's excited voice preceded her into the clinic as Clay McCord held the front door open. "I can't believe Rachel didn't tell me when we worked together the other day."

Closing the door, Clay followed her to the back, watching as she put away her coat. "She and Ginny had just learned the news themselves the day before. How did you hear?"

"Dirk Masters and Travis Dixon stopped at the boardinghouse for supper last night. The Pelletiers had told their ranch hands about Rachel and Ginny being pregnant. Everyone in the restaurant cheered."

"It is big news." His voice sounded far from enthusiastic.

Rosemary turned to him, her smile fading. "What's wrong?"

"It's not my business what my patients decide to do."

She leaned against the counter, the excitement of moments ago disappearing. "You think they should have waited to tell everyone."

"As I said, Rosemary, it's not my business what the Pelletiers decide to tell others."

"You have an opinion, though. How am I supposed to learn if you don't tell me what you think?"

Snatching his coat off a hook, Clay slipped it on, considering her question. "Given what happened before, it may have been wise for Luke and Ginny to wait a little while. I need to take care of some business at the bank. Will you be all right without me for a few moments?"

"The bank is just across the street. I'll find you if someone comes in."

"I won't be gone long."

Hearing the door close behind him, Rosemary started going through the supply cabinet, making notes of anything they needed to order. Finishing, she rinsed out a cloth, wiping down the counters while humming to herself.

"Doctor?"

Tossing down the cloth, she hurried to the front, stopping when she didn't recognize the man leaning against a wall, cradling his left arm. "May I help..." Her voice trailed off when she saw the blood. "What in the world happened?"

"Best I recall, I was shot." Although he swayed a little, his voice sounded steady.

"Let's get you in the back so I can look at it." It wasn't easy helping the man who towered over her, but they somehow managed. "Can you get on the table?"

"I don't recall being crippled, ma'am. Just shot." He leaned against the exam table, then pushed himself onto it with his good arm. "Probably just needs cleaning." He grimaced as she probed the wound.

"Well, Mr...."

"Adam Mackey, ma'am. My friends call me Mack. And you are?"

"Rosemary Thayer." Without asking, she gripped the sleeve of his shirt, ripping it open.

"Hey. This is a new shirt."

"Then I guess you shouldn't have gotten shot." Concentrating on the wound, she shook her head, taking a step back. Grabbing a clean cloth, she pressed it against the wound, glancing up at Mack. "This will need sutures. I'd better get Doc McCord."

"Can't *you* do something about it?"

"Sorry. I'm not trained for this. He's just over at the bank. It will only take a few minutes to get him."

Dashing outside, holding up her skirt, she dodged a couple wagons and several horses, doing her best to avoid the deep, water-soaked ruts in the road.

Clay walked out of the bank, spotting her. "Rosemary. Is everything all right?"

"A man came in with a gunshot wound."

"You didn't recognize him?" He took her arm, helping her back across the street.

"I've never seen him before. Introduced himself as Adam Mackey."

"He must be new in town." Pushing open the clinic door, he moved aside as Rosemary walked in. "Let's see what we can do for Mr. Mackey."

# Chapter Seven

*Big Pine, Montana Territory*

Brushing the dirt off his coat, Dutch stomped his boots on the boardwalk, his gaze settling on a restaurant not far down the street. He needed food, a room, and to get a telegram off to headquarters.

Taking off his hat, Dutch slapped it against his thigh, stepping through the door of the restaurant.

"Sit down anywhere." A woman with graying hair swept her hand toward the dining room.

Looking around, he selected a table near the front, the dirt-encrusted window providing a peek of the street outside.

"You have a choice of meatloaf or stew today. Both come with biscuits and coffee. What will it be?" The wafer-thin woman set a cup down, filling it with the thickest, blackest coffee Dutch had seen since the war ended.

Lifting his brows, he glanced up at her.

"I can make fresh if it's too strong for you."

He shook his head. "Don't bother. I'll have the meatloaf. Jam with the biscuits." Nodding, she left him alone.

Taking a sip of the murky brew, he winced, forcing himself to swallow it.

"You'll get used to it."

Dutch set down the cup, glancing up to see a wiry, older man with silver hair standing next to his table, a badge visible under his heavy coat.

"Don't think I've ever seen you in Big Pine." Without invitation, he pulled out a chair and sat down. "I'm Parker Sterling, the sheriff."

"Dutch McFarlin."

Parker nodded at the woman as she set a cup of coffee in front of him. "I've heard of you. Pinkerton Agency, right? Tom Horton, Luke Pelletier, and you helped bring in those outlaws when my deputies and me were in Moosejaw a couple years back."

Dutch nodded. "I had to leave before you got back."

"You have a reason for coming to town?"

"On my way to Splendor. Why? Are you expecting trouble?"

Chuckling, Parker studied his cup. "I'm always expecting trouble."

"Anyone specific you're looking for?"

The sheriff waited until Dutch's food was placed in front of him, then sat back, not answering the question, choosing to ask his own. "You have business in Splendor?"

"Thinking of visiting Luke. Have you been there?" Dutch dug into his food, unable to ignore the growling in his stomach any longer.

"Nope. My job here gives me little time to travel. I know the sheriff, his deputies, and several others who come here for supplies not available in Splendor." Parker leaned forward, settling his arms on the table. "Is your visit part of an assignment?"

Swallowing a bite of meatloaf, Dutch forced down another sip of coffee. "It is. The information I received from my boss makes it look like a simple job."

Parker snorted. "There are no simple jobs this far west. I'd suggest you check with Gabe Evans, the sheriff in Splendor. He's a good man." Shifting his gaze out the window, his body tensed, seeing two men enter the bank across the street.

"What is it?" Dutch followed his gaze.

Standing, Parker kept his gaze trained outside as he pushed his coat out of the way of his gun. "Nice meeting you, McFarlin. Come see me before you leave," he called over his shoulder as he walked to the door.

Dutch pushed his plate aside, tossed money on the table, then followed the sheriff outside. "What did you see?"

"Two men I've never seen before walked into the bank across the street. Something about them..." His voice trailed off an instant before they heard shots coming from inside the bank. Cursing, Parker pulled out his gun, hearing women scream, seeing pedestrians scatter at the sound of more gunfire.

"What do you want me to do?" Dutch slipped his gun from its holster and checked the cylinder.

Focused on the bank, Parker readied to start across the street. "I'll cover the front. You make your way around back." As he approached, the door swung open, the two men running outside. Parker took cover behind a wagon, Dutch coming up beside him. "I thought I told you to go around back."

"And miss all the fun?" Dutch trained his gun on the men, both shooting wildly as they tried to make it back to their horses. "Don't you just hate stupid men?" He fired, downing one man, then focused on the other, who'd turned to aim toward where he and Parker hid. Squeezing the trigger again, the second man screamed before collapsing to the ground.

Parker ran toward the downed men, holding his gun steady as he nudged each. Kneeling, he checked for pulses, then stood as Dutch stopped beside him. "Well, there's nothing wrong with your shooting, McFarlin. They're both dead."

He snorted. "I'm not known for wounding the men I aim at, Sheriff. Do you recognize them?"

"Never seen either one before."

Holstering his gun, Dutch reached down to grab a sack of money still clutched in the hand of one man. Feeling its weight, he handed it to the sheriff. "What made you suspect them?"

"Instincts. We've been expecting the Dawson gang to show up any day. You ever heard of them?"

Dutch shook his head. "Where are they from?"

"I don't know for sure. They were part of another group who went after one of the deputies in Splendor. From what I know, two citizens were wounded. Afterward, Louis and Clem Dawson formed their own gang. They've been going after banks, rustling cattle, and stealing horses. Indications are they're heading this way."

"Do you think these men worked with the Dawsons?" Dutch swiveled around, letting his gaze wander over the gathering crowd and nearby buildings. Seeing nothing, he turned back to Parker.

"They aren't Clem or Louis. Could be part of their gang, or raiders working on their own."

"Thank goodness, Sheriff." A balding man of medium build pushed his way through the crowd, coming to an abrupt halt at the sight of the two bodies. Pulling out a handkerchief, he patted his forehead, spotting the bag of money in Parker's hand.

"Put this where it will be safe, Watson." The sheriff held the bag out to the banker, looking around. "Anyone inside the bank get shot?"

"Two. Doc's with them now. The wounds don't seem too bad." Watson looked at the dead men again. "Better than these two anyway."

Spotting two of his deputies, Parker motioned them over. "Jeff, I need you to get the undertaker."

"Yes, sir." Jeff hurried off.

"Gideon, check these two for anything we can use to figure out who they are."

The young deputy nodded, dropping to his knees to look through the clothes of the first robber. Older, with gray stubble, he had a shocked look frozen on his face.

Wincing at the blood, Gideon checked the man's pockets, finding some money, tobacco, and an old photograph of a woman and child. Turning it over, he saw their first names scrawled in an uneven hand, but nothing to indicate the outlaw's name. Moving to the other body, he repeated his actions, finding a letter and pocket watch.

"I found something, Sheriff." He handed them to Parker, then stood to make room for the undertaker, who'd pulled his wagon to a stop.

Parker spoke to the undertaker before reading the letter Gideon found and checking the pocket watch. Turning to Dutch, he waved the letter in his hand. "Seems we have the name of one of the robbers. Nothing about where they're from, but at least there's something to mark the grave. We'll bury them next to each other. Maybe someone will come through Big Pine someday and tell us who they are."

"You don't think they're with the Dawsons, do you?" Dutch asked as the undertaker, Gideon, and Jeff loaded the bodies into the back of the wagon.

"Wish I could believe otherwise, but no. My guess is these two were on their own." He looked at the people still standing around. "Time to go about your business. There's nothing more to see here."

Dutch pushed his hat back, scratching his forehead. "Let me know if I can do anything more. If not, I'm going to send a telegram off to my boss, then find a room."

"The Imperial Hotel is the best place in town."

"Thanks, Sheriff. I'll stop by before I ride out tomorrow."

Parker held out his hand, grasping Dutch's. "I owe you, McFarlin."

Releasing his hand, Dutch shook his head. "You don't owe me a thing. Glad I could help."

*Splendor*

"I wasn't sure you'd gotten my telegram." Caleb shook Mack's hand, noting his bandaged left shoulder. "What the hell happened to you?" He indicated for Mack to sit in one of the empty chairs inside the jail.

Mack shook his head as he sat down. "Damned if I know. I was about two hours away from Splendor when someone took a shot at me. Next thing I know, I'm waking up on the ground, my shoulder on fire, my horse twenty feet away. As far as I can tell, whoever shot me didn't take anything. Left a hole in my shoulder and rode off." Anger and confusion laced his words.

"Nothing missing?"

"Nope, and I didn't see any tracks indicating they'd checked on me. It was almost as if they were using me for target practice."

Cash and Beau came in from outside, bantering back and forth, stopping when they saw Caleb talking to a man neither recognized.

"Cash, Beau, this is Adam Mackey. He served with me under Gabe. Mack, these are the other two deputies, Cash Coulter and Beau Davis."

"Call me Mack." He stood, shaking each offered hand

Beau walked over to the stove and filled a cup with coffee. "Help yourself, Mack. What happened to your arm?"

"Got shot on the trail from Big Pine."

Beau shared a look with Cash. "Did you see them?"

"No." Mack repeated what he'd told Caleb.

Beau glanced at Cash. "Do you think it could be the Dawsons?"

Cash shook his head. "From what Sheriff Sterling said, they're rustling cattle and robbing banks. Doesn't seem they'd shoot someone without trying to rob him."

"They're the same ones who shot Noah and Bull," Beau reminded him.

Cash poured himself a cup of coffee. "That was on orders from the Pendervilles. Still, I guess anything is possible. What brings you to Splendor, Mack?"

"I got a telegram from Caleb after he received Gabe's message." Mack shifted in his chair, resting his right arm over the back of it. "He mentioned the colonel needed two men, and I'd been considering a change."

Beau leaned his hip against the edge of the desk. "What were you doing before?"

"I was a deputy in Kansas City, Missouri. I'd already made the decision to quit and join Caleb as a Texas Ranger. Then I got his telegram."

The door banged open, Gabe entering, an irritated expression on his face. "What the..."

Mack stood, holding out his hand. "Colonel. It's good to see you again."

The scowl on Gabe's face turned into a broad smile as he grasped the outstretched hand. "Adam Mackey. Caleb said you might join us, but I didn't quite believe it." Shrugging out of his coat, he slipped it onto a hook, then turned back to Mack. "That why you're here?"

"Yes, sir. Assuming you're still in need of another deputy."

"Consider yourself hired." Gabe took a seat behind the desk, leaning forward. "What happened to your arm?"

Mack explained what he remembered, watching as Gabe's eyes narrowed to slits.

"You said it happened about two hours east of here?"

"Yes, sir."

Gabe stood, grabbing his coat. "I'm going to send a telegram to Sheriff Sterling, warn him about what happened. Could be just some drunken cowhands or a stray bullet."

Cash shook his head. "You don't believe that, do you, Gabe?"

"No. I don't know what happened, but I plan to find out."

"You'll join us at Suzanne's for supper tonight, won't you, Caro?" Isabella smoothed her hand over a bolt of fine fabric in Allie Coulter's shop.

"I don't know. You and Travis have so little time together. I hate to intrude." Caro stepped next to Isabella. "I believe you should purchase a piece of this beautiful brocade. The color is perfect for you."

Isabella smiled. "You're trying to change the subject. Travis plans for us to be there at five o'clock, and I expect you to join us." She turned to Allie standing at the counter, finishing with another customer. "Allie, I believe I need some of this brocade."

Allie walked over to the table, picking up the roll of fabric "Of course you do, Isabella. Do you want me to sew you a dress out of it?"

"That would be lovely."

Setting the roll down on a table, she measured a length, then looked up. "I have the perfect pattern in mind. Travis won't be able to keep his hands to himself."

Isabella's eyes danced with laughter. "You shouldn't be saying such things, Allie."

"I don't know why not. We all know how he feels about you. Why he hasn't asked you to marry him is a mystery to me." Allie crossed her arms, her gaze shifting to Caro. "I do believe you need a new dress, too. One that will make Beau realize the real reason you came back to Splendor."

Caro's mouth opened, then closed, her face flushing. There'd be no point in denying what Allie meant. She let out a sigh before raising her chin. "Beau isn't interested in me any longer."

"Nonsense." Allie shook her head, walking toward a display of new fabric. "Beau hasn't spared a look at another woman since you left."

Caro crossed her arms, tilting her head to one side. "What about Sarah Murton?"

Isabella stepped next to her. "I told you he has no interest in her."

"She's right, Caro. Sarah Murton is the one pursuing Beau. Definitely not the other way around." Selecting a roll of fabric to complement Caro's blonde hair and violet eyes, she walked past her friend. "Have you told him why you're here?"

Caro huffed out a breath. "Of course not."

Setting the fabric down, Allie stared at her. "And why not?"

"Because it just isn't done." Caro dropped her gaze. "At least not where I grew up. It would be humiliating to state my intentions."

"Especially after you turned down his proposal." Isabella covered her mouth the instant she realized her mistake.

Allie's eyes widened. "What? Beau asked you to marry him?"

Caro sent a disbelieving glance at Isabella, then nodded, her features showing the misery she felt at remembering that night. "I thought I needed the vibrancy and culture of a big city." She walked over to a beautifully upholstered chair and sat down. "I've never felt as awful as when I told him I wasn't ready to marry."

Isabella walked over, placing a hand on her shoulder. "You have time to convince him you were wrong. Beau is a reasonable man. I'm certain he'll give you another chance."

"Yes, he's reasonable, but he also has a great deal of pride. I wounded it a great deal by turning him down. It wouldn't have mattered how I phrased it. Saying no to him was still a rejection." She sucked in a ragged breath.

"Well, if our plan works, he won't be able to stay away from you."

Allie walked up to them, looking at Isabella. "What plan?"

# Chapter Eight

Caro finished her hair, then checked herself in the mirror once more. Supper at Suzanne's didn't require the same attire as if they were meeting downstairs in the more upscale Eagle's Nest restaurant in the St. James Hotel. Still, she wanted to look her best, even if her heart wasn't in spending an evening with Isabella and Travis.

The last few days had been busy. Caro had negotiated a deal with Noah to use his wagon as often as needed until he could build her one. Gabe had taken her to the Pelletier ranch to purchase one horse to pull a wagon and one to ride. Both were now at Noah's livery. Merritt and Gus had been working from dawn to dusk on repairs, already making substantial progress.

Through it all, she'd seen no sign of Beau.

"Caro, are you in there?"

She walked to the door, pulling it open to see Isabella waiting. "You didn't have to come here." She picked up her coat, gloves, and reticule, pulling the door closed as she joined Isabella in the hall. "I could've met you at Suzanne's."

They walked down the stairs to the lobby. "Travis wouldn't hear of it. He's thrilled about escorting two beautiful women to supper."

"Good evening, Caroline."

"Good evening, Travis. Thank you for including me tonight."

Travis stepped up to them, linking their arms through his. "We're glad you could join us. It will give me a chance to hear all about the progress at your new place."

The St. James Hotel and Suzanne's boardinghouse were at opposite ends of the main street. Walking past the Dixie Saloon, Caro couldn't help but glance inside, hoping to see Beau. Disappointed when there was no sign of him, she looked across the street at the jail, noting the light coming through the window, spotting no one inside. She wondered where he was and what he was doing.

"Here we are." Travis opened the door, stepping aside to let the women enter.

Suzanne walked up, smiling as she gave each of them a hug. "I have the table you requested, Travis." Motioning for them to follow, she walked to a table in an alcove at the far end of the dining room. Before they took their seats, Caro startled at a familiar voice behind her.

"Sorry I'm late." Beau glanced at Travis and Isabella, then shifted toward Caro, letting his gaze wander over her, a smile tugging at the corners of his mouth. "Good evening, Caro. You look beautiful tonight." He controlled the urge to lean down and brush a kiss across her cheek.

She shot a quick look at Isabella. "I didn't know you were joining us tonight, Beau."

"Travis invited me when we saw each other at the bank." His gaze narrowed. "I hope it isn't a problem."

"Of course not. It's a surprise, that's all."

"Isabella." Travis pulled out her chair, Beau doing the same for Caro before both men sat down.

Beau looked at Travis. "Did you hear Gabe hired another new deputy?"

"Bull mentioned a Caleb Covington."

"He also hired another man who served with him during the war. Adam Mackey. Caleb worked as a Texas Ranger, and Mack as a deputy in Kansas City. It's a relief to have two more men."

Suzanne approached with four cups of coffee, setting them down.

"I'm sure it's necessary. The town is growing." Isabella sat back, picking up her cup.

"Why don't I take your orders? We have venison stew or roasted chicken tonight."

After Suzanne took their orders and walked away, Travis crossed his arms, looking at Beau. "I heard Mack was shot on the trail between Big Pine and Splendor. Any idea who did it?"

Caro stiffened at the news. "Shot?"

Beau nodded. "Mack took a bullet in the shoulder. Unfortunately, he didn't see anyone."

Caro leaned toward him, a shiver running up her spine remembering when Noah and Bull were shot. "Gabe told me the Dawsons might be in Montana. Could it have been them?"

"Perhaps, but Sheriff Sterling hasn't seen them around Big Pine, and Gabe's certain they'll ride through there before coming this way." Beau sent her a reassuring nod. "It's best to stay vigilant."

"Here you are. I'll be right back to refill your coffee." Suzanne set down the plates, then hurried away, but not before noticing the somber expressions around the table, wondering what had them so concerned.

Caro moved the food around on her plate, taking an occasional bite, doing her best to ignore the man sitting next to her. She'd been gone much of the last few days, either at her new place or the Pelletier ranch. Her mind drifted to her time in San Francisco and the many nights she'd lain awake missing Beau.

She'd foolishly hoped returning to Splendor would erase the constant ache in her heart, the loneliness she felt at being away from him. A part of her had envisioned them going back to the way they were. Instead, she'd found a man who'd lost all interest in her and what they had. Caro knew he'd always be there for her, but the love they'd shared disappeared the same way she had when she made the decision to board the stage.

Glancing at Isabella, Caro's heart warmed at the encouraging smile on her friend's face. If they were alone, she had no doubt Isabella would remind her it would take time to break through the barrier he'd erected in her absence. The same as it had taken Caro time away to discover the depth of her love for Beau, he needed time to work through the anger he still carried at her leaving. Isabella had encouraged Caro to say something to him, tell him why she'd returned. Continuing to pick at her meal, casting an occasional glance at Beau, she finally accepted perhaps her friend was right.

Beau tucked into his meal, doing his best to ignore the beautiful woman sitting a foot away. It had been a mistake to accept Travis's invitation. He'd been upfront, mentioning Caro would be joining them. Instead of declining, his need to see her had been stronger than his ability to refuse the invitation.

He'd been by her place a couple times to check on Merritt and Gus's progress. Ty Murton had been right. The brothers knew what they were doing and worked fast. The first time he'd gone by, they'd already finished the front porch and were busy installing new windows. He'd been relieved, but also disappointed when he didn't see Caro. Gus had told him she'd gone with Gabe to the Pelletier ranch to purchase horses.

The second time he stopped, they were working on the front and back doors, also rebuilding the stoop outside the kitchen. Merritt figured they'd start work inside by the end of the week. Beau hadn't asked about her that time. The less interest he showed in the woman, the better.

Finishing, he pushed his plate away, seeing Caro had made little progress on her own meal. "Not hungry?"

Her eyes lifted as her hand stilled in the middle of shoving potatoes to the side of the plate. "I think I'm more tired than hungry." She shifted her gaze to Travis. "I'm sorry for my lack of appetite tonight."

"Don't think anything of it, Caroline. I've been known to miss a meal or two due to exhaustion." Travis set down his fork and pushed his own plate away.

Standing, Beau moved behind Caro's chair. "If you're finished, I'll walk you back to the hotel."

Feeling her heart quicken, she stilled, not sure she'd heard him right.

Not hearing her answer, Beau placed his hands on her shoulders. "Caro? May I walk you back to the St. James?"

"Why, yes. That would be lovely." Sucking in a breath, she cast a look at Isabella, noticing the sparkle in her eyes. "Thank you for a lovely supper."

Turning to Travis, Beau reached into his pocket, pulling out some cash. "This is for Caro and me."

Travis shook his head. "Save your money, Beau. Supper is on me tonight."

After helping Caro into her coat, he took her hand, sliding it through his arm. As they stepped outside, he lifted his gaze to the cloudless sky, seeing a brilliant moon and broad swath of stars.

"I remember when we used to walk behind town on nights like this, disappear into the trees so we could be alone." He guided her across the street and past the next block, where his small house sat empty, to an area behind town.

Caro's throat tightened, her heart pounding painfully at the vivid reminder and where he led her. "We'd take a blanket, spread it out so we could watch the night sky."

He chuckled. "Shooting stars."

She glanced up at him, a warm glow spreading through her. "Animals calling to each other."

Beau continued the game they used to play. "Water flowing in the creek."

"Owls screeching, searching for prey."

"A mother yelling for her child to come inside." He settled his hand over hers, forgetting they were no longer a couple.

Taking a few steps into the cover of the trees, he stopped. Swallowing the knot of regret, he stared into the distance, letting the quiet settle over them. He couldn't recall the last time he'd felt so at peace. Caro by his side had always felt right, as if they were always meant to be together. Listening, he could almost hear her heart pounding in her chest.

"I need to get you back to the hotel." He started to turn, stopping when she refused to budge. His brows furrowed in question. "What is it?"

Caro bit her lower lip, her breathing unsteady as doubt began to take hold. She knew this was her chance, the perfect opportunity to confess why she'd returned. Before, fear and anxiety at what he'd say kept her quiet. Sucking in a steadying breath, she turned toward him.

"Is it all right if we take a few more minutes?"

Beau studied her. She had no idea what being close to her did to him. It had been a bad idea to stroll to their old spot, conjuring up memories when they'd never be able to create new ones.

"It's dark, Caro. It would be best to head back now." He began to turn, then froze at her next words.

"I came back because of you."

Slowly, he shifted back toward her, his eyes cold and remote. "Then you made a mistake."

She reached out to him, drawing her hand back when he moved away. "The mistake I made was leaving you."

He stepped closer, his eyes boring into hers. "The mistake was me falling in love with the wrong woman." The cold, passionless response had her taking a halting step backward.

Caro could feel moisture forming in her eyes, her bottom lip trembling, and prayed he didn't notice. "Why are you so sure I'm the wrong woman?"

Crossing his arms, he planted his feet shoulder width apart, his eyes flashing in disbelief. "You turned down my offer of marriage, then got on the stage without a backward glance."

His voice was deceptively calm. "You never would have gotten on that stage if you loved me, Caro." Dropping his arms, he shifted away.

"It wasn't about love, Beau." Her response was barely above a whisper.

"No? Then tell me what it was about."

Finding it hard to hold his unyielding gaze, she turned away, pacing in a circle before turning to face him again. "I needed time to make my own decisions. My entire life has been about doing what my father and then my husband wanted. They expected their dreams to be mine, neither considering I might have a few of my own." She wrapped her arms around her waist. "I don't expect you to understand."

"Oh, I understand, Caro. A wealthy, young widow with a list of places she wanted to see, people she wanted to meet. Splendor was a stop along the way, and like me, not a real part of your dreams." Removing his hat, he ran a shaky hand through his hair. "You and I both know the part I played in your plans."

Her eyes searched his, having no idea what he meant. "I don't understand."

"Are you sure? It seems clear to me." He leaned down to within inches of her face. "You were a lonely woman, used to companionship, a man in your bed." His voice hardened more with each word. "You needed the passion I provided.

When you'd had enough time in my bed, you moved on."

Without thinking, her hand connected with his cheek. "How *dare* you reduce what I felt for you to something so vile and crude."

"The truth hurts, doesn't it, *sweetheart*?" He spat the last word out, not bothering to acknowledge the sting of her assault. "I'll bet few men have ever been honest with you. Well, I'm not one of those men. We were good together, Caro. Better than good. But it's over. I have no desire to repeat the mistakes of my past."

Her body shook as his disgust with her became clear. Taking an unsteady step away, she swiped at the moisture on her face, then turned her back to him. After several shaky breaths, she willed herself to find the strength to accept his ire.

"I'm going to spend a little more time out here. Please, do not wait for me."

Beau closed his eyes, pinching the bridge of his nose. "I'm not going back without you."

Spinning around, she glared at him. "I'm not going *anywhere* with you. As you so elegantly reminded me, I've gotten everything I wanted from you. Your services are no longer required."

Until he heard those words, he'd thought she could no longer cause him more pain. He took a step toward her. "Caro..."

"You're right. The past can't be repeated. We had our time and now it's over." When her voice began to break, she sucked in a deep breath before continuing. "Please, Beau. Go back without me."

He shook his head. "I won't leave you out here alone." He nodded to a large tree about twenty feet away. "I'll wait over there until you're ready, then I'll follow you back to the hotel." Beau held up a hand when she began to protest. "That's my only offer. I'm not leaving without you."

"Fine." Swiping at another tear, she pulled her coat tight around her, wrapping her arms around her waist. Without another word, she walked toward the hotel, putting as much distance between them as she could.

Feeling her body shake, Caro pushed down the urge to run. She would not let him see how deeply his words hurt, nor would she apologize for her hurtful response. They'd broken whatever tenuous connection they still had, crossing a line no amount of apologies could ever change.

True to his word, Beau stayed several feet behind her until she disappeared into the hotel. Caro hadn't looked back, didn't want him to see the pain on her face. All she wanted was to get to her room, close the door, and cry until she had no tears left. As much as she'd grieved for her late husband, the ache in her heart tonight was increased by tenfold.

He'd been wrong. She'd never experienced the same desire or passion for her husband as she felt for Beau. Never before felt as if she couldn't breathe when he stepped into a room, his intense gaze focused on her. Beau's face was the last image she saw before falling asleep each night, and the first that came to her mind each morning. Although no one knew, her time in San Francisco had been pure misery. She'd thought about him day and night, comparing all men to him. None came close to stealing her heart the way he had.

Closing the door to her room, Caro took off her coat, tossing it on a chair, then removed her hat. She could feel her hands shaking, her body trembling with each motion. Pulling a nightgown out of a drawer, she changed clothes, her movements stiff. Sitting at the dresser, she drew the brush through her hair, braiding it without thought, not daring to look at her reflection in the mirror.

After a few minutes, she walked to the bed, turned the wick down on the oil lamp, then blew out the flickering flame. Settling under the covers, she stared at the ceiling, unable to stop his hateful accusations from repeating over and over in her mind.

Caro had decisions to make, and they needed to be made soon. Thanksgiving wasn't far away, which meant snow would begin blanketing the ground any day. If she stayed, there would be no leaving Splendor until spring. The thought made her pause. Staying would mean moving into the house before Christmas, living miles from town with no one close by if she needed help.

Beau planned to build in the spring, which meant he'd be living in his small house behind the jail until his place was completed in late summer. Her heart squeezed. After tonight, even if he did live on his land, she could never depend on him to help her. He had made his feelings for her quite clear. He might not hate her, but he had no desire to spend any more time around her than necessary.

Caro had fallen in love with the house the instant Horace Clausen's wagon pulled to a stop in front of it. She hated the thought of leaving it unfinished. Furniture had already been ordered. Even after the hurtful events of this evening, Caro felt a reluctant smile tug at the corners of her mouth.

If she returned to San Francisco, she'd spend every day and night as she had the last year—with thoughts of Beau consuming her mind. Staying in Splendor would mean concentrating on her new home, making it her own in a way she'd never done before. Even in San Francisco, the house had come with most of the furnishings, items which meant nothing her. Here, every item would be uniquely hers.

Her late husband always told her she had more strength than she knew. If it were true, the time had come to prove it to herself.

Having made her decision, she pulled the covers up under her chin, feeling one last trickle of moisture trail down her cheek. Swiping it away, she vowed it would be the last tear shed for Beau Davis.

# Chapter Nine

Smashing the empty bottle of whiskey against the wall, Beau let out a string of curses before slouching back in his chair. He hadn't been this drunk since Caro left, believing he'd put this kind of behavior behind him. It had taken being alone with her, hearing her weak excuses for leaving, to push him back into his old ways. It galled him to realize tonight's argument hadn't been all her fault. He had to accept some of the blame.

The instant Caro said she'd returned because of him, he'd lost every ounce of control. Beau hated lies, and none more than those pouring out of the mouth of the woman he'd once loved—still loved, if his alcohol-filled brain were being honest.

No amount of whiskey could push away the image of the pain on her face when he'd accused her of wanting nothing from him other than time in his bed. He'd meant the words to cut deep, and they had. Nothing would ever purge the look of shock on her face at the accusations he'd so carelessly thrown at her.

Leaning forward, he rested his elbows on his thighs, then dropped his head into his hands, rubbing his tired eyes. Fatigue overwhelmed him. Tomorrow, he'd be able to function, but not by much.

Standing, his legs feeling as if they'd been encased in iron, he walked into his bedroom, falling back on the bed. Resting an arm over his eyes, he tried to push the image of Caro's stricken face from his mind. Drunk or sober, he couldn't purge her from his thoughts.

A loud pounding on his door shook Beau from his misery. He ignored it, believing the whiskey played tricks on his brain. When he heard the deafening sound again, followed by shouts, he mumbled a curse, pushing his body off the bed.

Grabbing the handle, he pulled the door open, bleary eyes boring into Cash, who stood on the steps with his arms crossed. "Do you know what the hell time it is?"

Cash took a good look at Beau, letting his arms drop to his sides. "You're a mess. Into the whiskey again?" Pushing past him, Cash walked inside. "Smells like a saloon in here."

Beau huffed out a frustrated breath, closed the door, and leaned against it. "It's after midnight. What do you want?"

"It's almost dawn, Beau. How long have you been drinking?" Cash glanced around, spotting the broken bottle on the floor, shards of glass everywhere.

Letting out a breath, he pushed away from the door, scrubbing his hands down his face. "Just tonight." Plodding to the kitchen, he opened a cupboard, pulling out a full bottle of whiskey. His hand stilled when Cash gripped his wrist.

"The Dawsons are in Big Pine."

Beau's eyes narrowed. "How do you know?"

Dropping his hold on Beau's wrist, Cash lowered himself into a chair. "Sterling sent a telegram saying one of his deputies spotted Louis and Clem Dawson in Big Pine last night. He followed them from a saloon to the biggest bank in town." Leaning down, he picked up pieces of broken glass, setting them on the table. "Bernie Griggs couldn't sleep. Went into the telegraph office early to do paperwork and happened to be there when the message came through. He woke Gabe to give it to him."

Taking a seat near Cash, Beau pinched the bridge of his nose, resigned to the fact he'd get no sleep. "What does Gabe want us to do?"

"We're to meet him, Caleb, and Mack at the jail."

Pushing himself up, Beau grabbed his hat, then slipped on his coat. "Then I guess we'd better get going."

"Beau, I want you and Cash to cover the bank. Caleb and Mack will be up by the lumber mill. That way, we cover both ends of town. You'll rotate shifts every eight hours. Beau and Caleb the first eight, then Cash and Mack the second eight, so there's one of us on guard at all times. I'll relieve each of you so everyone gets meals."

Beau nodded, glancing at Gabe. "What about Bull and Noah? You know they'll want to help out."

"Are those the two the Dawsons shot?" Caleb asked. He and Mack had heard all about the men who'd gone after Cash and his two friends.

"They are. Noah's still dealing with the injury to his arm." Gabe and Noah were close. Grew up together in New York, joined the Union Army at the same time, then rode to Splendor when they discharged out. "I'm going to wait a few days before telling either one."

Cash leaned against the desk, crossing his arms. "We could sure use both of their guns if the Dawsons show up."

Noah had been a Union sharpshooter during the war. Almost as skilled, Bull fought alongside the civilian Squirrel Hunters when he was in the Union Army. Neither backed away from trouble.

Gabe nodded. "We could, but I'd rather wait a few days before saying anything."

Mack chuckled. "They're going to see us and wonder what's happening. Seems it would be best to let them know now." He looked at Gabe. "Just my thought, Colonel."

"It's Gabe, and you may be right, Mack. I'll need to think it over a bit."

All five turned as the door opened, a large man with unruly red hair stepping inside. "I'm looking for Sheriff Evans."

"You found him." Gabe took a couple steps toward the man. "What can I do for you?"

"My name's Dutch McFarlin." He extended his hand for Gabe to grasp. "I met with Sheriff Sterling in Big Pine. He said I should look you up. If you have time, I'd like to speak with you...in private."

"I suppose we're done here." Gabe looked at his men. "Any questions?" When no one spoke, he nodded toward the door. "Then get on it." He waited until they left before gesturing for Dutch to take a seat. "What did you want to talk to me about?"

Dutch pulled out his badge, handing it across the desk. "I'm with the Pinkerton Agency. We've been hired to confirm the identity of an ex-Confederate officer."

Gabe sat back in his chair, his gaze narrowing on Dutch. "Why do you want him?"

Dutch shrugged. "Someone's looking for him. All I've been asked to do is verify the man is in Splendor. Sterling said you could help me."

Shaking his head, Gabe crossed his arms. "Depends. I'm a cautious man, McFarlin. If the man's in Splendor, I want to know what you plan to do with him."

Dutch didn't flinch at Gabe's statement. He'd feel the same if it were him. "As I said, Sheriff, my boss didn't tell me why the client wants to be sure the man I'm looking for is the one they believe to be in Splendor. Once I confirm he's here, I'm to send a telegram to Pinkerton. They'll either keep me on it, letting me know why they want the man, or they'll put me on another case."

Gabe studied Dutch, believing the agent didn't know more than what he'd said. "What's the name?"

"Beauregard Davis."

Thanking his years of service as an officer, which taught him how to keep his face neutral and emotions under control, Gabe didn't immediately respond.

"Have you heard of him?"

Standing, Gabe grabbed his hat and coat. "We need to take a ride."

Confusion washed across Dutch's face as he stood. "Where are we going?"

"To visit a friend of mine."

Beau took a position outside the bank, trying to look inconspicuous as he leaned against a post, his gaze focused on the main street. Two more weeks remained in November and the weather had turned downright cold. Rubbing his hands together, he shoved them in his pockets, glancing up at the darkening sky. It was still morning, but if he wasn't mistaken, it felt like they were in for rain. If the temperatures dropped, he'd be keeping watch in the snow.

"Here. You look like you could use this."

Beau shifted, a grin tugging at his lips at the sight of Allie Coulter holding out a cup of coffee. "Cash told me what Gabe asked you to do and that he'd be taking your place in a few hours."

Reaching out, he took the cup, wrapping both hands around it. "Thanks, Allie."

"If you want more, I'm just inside." Across the street from the St. James Hotel, her seamstress shop butted up against the bank and had a good view of the town. "Caro came by the shop this morning."

Beau looked over the rim of his cup, his expression neutral. "That so?"

Allie nodded. "She asked me to make her a new dress. It will be gorgeous on her." After Caro and Isabella left her shop the week before, she'd understood much more about what happened between Caro and Beau.

"I'm sure it will."

"She also asked me to make curtains for her new place. I'll be going out there to take measurements. Seems to me she plans to stay in Splendor."

Beau didn't want to know about Caro's plans, whether she planned to stay or leave. After their last conversation, he figured she'd want nothing to do with him.

He tipped up the cup, drinking the last bit of coffee. "Thanks for the coffee."

"Let me know if you want more, and please, come inside if you need to warm up." Taking the cup, she turned to leave, stopping when she heard someone shouting her name.

"Allie. I thought that was you." Hurrying across the street, Caro stepped onto the boardwalk, not noticing Beau standing a few feet away. "I'm riding out to the property. Would you like to come along?"

Allie glanced behind Caro, seeing Beau take several steps away, turning his back to them.

"Now would be fine. Come inside while I get my coat."

The instant he'd heard her voice, Beau felt his chest constrict, his hands fisting at his sides. His head still pounded from too much whiskey, a weak attempt to numb the pain of criticizing her the night before. He thought he'd dealt with his anger, the pain of her leaving, shoving it aside as he focused on his job and the house he'd be building come spring. The worst part of how the night ended was the realization he still loved her, might never be free of how she owned his heart.

Hearing the door to Allie's shop open, Beau walked down the boardwalk, getting as far away from the sound of Caro's excited voice as possible.

"We'll take the wagon, Allie. I'm so glad you're able to ride out now. It shouldn't take long. I think most of the windows are the same size."

"I've been wanting to see the house since you bought it. Mr. Clausen told me it had been beautiful before the family moved away."

Their voices faded as the women crossed the street toward the wagon Caro had waiting. A tug at Beau's heart caught him by surprise when Caro settled onto the wagon seat and took hold of the lines, just as he'd taught her.

He'd like nothing more than to start yesterday over, force himself to listen to what she said without his vicious response. Never one to let emotions dictate his actions, he cringed at how easily her excuses undermined his intentions to understand why she'd left. What surprised him most was how much he wanted to go to her and apologize, ask her more about why she'd come back to Splendor.

"What are you doing huddling outside the bank?"

Beau glanced up, realizing he'd been so focused on his own thoughts, he hadn't noticed Bull step next to him. Hell, he wouldn't have seen the Dawsons if they rode right by him.

"Checking the town, trying to keep warm." He noticed the roll of paper under Bull's arm. "Are you working on the plans for the clinic?"

Bull nodded. "I'm about finished with it. Depending on the weather, we're hoping to start building after Christmas. I'll be finishing the plans for your house right after Thanksgiving. Which reminds me. Rachel wanted me to tell you she expects you at the house for Thanksgiving supper."

"I'll do my best." He couldn't tell Bull what was going on with the Dawsons. Not until Gabe made the decision to tell him and Noah. If it were up to him, they would've already known about the gang's arrival in Big Pine.

Bull shook his head. "That won't be good enough for Rachel. The Pelletiers expect you. Don't make me have to ride into town to get you."

Beau chuckled, holding up his hands. "All right. Tell her I plan to be there."

"Good." Bull looked over his shoulder at the St. James. "Have you seen Caro this morning?"

"She rode out to her place with Allie. Why?"

"She wants me to ride out and look at the kitchen. Guess she's hoping to expand it and wants my thoughts. Sure seems she plans to stay in Splendor."

Beau sucked in a breath. The news should've pleased him, and it would have a few days ago. Right now, it felt like a weight bearing down on him. "Maybe."

"I suppose it would be best to head out there now. I'd like to meet her two men. Caro said they're real good workers, and we're going to need all the men we can get to build the clinic."

Looking up the street, Beau focused on two men riding past the church. He didn't recognize either, but they didn't look like the images on the posters Gabe had of the Dawson brothers. That didn't mean they weren't part of the gang.

Taking another look, his gaze took in their attire, the guns strapped on their hips. Neither had the appearance of a gunslinger, but he'd been fooled before. Watching as they stopped in front of the Dixie, he wondered what drew the men into the saloon in the middle of the morning.

Beau turned to Bull. "I'd better get going." He started to move toward the saloon, glancing at Bull as he walked away. "You might want to ride out now if you want to catch Caro at the house." Without thought, his hand moved to the butt of his gun. He knew it was loaded and ready.

Crossing the street, he raised a hand, acknowledging Caleb, who stood at his position down the street at the lumber mill. From several doors down, he saw Mack approach, nodding as Beau stepped inside the Dixie.

He spotted the two men at the bar, downing whiskeys, setting their glasses down for more. Taking a seat at a nearby table, Beau saw Mack slip inside the saloon. There were few others around at this hour, which made watching the men both easy and difficult. Beau didn't move as they continued to down one drink after another until they swayed on their feet, their voices growing louder as more alcohol streamed down their throats.

His gaze narrowed as one of the men slapped the other on the back, cackling.

"Hell, that wasn't you. I'm the one who fired the shot."

Beau and Mack straightened in their seats, senses on alert as the men's bantering grew louder, more belligerent. Catching the bartender's attention, Beau motioned for him to stop pouring the whiskey, hoping the two would settle down. Instead, Paul's refusal to pour another round angered both.

"Don't take that bottle away." One of the men held his glass out, almost leaning over the bar.

Paul turned toward them, setting the bottle on a shelf under the back counter. "I think you've had enough."

Before either Beau or Mack could react, one of the men drew his gun, firing at Paul, missing by inches and hitting the mirror behind the bar. "I'd like that bottle." He pointed the barrel of his gun at the whiskey under the counter, unaware of Beau and Mack moving up behind him, guns drawn.

"I'll take that gun." Beau nudged the man in the back with his revolver.

"Don't do it," Mack said as the second man reached for his gun.

"Both of you set your guns on the bar, then put your hands in the air." Once they complied, Beau's slight nod to Paul had the bartender grabbing the guns, setting them on the counter behind him. "Turn around and let's go outside. The jail is across the street. You can't miss it, boys. It's the one with the big sign on the roof."

Walking behind them, Mack glanced at Beau. "These boys sure have given us some choices—disorderly conduct, public drunkenness, damage to personal property. What are you going to charge them with?"

"All of it, plus being just plain stupid." Beau shot him a devious grin.

# Chapter Ten

"What do you think?" Caro led Allie into the parlor after showing her the upstairs.

Turning in a circle, Allie took in the large room with several windows and sighed. "It's going to be beautiful." She turned to look at Caro. "I can just imagine it with furniture. You're going to be able to have the most wonderful parties here."

Caro laughed. "First, I have to learn how to cook."

"You can always hire Suzanne to cater until you learn. In fact, she'll probably be happy to teach you, and I'll do all I can, although my skills aren't as good as some of the other women." Allie tapped a finger against her lips. "You know, Cash once told me Beau is a pretty good cook. Maybe he'd be willing to come over and help."

"Oh, no. I could never impose on him. He's busy with his job and will be building his house in a few months." She wouldn't burden Allie with the truth.

After the horrible argument with Beau the night before, she didn't believe he'd ever be willing to help her again. His feelings for her were clear. Beau believed her to be a woman who took what she wanted, then abandoned her friends without a backward glance. She'd be fortunate if he acknowledged her on the street, which he hadn't been willing to do today.

When she'd looked out the hotel window to see Allie hand Beau a cup of coffee, she'd quickly slipped into her coat, hoping to talk with him, possibly salvage a badly damaged friendship. The opportunity disappeared the instant he turned his back and walked several feet away, hoping she wouldn't notice him. The pain to her heart had been swift and deep.

"Caro?" Bull stepped inside, taking off his hat as he walked toward the women.

"Bull. It's so nice to see you. Allie and I were just discussing changes to the house. Would you like to see the kitchen?" Caro headed toward the hall, knowing Allie and Bull would follow.

"That's why I rode out. Beau said he saw you two leave."

Bull didn't notice the catch in her step at the mention of Beau. It confirmed what she already knew—avoiding her had been intentional. She stopped inside the kitchen, sweeping an arm around the room.

"Here it is."

Bull moved about the room, noting the size, where the stove had once stood, the door to the outside, and the windows. "You mentioned enlarging it."

"Yes. The home I grew up in had a table and chairs for informal meals. I'd like to have the same here, but there isn't enough room."

"I walked around the outside before I came in. I don't see why you can't add the needed space. I'd suggest creating a nook for a table and chairs over there." He took a few steps, indicating a wall with an existing window.

"That would be perfect."

Bull nodded. "Good. I'll draw up plans and have them to you next week."

Caro clasped her hands in front of her. "Wonderful, Bull. I look forward to seeing them."

He scratched his head. "I almost forgot. Rachel wanted me to remind you and Allie about Thanksgiving supper at the ranch. Says she's expecting you."

"Cash and I wouldn't miss it. Caro, you must come with us."

"I'd love to."

Bull looked between the two women. "If you ladies are ready to start back, I'd be happy to ride along with you."

Keeping her attention on the trail ahead, Caro adjusted the lines, leaning forward. After having Bull and Allie at the house, witnessing their enthusiasm, hearing their ideas, she felt as if a huge weight had been lifted. She'd never been in charge of a project this large, never hired men, other than a butler or carriage driver. Instead of fear, the entire experience left her invigorated.

"You are doing real good with the wagon, Caro."

She shot a quick look at Bull, a grin curving the corners of her mouth. "It's easier each time I come out here. I'm looking forward to getting the wagon Noah's building for me."

Bull nodded, keeping pace alongside the wagon. "I have no doubt you'll be pleased with his work. Noah is more of an artist than a builder."

Glancing up the trail, he spotted two men riding toward them. Neither were familiar. "Caro, I want you to pull up the wagon for a minute. Do you have a rifle?"

She drew back on the wagon lines, her gaze focused on the men ahead. "I do. It's under the seat."

"Good. I'm going to see what those men want." He didn't elaborate as he rode forward, putting as much distance as possible between the riders and the women. Reining Abraham to a stop, he settled a hand on his thigh, close to his gun. "Gentlemen."

They stopped, glancing at each other before the oldest acknowledged him.

"We're looking for the Iverson place. Heard she's looking for some men."

"You're headed in the right direction, but as far as I know, she's already hired the men she needs." He kept his gaze trained on their movements, noting neither made any attempt to reach for their guns. Shifting in the saddle, he motioned for Caro to come forward. "That's Mrs. Iverson driving the wagon. Why don't you ask her?"

She pulled up beside Bull, narrowing her gaze as she studied the two men. Her thoughts moved to Beau and the advice he'd given her about being cautious when on the trail. Although they appeared older, she guessed them to be in their mid-twenties.

"These two men heard you might still be hiring."

"I see." She turned her attention to the riders. "I'm Caroline Iverson."

Both men removed their hats, the oldest addressing her. "I'm Matt Volker. This is my brother, Nolen."

"What kind of work are you looking for, Mr. Volker?"

"Whatever you need, ma'am. We build, work cattle, plow fields, bring in crops. We just need work."

"Where are you from?"

"Kentucky, ma'am." He looked away for a moment, his gaze clouding before he focused back on her. "Had a farm. We joined the Union Army, fighting until the end." He glanced down at his hands resting on the saddle horn. "We may have won the war, but we lost our farm in the process. Came out this way hoping for a new start." The desolation on their faces broke her heart.

She took her time, considering her answer. "I have men already working for me. It doesn't mean I won't need more, but I won't know for several days."

Bull cleared his throat. "I'm going to need men to build a clinic in town. We don't start until after Christmas, though. Until then, there might be work out at Redemption's Edge. It's a ranch north of town."

A thread of hope passed across Matt's face, while Nolen's features remained distant. "As I said, whatever work you have, we'll take it."

Bull turned his attention to Caro. "I'm pretty certain Dax and Luke can use the extra help until you know if you need them. If it works out, I'd like to use them for the clinic, then maybe Beau's house."

"That's fine, Bull." Unbidden, her mind shifted to Beau and the house he'd be building a few miles away. Once again, her spirits sank at what had transpired between them the night before.

She wanted to speak with him this morning. It wasn't her way to let anger simmer, creating bigger issues and more pain. His actions made it clear he wanted nothing to do with her, which presented a problem.

She'd made the decision to stay in Splendor and become part of the community, which meant getting to know more of the townsfolk, attending church, hosting suppers, and stopping by the jail to speak with Gabe Evans, her childhood friend. It also meant seeing Beau, being continually reminded of what she'd lost.

Caro mentally slapped herself. She'd been through worse and survived. Lost her husband and, weeks later, her unborn child. After numerous discussions and arguments with family and friends, she'd made the hard decision to sell her home and travel west—alone, with a vague idea of where she wanted to settle. Beau hadn't been a part of her plans then, and sadly, he wanted to play no part in them now.

Straightening her spine, Caro tightened her hands on the lines, leveling her gaze at Matt and Nolen.

"Gentlemen, I'd suggest you follow us back to town. The sooner we get going, the sooner Bull can arrange for you to get to work."

*Redemption's Edge*

"The way I understand it, Allan doesn't know why the client wants to locate Beau, right?" Luke sat in a leather chair in the study of the Pelletier ranch house, his gaze fixed on Dutch.

They'd greeted each other as old friends would, spending time catching up on what had transpired since they'd seen each other last—when Luke still worked for Allan Pinkerton. His life had certainly changed since leaving the agency and marrying Ginny. Now they expected their first child.

"The reason hasn't been shared with me." Dutch took a sip of coffee, glancing at Gabe sitting next to him. He had yet to meet Dax Pelletier.

Gabe set his own cup down, lifting a brow. "Isn't that somewhat odd, McFarlin?"

"I won't deny it. This is the first time I've been given an assignment to find someone who isn't wanted. Usually, it's for robbery, fraud, murder. I've never been asked to simply confirm a man's identity and location."

Luke leaned forward, resting his arms on his legs. "It sure doesn't feel right, Dutch. No one goes to this much trouble unless they have something specific in mind. You already know Beau lives here and works for Gabe. He owns some land south of town with plans to build a house in the spring. The man is honest and honorable. And he's good friends with a man Dax and I grew up with."

Dutch nodded. "Cash Coulter, one of the other deputies."

"I've known Cash my whole life and trust his judgment. If he rides with Beau, that's all I need to know." Luke stood, pacing to the window, staring at the barn. "When do you have to report back to headquarters?"

"Now that his identity has been confirmed, I should send them a telegram. Why?"

Luke turned toward him. "I'd like to talk to Beau."

Dutch shook his head. "You know that isn't how it's done, Luke."

"I also know nothing about this assignment of yours makes sense."

"I agree." Gabe had stayed quiet, listening to them go back and forth. It was his deputy they discussed. His friend. A man he trusted with his life. "There's no reason to locate someone out of curiosity. There's more to this than a mere inquiry, and I want to know what it is."

Beau tried to concentrate on the telegram he needed to send, grimacing at the loud banter between the two prisoners in the back. It had been too long since he'd written his family a letter. Longer since he'd visited. For now, a brief telegram would have to do.

Resting his back against the chair, he folded his hands in his lap, closing his eyes, wishing today's image would be different. It never was.

His younger sister, Genevieve, ran in circles around him, laughing, begging him to let her climb a nearby tree. At twelve, Beau had always felt responsible for the precocious eight-year-old, even with servants.

Their parents had been older when they had their two children. Although thrilled, they never had the vigor to oversee such energetic and inquisitive children.

Beau sucked in a breath as the image changed. His attention momentarily shifted to an animal making its way toward a stream yards away. The animal stopped, glancing over its shoulder, then continued until its tail disappeared. Almost as if it were happening now instead of years before, the scream rocked through him. Jumping to his feet and shifting toward the tree, Beau spotted his sister. Genevieve lay on the ground, unconscious, her head and legs at odd angles.

"Hey, Deputy. Can we get some food back here?"

A shout from the back ripped his attention to the present. Scrubbing a shaky hand down his face, Beau leaned forward, resting his arms on the desk, hanging his head.

"You out there, Deputy?"

Irritation replaced internal pain as the prisoners fought for his attention. Once the two had been secured in cells, Beau resumed his post at the bank until Cash relieved him. Listening to the still drunk men now, he was tempted to volunteer to take his friend's place outside.

"Whew. The temperature is dropping fast out there." Caleb closed the door, walking toward the stove, making no move to remove his coat or hat. Hearing the noise in back, he lifted a brow. "What the hell is that?"

Beau shook his head. "Those two rascals Mack and I arrested at the Dixie. They haven't stopped yapping since we brought them in. I may have to shoot them just to shut them up."

Caleb chuckled. "Something to consider." Shoving more wood into the stove, he closed the metal door, rubbing his hands together. "You plan to release them when they've sobered up?"

"Wish I could. They pulled a gun on Paul at the Dixie. It's doubtful Gabe will want to put them back out on the street."

"Probably not." Caleb grabbed the back of a chair, turning it around to straddle the seat. He glanced over his shoulder at the sound of the door scraping open. Gabe walked in, followed by Luke and the man who'd wanted to talk to Gabe earlier.

"Hey, Luke. Didn't expect to see you in town today." Beau nodded toward Caleb. "Have you met the new deputy?"

Luke nodded. "A few days after he took the job. Good to see you, Caleb."

Settling his gaze on Beau, who folded a piece of paper and slipped it into a pocket, Gabe removed his hat, hanging it on a hook. His head lifted when he heard the loud chatter coming from the back. "Who's back there?"

Beau gave a brief explanation, then stood, letting Gabe take his usual seat. As he leaned against the edge of the desk, his gaze returned to the man who'd walked in with Luke and Gabe, curious as to his business in Splendor.

Gabe glanced at Caleb, then Beau. "I don't think either of you met Dutch McFarlin when he showed up this morning."

Caleb held out his hand, clasping Dutch's, then stepped back as Beau did the same.

Luke crossed his arms, leaning against a wall. "Dutch and I worked together when I was still with Pinkerton."

Dutch grinned. "Right before he met Ginny and decided to give it all up to concentrate on the ranch."

Luke nodded, smiling. "Best decision I ever made."

"What brings you to Splendor?" Caleb asked, echoing Beau's thoughts.

"Finished an assignment in Omaha. Pinkerton sent me out here to confirm some information." His gaze shifted to Beau, then quickly moved away.

Beau studied Dutch, his instincts insisting something was amiss. "And just what is your assignment?"

Dutch's jaw hardened, his expression blank as he considered his response. He saw no reason to hide the truth. "I'm to verify one Beauregard Davis resides in Splendor."

# Chapter Eleven

Caro's back and feet hurt. Surprisingly, the soreness didn't bother her. The pain filled her with a sense of pride, doing tasks that were always entrusted to others in the past.

She'd been working inside the house since not long after sunrise, helping remove items Bull would replace when he repaired the kitchen. Merritt and Gus tried to convince her to let them do it, but she'd refused. Rather than watch it all take shape, she had to be a part of this beyond making decisions.

The sun now sat high in the sky. Her stomach growled, reminding her she'd only eaten a slice of toast and one egg for breakfast. Rubbing dirty hands down the wool dress she wore, Caro stifled a laugh. Her parents would be aghast at the condition of her filthy clothes, a dress costing more than most women in Splendor could ever imagine. She made a promise to herself to stop by Stan Petermann's general store to buy practical clothes, the kind worn by women who worked alongside their men.

"Mrs. Iverson, would you have a minute to take a look at something?" Merritt stood in the open front door, glancing around. "You sure have gotten a lot done, ma'am."

Caro couldn't contain her smile. "I'm quite excited about how this will look when we're finished."

Merritt held out a hand, helping Caro step over an open area in the porch.

"My goodness. You've gotten so much done since this morning." She'd been so busy with her own work, she hadn't thought to look outside.

"We expect to finish this by tomorrow night, then we'll start inside, if that's all right with you, ma'am."

She breathed in the cold air, glancing over the wide expanse of land, feeling a sense of joy she never expected. Taking a step back, she inspected the men's work.

Since Merritt and Gus had started, she learned a little about the two brothers. In their late twenties, neither had married, no longer having strong ties after their service to the Union Army ended. They'd heard about the vast opportunities out west, making the decision to leave behind what little they had. She thanked God every day for their decision.

Glancing over his shoulder, Gus straightened, nodding toward the trail from town. "Rider coming."

Shielding her eyes, Caro focused on the lone rider, her breath hitching in recognition. Beau rode toward the house, his gaze fixed on her. Letting go of the rail, she walked down the new steps, hugging her arms around her waist as she worked to control the incessant pounding in her chest.

"Caro." He didn't smile as he reined Smoke to a stop, nodding at Merritt and Gus. Beau made no move to dismount.

"Hello, Beau." She took a tentative step toward him, keeping her hands around her.

"Appears you're making progress."

"Um, yes...Merritt and Gus are doing a wonderful job."

Beau studied the finished front steps and the progression of the porch, his jaw tightening before it relaxed. His gaze moved back to her, a hand reaching back to touch a saddlebag.

"Suzanne stopped me as I rode out of town. Asked if I could bring something to you."

Walking forward, she held out her hand. "All right."

"She made enough for both of us. Do you have time to stop for a bit?"

Catching her bottom lip between her teeth, she nodded once.

He reached down. "Swing up behind me and we'll take a ride."

She licked her lips, not sure what to do. Anger still simmered at the way he'd ignored her the day she'd ridden out with Allie. Keeping her distance seemed the best choice, not riding behind him with her arms around his waist.

"I won't bite, Caro."

Snorting at his reference to a night long ago when he'd invited her to his home for supper, she shook her head. "As I recall, the last time you said that to me, you *did* bite."

"Yes, I suppose I did." He grinned. It was the first time they'd made love. There had been no awkwardness. Their time together had been natural, as if they'd been made for each other, neither wanting the sun to rise above the eastern range. But, of course, they both knew it would. The trick had been getting her back to her room at the hotel before dawn without anyone seeing. He thrust his hand out again. "So, what will it be?"

"All right." Taking his hand, she swung up behind him, gripping the cantle at the back of the saddle.

When he didn't feel her arms around him, Beau looked over his shoulder. "No, Caro. You've got to hold onto me, not the saddle."

Stifling a groan, she did as he asked, slipping her arms around his waist, feeling instant heat through his thick coat. "Satisfied?"

Chuckling, he clucked, moving Smoke forward. "Yes, ma'am."

Beau felt as if he were straddling heaven and hell. After meeting Dutch and hearing his reason for being in Splendor, Beau needed space. He didn't know why, but his first thought had been of Caro. He needed to see her. She'd always been able to sort through the spider webs in his brain, helping him figure out the good ideas from bad. Her calming presence settled the ghosts lodged in his brain. Ghosts that haunted him since he'd heard Genevieve scream.

"Where are we going?"

"To a spot along the river. The sun shines all day and you can see for miles." Beau felt her arms tighten around him. Something he never imagined experiencing again.

As good as having her close felt, he refused to delude himself. A future together would never happen. Caro wanted what he couldn't provide. Her leaving for San Francisco had made it clear she needed a rich social life, access to fine clothes and food, friendships with influential people. He knew how she felt. He'd once believed in all those himself.

The war had changed what mattered to him. Seeing comrades fall, hearing their screams, replacing them with men who faced the same fate, he realized how little material possessions counted. Lives were permanently changed, families destroyed, and neither wealth nor social status could reverse the carnage. Friendships forged in hard times, a good job, warm clothes, and hot food now defined him, and he made no excuses for any of it. Caro buying a house and making repairs meant nothing. She had the means to leave at any time, and he had no doubt she would.

Beau left the trail, making a few turns, ending up in a clearing. "Here we are." He slipped off Smoke, then helped Caro down. Untying the leather thongs around the blanket, he handed it to her, then lifted the food out of the saddlebag.

"Is this all right?" Caro shook the blanket out near the edge of the river.

"It's perfect." He let her settle on the blanket first, then took a place at the other end. Unwrapping the food, he spread it out between them.

Caro's mouth watered. "Chicken, biscuits, fruit, and spice bread. I can't believe Suzanne did this." She picked up a chicken leg, taking a bite. "Mmm...it tastes so good."

His chest squeezed at the pleasure on her face. Beau wouldn't tell her he'd requested it, wanting an excuse to ride out. "She was happy to do it."

Caro chewed, then picked up a biscuit, glancing up at him. "Aren't you going to eat?"

He pulled his gaze away, looking down at the plate of chicken and selecting a plump breast. They ate in silence for several minutes, listening to the water a few feet away.

"I met a Pinkerton agent today. Dutch McFarlin."

The biscuit in her hand stopped midway to her mouth, her brows raised. "Is he a friend of Luke's?"

"He is, but that's not why he came to Splendor."

Setting her food down, she laced her hands together in her lap. "Why is he here?"

Beau tossed a chicken bone into the brush, picking up another piece, turning it over in his hand. "He was sent to confirm I live in Splendor."

"For what purpose?"

"McFarlin says he doesn't know."

She leaned forward, her eyes flashing. "He doesn't *know*? That's preposterous. Allan Pinkerton does nothing without a reason."

Beau's eyes narrowed. "How do you know what Pinkerton would do?"

Caro shifted, repositioning her dress, clearing her voice. "I've met him more than once. He and my late husband were friends."

His mouth twisted into a wry smile. "Sometimes I forget about all your social contacts."

She couldn't miss the sarcasm in his voice. "Frankly, it doesn't matter what you think of my social connections. There are times they become quite useful."

"This isn't one of those times, Caro." He glared at her a moment before taking another bite of chicken. Chewing, he swallowed, never taking his gaze from hers. "I'll find out the reason an agent was sent to find me. You're not to get involved."

She raised a brow. "Ordering me around, Mr. Davis?"

He threw the bone toward the same place as the other one. "I'm saying this is my business and you aren't to do anything unless I ask."

Sighing, Caro relaxed her shoulders. "I don't like it, Beau. He's here for a reason beyond finding you. Why would someone want to know where you live?"

"There are reasons."

She sat a moment, touching a finger to her lips. "I suppose so." Glancing up, she bit her lower lip. "A relative? You still have family back east. Maybe they're trying to find you."

"They know I'm here. It isn't that."

One brow rose. "Perhaps a past lover? A woman who can't get you out of her heart?"

Beau snorted. "Trust me, sweetheart. No such person exists."

Caro felt her heart flutter, but didn't respond. She knew of one such woman. "All right. What about someone who has a score to settle? Someone out for revenge?"

Beau's features stilled. He thought of the war and the men he'd killed, all part of his duty to the Confederacy. The one death that bothered him, would always haunt him, was the killing of one of his own men.

Lieutenant Perry Eldridge had been a good officer, loyal to the cause, and a man Beau could count on—until the day he executed a fellow soldier, planning to execute others based on his own suspicions. A hearing cleared Beau, his superiors agreeing with his decision to shoot Eldridge when he refused to lower his weapon. They said he'd done everything right. After their own hearing, the men Eldridge threatened were cleared of charges of desertion. The decisions did little to heal the personal agony of killing a fellow officer. Beau had never heard a word from the lieutenant's family.

"No. There is no one."

She shook her head. "Are you sure, Beau? You and Cash were bounty hunters after the war. It's hard to believe there aren't people who hold a grudge."

"I suppose so, but going to Pinkerton isn't what they'd do. If someone set out to kill me, they'd ride out themselves, take care of it, and leave. It's a fact both Cash and I live with every day."

They quieted, each lost in their own thoughts. After a while, Caro dabbed the napkin at the corners of her mouth, then wiped her hands. Watching as Beau did the same, she clasped her hands in her lap.

"Why did you really come out here, Beau? We both know it wasn't to deliver food or discuss Dutch McFarlin." She'd told herself not to ask, to let their time together be whatever he wanted. Being so close, wishing for what she might never have again, she couldn't contain her curiosity any longer.

His gaze locked on hers. "I'm not your enemy, Caro."

Her stomach clenched. "I never said you were."

"What I said before you left was true. I loved you. Even though that time has passed, if you'll let me, I still want to be your friend."

*Friend.* The word weighed on her heart. She wanted to respond, tell him being his friend was fine, but it would be a lie. She wanted so much more.

He continued, unaware of the pain his words caused. "I'm sorry for what I said the other night. None of it was true. You had a dream. As much as I wanted it to, it didn't include me."

She ignored the lump in her throat, the burning pain in her stomach, hoping he didn't see the dampness in her eyes.

"Beau, I..." She could barely get the words out. Beau's thoughts and what she felt couldn't be more different.

"Caro, it's all right if you can't accept my apology. If it were reversed, I'm not sure I'd accept yours."

Standing, she turned from him, taking several steps away. She had to stop the tears, not let him see how his words stung. She needed time to accept the finality of his decision, accept she'd never have more than what he offered today.

Sensing him come up behind her, Caro tensed when she felt his hands on her shoulders. She had to tell him the truth, let him know the depth of her feelings. She stepped away from his touch, spinning around to face him. Lifting her chin, she willed her voice to stay calm.

"If friendship is all you have to give, then I'll take it and learn to live with it." Stepping around him, she bent to pick up the blanket.

His jaw dropped, mind reeling at her words. Reaching out, he gripped her arm, turning her to him. "What the hell does that mean?"

She glared at him. "It means I still love you. I came back to Splendor to tell you I made a mistake." Yanking her arm from his grip, she let her gaze fall to the ground.

Beau stared at her, disbelief and anger coloring his features. Grasping her chin, he forced her to look at him. "I gave my heart to you once, Caro, and you turned it down. I'm not going to offer it again just to have you toss it back in my face." He dropped his hold, taking a step away, his hands clenched at his sides. This wasn't going at all as he had planned.

Caro could see the misery on his face, the damage caused by her leaving. She couldn't blame him. The worst decision she'd ever made had become her biggest nightmare.

Glancing around, she focused on a tree behind him, unable to meet his stare. "I'm sorry for all the pain I caused, Beau. I know you won't believe me, will never trust me again, and that alone devastates me." She took a step forward, her hands outstretched. "I loved you then, and I love you now. They're only words, but they're all I have. If you can find it in your heart—"

"I can't, Caro," he ground out before letting his voice soften. He glanced up at her, his eyes full of sorrow. "I'm sorry, but I just can't." Stepping around her, he picked up what was left of their food, glancing over his shoulder. "Friendship is the best I can offer. I hope you'll consider it."

The ride back to Splendor seemed to take longer than the trip from town to Caro's. His heart heavy, mind a mess, he tried to sort out what she'd said, the confession she'd made. The look in her eyes and plea in her voice slashed through him, making him want to believe her words. If he were another man, a better man, perhaps he could.

She'd ridden behind him on the trip back to her place, insisting on holding the saddle's cantle, not wrapping her arms around his waist. At first, he'd argued, telling her it wasn't as safe. Then he relented, not wanting to worsen their already damaged friendship. Once they reached her house, she'd slid off Smoke without a word, calling out to Merritt and Gus as she walked toward the house, not looking back. Beau sat a few moments, finally accepting her cool departure before turning his horse toward Splendor.

Doing his best to focus on the trail ahead, he remembered the telegram he needed to send to his parents. Reaching into his coat, Beau patted his pocket, feeling the piece of paper where he'd scrawled his message.

Guilt washed over him. He'd been remiss at contacting his parents over the last few months. Short telegrams weren't enough to satisfy his family. At some point, he'd need to go back, make sure they and his sister were cared for, which he couldn't determine through letters sent from hundreds of miles away.

Entering the outskirts of Splendor, his gaze sought out Cash. Beau needed to replace him in front of the bank, taking his own eight-hour shift. After Gabe, then Mack had questioned the two men sitting in jail, they were certain neither were part of the Dawson gang. They'd all hoped otherwise, wanting to find some connection to the outlaws moving their way.

Riding to the other end of town, he dismounted at Noah's livery, intending to take Smoke to the stables in back. The sound of the stage coming through town and coming to a stop drew his attention. Watching as the driver climbed on top, tossing baggage to the guard on the ground, he caught sight of a woman stepping to the ground. Wearing a yellow dress, matching hat, and parasol, her bright eyes scanned the street, halting when she saw him.

She walked straight toward him, tendrils of deep red hair falling loose below her hat, touching her shoulders.

"May I help you, ma'am?"

"I hope so. I'm looking for someone. Gabriel Evans. Do you know him?"

"I do. Gabe is the sheriff. I'm Beau Davis, one of his deputies." Beau glanced over her shoulder toward the jail. "If he knew you were coming, I'm surprised he wasn't here to greet the stage."

"Oh, he's not expecting me. Would you have a moment to take me to him?" She flashed him a devastating smile. If he hadn't still been in love with Caro, he might have found himself interested in the beautiful woman.

"I'll be glad to. Let me put my horse away." Turning, he spotted Noah walking toward him.

"Who is she?" Noah reached out his hand, taking Smoke's reins from Beau.

"Don't know. She came on the stage and is looking for Gabe. Have you ever seen her?"

Noah and Gabe grew up together. He knew everyone in Gabe's family, had been to more suppers at their home than his own. Glancing around Beau, he shook his head.

"I've never seen her before. Why don't you take her to Gabe and I'll put Smoke away."

"Thanks, Noah. This ought to be interesting." He walked back up to her. "He's probably in the jail." Taking her elbow, he guided her across the street, then up on the boardwalk, passing the Western Union building and Wild Rose Saloon before stopping outside the jail. "Here we are." Pushing the door open, he stepped aside, allowing her to enter first, then followed, closing the door.

Gabe sat at his desk, a pen in his hand. Looking up, he noticed the woman and stood, moving toward her.

"She got off the stage, Gabe. Said she was looking for you."

Gabe let his gaze wander over her without a hint of recognition. "I'm Sheriff Evans. May I help you?"

She swallowed, showing a bit of uncertainty for the first time. Taking a shaky breath, she nodded. "My name is Nora Evans. I'm your sister."

# Chapter Twelve

Gabe stared at the young woman, working to control his shock. He had three brothers, all with similar features and dark hair. They didn't have a sister. Crossing his arms, he leaned against his desk.

"I don't know what you expect to accomplish, but I don't have a sister."

Nora bit her lower lip, placing a hand on her stomach. Glancing at Beau, who stood a few feet away, she swung her gaze back to Gabe. "Didn't Father send you a telegram?"

Gabe snorted. "Whose father? Yours or mine?"

She blinked a couple times, noticing the hard set of his face. "They're the same person."

"They certainly are not." He pushed away from the desk, taking a step toward her. Gabe towered over Nora. He stood over six feet tall, the same as his brothers and their father. Their mother was also tall, certainly not as short as the woman before him.

Nora lifted her chin, refusing to cower under his glare. "They *are*. I'm sorry if he didn't send a message, but I assure you, I am his daughter."

"Uh, Gabe? Would you like me to leave?" Beau listened to the exchange, growing more uncomfortable with each comment.

"No," Gabe barked back, then took a deep breath. "Miss *Evans* and I are going to the St. James. I'd appreciate it if you'd stay here."

"I need to let Cash know." Beau should be relieving him. Instead, he'd been witness to a conversation he wished he hadn't heard.

"I'll tell him." Grabbing his coat and hat, he looked at Nora, nodding toward the door. "Let's go."

She took a step away, crossing her arms. "I'm not going anywhere with you."

Taking hold of her elbow, he turned her toward the door. "Oh yes, you are, and you'll do it without making a scene."

Beau blew out a relieved breath, glad he didn't have to be anywhere near Gabe right now.

Gabe walked past his stunned wife, Lena, and his business partner, Nick, seeking a private table in the hotel restaurant. Spotting one, he headed toward it, setting his hat on a chair.

"Sit." He pulled out a chair for Nora. Once she sat down, he took a seat next to her, his gaze on Lena and Nick. Seeing the questioning look on their faces, he shook his head slightly.

Nora fiddled with the buttons of her coat, not looking at Gabe. She'd recognized him right away, having seen an old photograph her father had in his wallet. He had one picture of her when she was much younger, her mother at her side. He'd never given them a photograph of himself. Right now, she wished he had.

"Good afternoon, Sheriff Evans. What may I get you?" A young man stood at the table, an anxious look on his face. As one of three owners of the hotel, Gabe had become used to their workers being a little nervous when he appeared.

Gabe looked at Nora. "Have you eaten?"

She shook her head.

"Bring each of us whatever the cook recommends. And coffee."

"Yes, sir."

Waiting until the server left, he leaned forward, placing his arms on the table. "Now, tell me who you really are."

She clasped her hands in her lap, keeping her back straight and chin high as she met his gaze. "My name is Nora Reeser Evans."

His hard gaze didn't waver. "How old are you?"

"Twenty-six, a couple years younger than you."

Gabe's eyes widened before he steeled his features. "How do you know my age?"

"Father told me. I also know of my other brothers, although I've never met them. Mother and Father never allowed me to get too close."

Gabe's anger rose as she told one lie after another. "My mother is Florence Evans. Who is yours?"

Nora pushed aside the ache lodged deep in her heart and cleared her throat. "Her name was Anna Marie Reeser Evans. Our father, Walter Evans, married her right after I was born."

Gabe's nostrils flared as his hand slammed down on the table. "That's a lie. *My* father has one wife. My mother, Florence Evans." He sat back, waiting until the server set down their meals.

"Anything else, Sheriff?"

"No. That will be all." Gabe studied the food, having no desire to eat a bite.

"I'm sorry, Gabe. I know this must be a horrible shock. Believe me, I never would have come to you if Father hadn't assured me he'd let you know about me and my mother." She glanced away, taking a ragged breath, her next words a whisper. "He *promised* me he'd let you know. Then again, he made many promises over the years."

Gabe closed his eyes, praying what she said wasn't true. "Are you saying my father was married to my mother and yours at the same time?"

Licking her lips, she nodded, focusing on her hands in her lap. "At first, my mother didn't know about his other wife, or his children. Neither ever explained what happened, but our neighbor was more than happy to tell me all the details." Lifting her head, she let her gaze meet his. "I'm not sure you want to hear."

Gabe didn't, but that wasn't how he was built. No matter who she turned out to be, he needed to hear the story, decide for himself if it was a lie or the truth.

"Tell me, and don't leave anything out."

An hour later, they still sat in the restaurant, Gabe's head spinning from what Nora told him. If she were to be believed, his father had an affair with her mother not long after his birth, continuing through Nora's birth and those of Gabe's three younger brothers. Walter Evans had married Anna Marie, even though it was illegal. He loved her enough to do what she needed, uncaring if it created dire consequences later.

Their relationship ended with the death of her mother when Nora was fourteen. Almost immediately, Walter enrolled her in a girl's school in Pennsylvania, where she later became a teacher. A few years ago, he provided her an apartment in New York, where she lived a quiet life until confronting their father about his other family. His solution was to send her west to his oldest son, Gabe, her half-brother.

"He made certain I had access to funds, so I won't be asking you for money if that's what worries you."

When her words registered, Gabe's head snapped up. "Money isn't what bothers me. It's the fact my father had two wives, two families for years, and no one knew."

"My mother knew." She shook her head. "I won't pretend to understand it. He promised my mother he would get a divorce. Of course, he never did. He did provide for us, though, for which I'll always be grateful." Glancing up at him, he could see her fighting off the moisture in her eyes.

Gabe could appreciate the brave front Nora tried to present, not wanting her defeated tone to bother him. In his late twenties, he'd been allowed every privilege possible, allowed access to social circles most dreamed of. In the end, he walked away from it all. Nora had been born to the same man, yet her life had been lived in the shadows. Still, the rage he felt toward their father won out over the compassion he knew he should be feeling for the woman sitting next to him.

Standing, Gabe moved behind her chair. "You need to get settled. I'll speak to the concierge about a room in the hotel."

Shock flashed across her face. "Oh, no. Father may have been generous, but I can't waste funds on such an extravagance."

"Don't worry about the cost. My wife and I are two of the owners." He signaled Nora to follow him to the front desk, halting when Bernie Griggs came through the front door, waving a piece of paper.

"Afternoon, Sheriff." Bernie held out the telegram. "Sorry this took so long. Between the stage and mail delivery, I didn't have a chance to get this over to you." He tipped his hat to Nora. "I have to head back, but I'll be there 'til dark if you want to send a reply."

Gabe took a step away, expecting the message to be from Sheriff Sterling in Big Pine. He'd been waiting for any additional information the sheriff had on the Dawson gang. Opening it, he scanned the message, his face tightening. He didn't bother reading it a second time.

"I hope it isn't bad news."

He looked at her, knowing she wasn't at fault for the sins of their father. "It's from Father."

She placed a hand on her stomach, doing her best to ignore the building ball of uncertainty. "What did he say?"

Folding the paper, he stuffed it into a pocket, taking her shoulders, forcing a smile. "Welcome to the family, Nora."

Beau bent over the rifle on the desk, taking his time cleaning it. His revolver would follow, then he'd sit back and wait for Gabe to return. Caleb had stopped by after Mack relieved him, then left for a late dinner. If Gabe still hadn't returned when he was finished, Caleb would take his place in the jail so Beau could relieve Cash. Normally, it would bother him, letting his friend take a double shift. Knowing Cash surveyed the street from inside his wife's shop, Beau didn't feel quite so bad.

Hissed whispers from the back had him sitting up, straining to hear what the two men said. After the effects of the alcohol wore off, they'd been quiet, becoming ideal prisoners. Even so, Beau hoped the circuit judge would arrive soon. The city leaders had discussed the need for having their own judge. The territory had grown, requiring them to wait long periods before the judge made an appearance.

Leaning the rifle against a wall, he slid the revolver from its holster, setting it on the desk. The work relaxed him, even if it didn't clear his mind of Caro. Her admission of wanting more than friendship still sat like a burning ember in his gut. Loving her wasn't the issue. He couldn't imagine ever loving a woman the way he did Caro. Trusting his heart to her again caused a cold chill to wash through him.

He'd been so certain she'd change her mind about traveling to San Francisco and accept his offer of marriage. Caro's refusal had cut through him, as if he'd been impaled with a sword. Her return had strengthened his resolve to never be at the mercy of his heart again.

Beau finished cleaning his gun as the door swung open, a tired Gabe stepping inside. "The prisoners give you any trouble?"

"Nope." Standing, he vacated Gabe's chair, taking one across the desk. "Did you get it all worked out with the woman?"

Gabe let out a deep sigh. "That woman is my sister."

Rubbing a finger across his brow, Beau shook his head. "She told you the truth?"

"It's a long story, but yes. It was confirmed by a telegram from my father."

"Must've been quite a shock." Beau didn't know what else to say.

Dropping into his chair, Gabe scrubbed a hand down his face. "You've no idea. Someday, we'll share a bottle of whiskey and I'll tell you all about it." He glanced at the door as it opened.

"Sorry, Sheriff. Another telegram came for you." Bernie scurried across the floor, holding out the paper.

Gabe read it, scribbled a few words on the back, then handed it back. "Here's the reply, Bernie. Thanks for bringing it over."

"No problem, Sheriff. I'll get this right off."

"I'm headed out to relieve Cash. Anything I should tell him?" Beau asked Gabe the instant Bernie closed the door.

"The message was from Sheriff Sterling. No sign of the Dawsons. The guard and driver on the latest stage between Splendor and Big Pine saw no sign of outlaws. Sterling thinks they left the territory."

Beau's brows drew together. "Not that I'm not grateful, but it's surprising. I don't know that I believe it."

Gabe thought about the odds, wondering what would cause them to ignore a town such as Splendor. It was no secret the bank held a good deal of money due to the success of several ranches, including Redemption's Edge. "Could be they wanted to avoid the harsh winter. Might have lost some men. Or they may have found better opportunities in Colorado, Wyoming, or even Utah."

"Sterling could be wrong. They may be holed up somewhere, waiting until the time is right."

Gabe sat back, crossing his arms. "That's why I'm going to have you and the others stay in place a few more days. We can't afford to be caught unaware."

Beau pushed up, slipping on his jacket and hat. "I'm headed out."

Beau felt the chill rush through him the instant he stepped outside. The temperature dropped as the sun began its descent behind the western hills. Soft rain fell, turning to flakes of snow before reaching the ground. The ground began to freeze, turning mushy ruts into deep, treacherous channels of hardened mud.

Pulling up the collar of his coat, he walked down the boardwalk toward the bank, his steps faltering when he saw Caro coming toward him. She looked strong and confident handling the lines of the wagon. He stepped to the edge of the walkway, holding up a hand, surprised when she saw it and brought the wagon to a stop.

Still holding the lines, she rested her hands on her lap, a bland expression on her face when she looked at him. "Did you want something?"

Beau walked toward her, not liking the strain on her face she tried to hide. "I didn't have a chance to thank you for taking the time to go to the river with me."

Caro shrugged, making no further effort to respond. Swiping a hand across her forehead, she tucked a strand of hair behind her ear. Tightening her grip on the lines, she turned away from him.

"Caro, wait." He could see her struggle, knowing she had no desire to be around him.

Letting out a breath, she glanced at him. "What?"

"If you ever need my help—"

"I won't. If you're finished, I need to get the wagon back to Noah." She waited a second, then slapped the lines, moving away from him.

Beau's hands slipped into his pockets, regret enveloping him, making it hard to breathe. Her reaction surprised him. This time, *he'd* been the one to turn *her* away. So why did he feel as if he'd tossed aside all that was important in his life?

The answer shouldn't have been a mystery. No matter how much he wanted to deny it, the only woman he wanted was Caro. There'd never be another, and he'd spurned her. Not once, but twice since her return to Splendor. He wondered if he'd made a mistake not giving her a second chance. If he could just believe she returned because of him, still loved him, and planned to stay. But he couldn't be certain and didn't want to consider his reaction if he were wrong a second time.

"About time you came to relieve me."

Beau looked up to see Cash standing outside Allie's shop. "Got a little delayed."

"Gabe came by and told me. Who was the woman with him?"

A grim smile turned up the corners of Beau's mouth. "His sister."

"Sister? I didn't know Gabe had a sister."

"Neither did he."

# Chapter Thirteen

Caro slipped into the tub, letting the warm water soothe her aching muscles. They'd made considerable progress, Merritt and Gus finishing the front porch. Tomorrow, they'd start inside. She felt a sense of accomplishment at her part in it. The difficulty had nothing to do with the work itself. The problem had been focusing after Beau left, shattering her hopes of reconciling their differences.

She'd done her best to push the disappointment aside. His request they be friends weighed heavily. It had been reasonable, all he could give her, yet was so much less than she wanted. Ignoring his offer had been petty and immature, haunting her all the way back to town. She could at least offer him something.

After leaving the wagon with Noah, she'd stopped by the Western Union office, sending a telegram to Allan Pinkerton. It pushed their friendship, and he could refuse, but she wanted to know who had hired the agency to locate Beau. She doubted Allan knew the true reason his client wanted to find him. A shrewd and cunning man,

Pinkerton would refuse work inconsistent with his beliefs and values.

"Mrs. Iverson. I have your supper."

Sighing, she stood, letting the water drip off her as she stepped onto the carpet and grabbed a towel. "Just a moment."

"Take your time," the cheery female voice responded.

Drying, she tossed the towel aside, slipped into a wrapper, then opened the door. "Please, come in." Her stomach growled as the rich aroma of cooked meat assaulted her.

The young woman set the tray down, then turned to leave. "Please, let me know if you need anything else."

"Thank you." Caro nodded, closing the door. After returning to the hotel, she was too tired to clean up, dress for supper, then sit alone at a table in the restaurant, eating in silence.

Placing the tray on the bed, she sat cross-legged, removing the cover. Picking up her fork, Caro took a bite, chewing slowly, pushing away the hurt from today. As she forked another piece of meat, a knock stopped her. Moving off the bed, she opened the door a crack, expecting to see the same young woman.

"Did you forget..." The words died on her lips. Beau stood in the hall, his fingers worrying the brim of his hat. The shock was so great, she found herself unable to move or talk.

"I wondered if you might have a few minutes to talk."

She stared at him, surprised and unsure of what to do. Men did not come to the room of a single woman, even if she were a widow. They'd meet in the lobby or restaurant, never alone. It simply wasn't done, yet here he was. She pulled the door wide, motioning him inside, bracing herself for whatever he might have to say.

Standing in the hall, Beau knew it was a mistake to come here, would understand if she refused to see him. It didn't stop him from knocking, hoping for a different response. He hadn't expected her to open the door clothed only in a thin wrapper that clung to every curve, her blonde hair cascading around her shoulders, her lips parted in disbelief. Stifling a groan had been almost impossible.

Reasonable thought eluded Beau when she motioned him inside. When the door clicked shut, he set his hat on a table, turning toward her.

Caro kept her hands clasped in front of her, tilting her head to the side. "Would you like to sit down?" She indicated a chair across the room.

Beau swallowed the doubt, shaking his head. "No. I'd better stand."

He'd been near the bank, keeping watch, when Gabe walked up. For reasons he didn't share, Gabe volunteered to take Beau's place for a couple hours. At first, he'd hesitated, knowing Gabe had other issues to deal with, then relented when his boss revealed he needed time to clear his head.

Beau had been left with little to do, except perhaps see the one person he couldn't push from his mind. He'd seen Caro return to the hotel after leaving the wagon with Noah, the now familiar ache growing in his chest as she vanished inside.

Walking into Suzanne's, he'd eaten little of the food she placed before him, unable to reconcile the quarrel he and Caro had earlier. If Beau could roll back time, he'd respond differently to her question about his true reason for wanting to see her. He'd hoped to explain how much he still cared about her and cherished her friendship. He'd been honest when he said friendship was the best he could offer...for now. It didn't mean he couldn't offer more at some point. He just needed time. No matter what had happened, he still loved her, wanted to marry her.

Pushing the emotion aside, Beau had to be certain she planned to stay in Splendor, build a life here because she wanted to, not because she thought it would mend the rift between them. Caro had to desire a life in the growing frontier town as much as he did. Beau didn't want to be the only reason she returned. If missing him was why she'd come back, he feared even his love wouldn't be strong enough to make her stay. Then he'd go through losing her all over again.

He'd come here to explain. Standing before her, his gaze taking in her familiar curves, seeing the hope on her face, he found it hard to form a coherent sentence.

Without thought, he stepped closer and reached out, running a hand down her arm, letting it stop at her wrist, drawing her to him.

"Beau?" The question was no more than a whisper, perhaps a plea, although she made no attempt to resist.

Inches apart, his other hand stroked her cheek, her wary eyes widening, her lips parting. Lowering his head, praying she wouldn't push him away, he brushed his mouth across hers, feeling an immediate jolt. It had always been this way with Caro. He let the passion flare, losing himself in what he felt for this woman.

Pulling back on a ragged breath, he waited until she opened her eyes. "There's so much I want to say, but not this way, not here. I shouldn't have come."

She placed a finger across his lips. "Shhh. We'll have more than enough time to talk." Wrapping her arms around his neck, she drew him down, their lips touching before he took control, settling his mouth over hers in a heated assault.

All the reasons they shouldn't be doing this fled as Beau aligned his body with hers, pulling her close. He'd missed this, missed her. His hands roamed intimately over the familiar curves, his body throbbing. Moving her backward, he slowly eased her down onto the bed, lying beside her as he slipped the wrap off her shoulders and down her arms. Caressing her, his lips trailing down her neck, he kissed the hollow at the base of her throat, smiling as she arched into him.

"Beau..." She breathed out as his kisses became more urgent.

Raising his head, Beau gazed into her eyes, his breath hitching at the desire he saw. "Do you want me to stop?" He prayed she didn't, knowing he would if she asked.

Shaking her head, she moved her hands between them, releasing the buttons of his shirt.

"Don't you dare," she breathed out as she opened his shirt, spreading it wide. "I won't survive if you stop."

Although her answer was what he'd hoped to hear, a measure of guilt rested in his gut. A nagging voice sounded in his ear, telling him to stop.

Shaking off the niggling of doubt, focusing on his desire for Caro, a soft smile curved his lips as he captured her mouth again. Groaning as her small hands explored his chest, then moved lower, all he could think about was the woman in his arms and how much he loved her.

"Can you stay?" Her soft breath tickled the hairs on his chest as he stroked her back.

A thread of regret washed over him. "Not tonight. Gabe offered to take my place on watch for a few hours. It was an impulse coming up here to talk with you."

Her fingers stilled on his chest, remembering his words about needing to talk. She'd ignored him. Doubt now took hold, making her wonder if she'd made a mistake in not hearing what he wanted to say before they'd made love.

She pushed up, her concerned eyes locking with his. "Do you want to talk now?"

He drew in a deep breath, nodding. Lifting so his back rested against the wall, he settled an arm across her shoulders, bringing her down so her head rested on his shoulder.

"I didn't like the way today ended between us. I'd hoped by coming up here, maybe we could put aside what happened in the past." He sighed. "I'm not your enemy, Caro."

Her chest tightened. "What are you?"

"Your friend. I'll always be your friend."

"Friends." The word pushed through her lips, understanding gradually hitting her. She looked away, turning her back to him, and grabbed her wrapper. "This wasn't supposed to happen, was it?" Standing, she slipped on the sheer fabric, crossing her arms to hold the front closed, stepping away from the bed.

Climbing off the bed, he grabbed his shirt, unable to stop the pain he'd caused by letting his desire rule him. Beau knew his love for her was real, a throbbing need he couldn't escape. What he didn't know was if he could ever believe she came here to stay, be able to find happiness with him in a wild frontier town.

He'd come here to talk, to mend their friendship, not make love. Taking a step closer, he reached out, caressing her cheek. "No, it wasn't."

"I see." Her voice broke, her hand fisting at her mouth as the reality of what they'd done crashed around her. The passion she'd felt minutes before dissolved as anger swelled. Whipping around to face him, she took a step forward. "It's time for you to leave." Picking up his hat, she tossed it at him before walking to the door.

"Don't do this, Caro. Let me explain."

She couldn't look at him as she gripped the knob. "There's nothing further to say."

"There's a lot to say if you'd just let me explain."

She ignored the plea in his voice, opening the door a crack. "Get out, Beau."

"At least listen to me."

"I've listened enough. You used me." She closed her eyes, pulling the door wide.

"That's *not* what happened."

"Do you love me?" she challenged.

"You know I do."

"Do you still want to marry me?"

His jaw clenched, a muscle in his neck pulsing. Looking down at the hat in his hand, he shook his head. "I wish I could say otherwise, but I just don't know."

She let out a slow breath, the pain of his confession more than she could endure. He loved her, but no longer wanted her as his wife. "It's best if you leave."

He couldn't get his feet to move as he studied her face, guilt overwhelming him at the pain and disappointment he saw there. "Caro, you need to understand why I'm not ready to offer marriage again."

Closing her eyes, she shook her head. "Please. Just go."

It couldn't have hurt more if she'd run him through with a sword. Letting out a shaky breath, he settled his hat on his head. "I'm sorry."

Stepping into the hall, he turned at the sound of the door closing behind him. She'd made no secret of how she felt, what she wanted from him. He'd been the worst kind of rake, knowing he hadn't made a decision about their future, yet allowing himself to come to her room, lose control, and take what he needed. Now she might never give him a chance to explain.

Walking down the hall, he shook his head. One more regret when it came to Caro.

Sitting on the edge of the bed, Caro covered her face with both hands. It had been over an hour since she'd insisted he leave, refusing to hear his excuses. She berated herself for her rash actions.

If only she hadn't been so upset, he might still be with her, explaining how he could still love her, yet no longer want her for his wife. His reasons might have made sense, if only she'd listened.

Caro knew it wasn't right to blame him for what happened. She'd ignored the warning in her head when he'd wanted to back away and talk. It had been too long, her need blinding her to the consequences of their actions. She'd never been a woman to make rash decisions. Then she'd fallen in love with Beau.

He made her feel beautiful without pampering her, seeing her as an equal, not a woman to be placed on a pedestal. Her father and late husband had never seen her as anything more than an extension of themselves. Unlike them, Beau never tried to stop her from voicing her opinions on matters of money, politics, or other issues much of society believed could only be discussed intelligently by men. He'd treated her as an intelligent, resourceful woman, wanting her for his wife.

She'd thrown it back at him, too eager to follow her own dreams. It had been the worst mistake of her life. It had taken time and being miles apart for her to realize only one dream mattered—being with Beau.

Groaning, she stood and walked to the window, pulling back the curtain. Her breath faltered when she saw Beau leaning against the wall of the bank. Even in the dark, she could see the determined look on his face as his gaze moved up the street, then back down. She didn't know what he looked for or why Gabe wanted him to take that position all night, but knew it had to be important. Beau would always do what was required to protect the people of Splendor.

Knowing there was nothing more she could do tonight, Caro walked to the wardrobe, replacing the wrapper with her nightgown. Turning down the light, she slipped under the covers. She stared at the ceiling, pushing aside the image of how Beau had held her in this same bed a couple hours before.

Taking a deep breath, she forced herself to remember his comments before she'd left him standing alone in the hall. He'd been firm, admitting he still loved her.

Closing her eyes, she clutched the blanket to her chest, repeating his words over and over, imprinting them on her heart. He might not want to marry her now, but he still loved her. The thought gave her hope, making her realize she might still have a chance to change his thoughts about marriage.

She'd give him what he seemed to need— time.

There was still much to do to finish her house. She'd hoped Beau would be by her side. Tonight, those hopes had been dashed.

For now, Caro would work alongside Merritt and Gus, possibly hire a couple others. She'd already made the decision her life in San Francisco ended with her return to Splendor. Whether or not Beau ever changed his mind, she'd stay, build her life here, and not look back.

# Chapter Fourteen

Dutch sat at the front window of the restaurant in the boardinghouse, sipping coffee, watching snow blanket the town. It had been this way for two days. As was the case in some eastern cities, the weather did nothing to change the pace of the townsfolk. Wagons still rolled down the street, the lumber mill filled orders, and Noah worked in his livery and blacksmith shop. People shuffled in and out of stores, the stage continued to arrive and leave, and Gabe's deputies kept the town safe. Dutch hadn't been in a place he enjoyed this much in a long time.

He chuckled, watching a group of young boys go at each other in an impromptu snowball fight, remembering when he'd done the same at their age.

"Mind if I join you?" Beau stood with his hand on the chair next to Dutch.

"Be my guest."

Beau sat down, following Dutch's gaze. "There are times I wish I could roll back time and be young again."

Dutch nodded. "Don't we all."

"Breakfast, Beau?" He looked up as Suzanne placed a cup of coffee in front of him.

"Whatever you have will be fine."

"Bacon, eggs, potatoes..."

"Sounds good, Suzanne. Thanks." He picked up the cup, blowing across the top, then took a sip. "Any word from Pinkerton?"

"Nothing other than he doesn't have another assignment and wants me to stay here until contacted." Shifting, he looked at Beau. "Wish I had more for you, but Allan isn't sharing information on who retained my services."

"It's what I expected."

"He may relent, especially if he gets the sense the client has a nefarious reason for finding you." Dutch rested his arms on the table, leaning forward. "By the time he'd learn of their reasons, though, it might be too late."

Beau's eyes narrowed. "What do you mean?"

Dutch waited until Suzanne set down Beau's plate, then lowered his voice. "You already said your family knows where you are and there's no one else you can think of who'd be trying to track you down, including a former lover, right?"

Beau nodded. Although he'd been with many women, none became important to him. The only woman he'd describe as a lover, someone he'd been serious about, lived in the hotel a few doors away. After the other night, he wasn't certain he'd use the word *former* to describe Caro. He didn't know *how* to describe her.

Dutch crossed his arms, leaning back. "That leaves someone looking to find you for other reasons. I have to wonder what those reasons are."

Beau thought of Caro and how she believed the same. She'd mentioned enemies he may have made during his days as a bounty hunter with Cash.

"I used to be a bounty hunter."

Dutch sat up straighter. "I haven't heard much about families of outlaws tracking someone down through Pinkerton, but the idea makes sense. Any you can think of who threatened you?"

Beau ran a hand through his hair, trying to recall the men he'd hunted. It wasn't a big number compared to more notable bounty hunters. Still, the men he brought in—alive or dead—probably had family. The truth was, he'd never thought about it. He slipped the reward money into his pocket, then rode off to find the next outlaw. Coming to Splendor had broken the pattern.

"I'm sure there must be a number of people who'd like to see me dead." He offered Dutch a wry grin. "It's never easy for family to admit their kin went bad." Looking out the front window, Beau tried to go through the people he'd tracked down, shaking his head. "I'm not saying there aren't any, but I can't think of anyone in particular."

Dutch stood, reaching into his pocket to pull out his money. Tossing it on the table, he grabbed his hat. "You think about it. Give me whatever you can and I'll go back to Pinkerton."

Their discussion left Beau with more than he expected. The same as Dutch, Caro worried someone from his past wanted revenge. Beau couldn't ignore the possibility.

Standing, he paid for his meal, then stepped outside, looking down the street where Cash stood outside the bank. In a couple hours, he'd take his place. In the meantime, Beau would create a list and run it by Cash. The results might surprise him. Revenge was a strange thing. You might never know who sought vengeance—until it was too late.

Caro brushed her dust-encrusted hands down her dress, stepping back to admire the repairs she helped make in an upstairs bedroom. She'd wanted to stay inside her warm room at the hotel, letting Merritt and Gus work alone in the freezing weather. Her indecision lasted a few seconds before she slipped into what had become

198

her work dress, then put on the warm boots purchased at Petermann's general store.

Noah couldn't hide his shock when she'd rushed into the blacksmith shop, brushing off the snow. He'd tried to talk her out of making the trip, concerned the weather could turn into a blizzard without warning. Noah had seen it over and over during his time in Montana. She brushed off his concerns, although she did agree to ride her horse rather than take the wagon, letting Noah's helper, Toby Archer, accompany her. Noah told her she could either accept Toby's help or he'd find Beau. Poor Toby hadn't known what to expect, but got right to work, not stopping until she insisted they break to eat.

Not long after they arrived at the house, the weather had cleared, the temperature warming enough to make the ride back to town easier. Exhausted, she returned her horse to the livery, wanting nothing more than a hot bath and bed. Food had become secondary, many of her clothes hanging loose on her body. She didn't care. The joy she got from repairing her house overshadowed everything else, except her regrets over Beau.

Caro pulled her coat tight around her body as she walked across the street, stepping onto the boardwalk. Tomorrow was Thanksgiving. She'd agreed to ride to the Pelletier ranch with Cash and Allie, so there'd be no time to work on the house. Caro couldn't consider attending a supper without bringing something. Opening the door to the boardinghouse, she spotted Suzanne.

"You didn't go out to the house in this weather, did you?" Suzanne walked up to her, crossing her arms.

Caro smiled. "The work needs to get done. Noah insisted Toby ride out with me, so it wasn't bad. He worked all day and never complained."

"Allie mentioned you're going to the Pelletier's tomorrow with her and Cash."

"That's the reason I'm here. I can't go out there without bringing something."

Suzanne laughed. "Of course you can, but I know how you feel. I'm making extra pies."

"Perfect. I'd like two. May I take them now?"

"Let me wrap them. I'll be right back."

Caro stood in the small alcove to the side, gazing out the window as she waited. There was so much to do on the house, she almost hated taking a day off for a social visit. She smiled, remembering how supper with friends used to be the most important part of her day, something to look forward to. Given the life she'd led, this was a refreshing change.

"Mrs. Iverson?"

Turning toward the entry, she saw Bernie Griggs walking toward her.

"Good evening, Mr. Griggs. Were you looking for me?"

Reaching into his coat, he pulled out a telegram. "I almost took this to the hotel, but Noah came by to send a telegram and told me you'd come in here to see Suzanne. Thought you'd want this."

Taking it, she quickly read the message, her eyes growing wide.

"I hope it's good news."

Nodding, she looked up. "It very well could be."

"Well, if you'll excuse me, I need to get back to the office." He hurried out, leaving her to ponder what to do with the information she'd received.

"Here you are." Suzanne handed her the wrapped pies. "I'll put it on your monthly tab, Caro. I have more pies to make before the supper rush." She hurried back to the kitchen.

"Thank you, Suzanne." Her mind had already gone elsewhere. Perhaps it would be best to tell Gabe what she'd learned, instead of trying to have a conversation with Beau. As exhausted as she felt, she simply didn't have the strength to talk with him right now.

Clutching the message in her hand, she walked outside and into the frosty air, glad the snow had stopped. Traffic on the street had dwindled to a few wagons and men on horseback. Oil lamps began to shine through several windows, giving the town a warm feeling.

Crossing to the other side, she stepped onto the boardwalk and pushed the door to the jail open, coming to a stop. The first voice she heard belonged to Beau. She did not want to see him. Caro wanted to share the contents of the message with Gabe, then leave.

"Good evening, Caro." Gabe stood as Beau turned to face her, his features guarded.

Ignoring him, she turned her attention to Gabe. "I wonder if you'd have a moment to speak with me?"

"Of course. Please, sit down." He motioned to a chair next to where Beau stood.

"Alone."

Beau's expression didn't change as he settled his hat back on his head. "I need to get going." He didn't acknowledge Caro as he stepped around her, closing the door as he left.

She wished his actions didn't bother her, but they did. Then again, he probably thought her rude for excluding him from the conversation. No matter what happened between them, it never ended well.

"You wanted to see me, Caro?"

She turned to see Gabe staring at her, his right brow raised a fraction. "Yes. A telegram came for me today. I thought you'd be interested in reading it." Handing the message to him, she took a seat, folding her hands in her lap.

His eyes widened a little as he read the contents. "I didn't realize you knew Allan Pinkerton."

"My late husband and Allan were friends. I wasn't sure he'd respond to me as we'd only met a few times."

"Does Beau know you sent Pinkerton an inquiry?"

"No, and I'd rather he didn't. We're, um...not getting along too well right now." She lowered her gaze to her lap, hoping he didn't ask any other questions about their relationship.

Gabe blew out a breath. "I see." He stroked his chin, setting the telegram down. "And how do you suggest I explain to Beau how I got this information?"

"Well...I hadn't thought about it." She glanced up at him, a mischievous smile curving her lips. "Have *you* ever met Allan?"

Without thought, he nodded, then stared at her. "Just once. He probably doesn't even remember. So no, I won't tell Beau I sent the inquiry."

"What about Nick or Lena?"

He cocked his head in question.

"Maybe one of them knows Allan."

Gabe shook his head, his lips twisting into a wry grin. "I don't think so." Sitting down, he rubbed the back of his neck. "I'll simply leave out how I received the information, tell him my source is confidential."

"He's smart. He'll figure it out."

Gabe chuckled. "Of course he will. The point is, he'll be focused on the name in the telegram. He might ask you at some point. It will be up to you how to respond, Caro."

She nodded, swallowing the slight sense of dread at Beau confronting her on it. "Do you recognize the name?"

"No. Maybe Beau won't, either. There's only one way to find out, and I'd rather learn the answer as soon as possible." Standing, he picked up the message, handing it back to Caro. "No sense having a telegram addressed to you on me."

Caro stood, a grateful smile on her lips. "Thank you, Gabe."

Walking up to her, he placed a hand on her shoulder. They'd grown up together in New York. At one point, their affluent families believed they might eventually marry. When he left to join the Union Army, she'd met her future husband, marrying him while Gabe was still fighting the war.

"Are you all right?"

Letting out a weary sigh, she nodded. "I will be. The house keeps me busy." Her mouth curved into a smile as she turned her face up to his. "I find there's a lot of joy in working with my hands."

His hand dropped on a deep laugh. "Ah, Caro. What would your parents say if they saw you now?"

Her smile broadened. "Probably the same as your parents if they saw you wearing guns and a star."

Nodding, he opened the door for her. "The difference is we each have the means to live the same as our parents. Instead, both of us have chosen to make a life in Splendor."

Walking past him into the chilly night air, she breathed deeply. "I do believe you are right, Gabe, and I'm certain we've made the right choice."

"Edmond Eldridge? No, I don't know the man. Why?"

Gabe had found Beau next door in the Wild Rose Saloon, one of two Nick, Lena, and Gabe owned. Sitting down, he'd mentioned the name, hoping for recognition.

Gabe sat back, crossing his arms. "He's the client who hired Pinkerton to find you."

Beau tossed back the rest of his whiskey, his brows knitting together. "Edmond Eldridge..." He searched his memory, a jolt of recognition passing through him. Letting out a mumbled curse, he leaned forward. "Percy Eldridge," he breathed out, regret building in his chest. "I never thought I'd say that name out loud again."

"Who is he?" Gabe signaled for the bartender to bring him a glass.

Beau shook his head, rubbing a hand across his brow. "A lieutenant who served under me. A good man—until he lost his mind one day before a battle. Accused men of desertion and started executing them."

Gabe swore, shaking his head. "Without a hearing?"

Beau's haunted gaze met his. "Without anything. If I hadn't stumbled onto them, he would have shot them all." He blew out a breath, pouring another whiskey from the bottle on the table. "He refused my order to lower his weapon. I had no choice but to shoot him."

Gabe picked up the bottle, filled his glass, then took a long swallow, letting the liquid burn down his throat. "What happened afterward?"

"I was cleared of any charges. The men testified for me. A sergeant who wandered onto the scene after I shot Eldridge testified he thought I'd done it out of anger, but no one believed him. My history with the men was too solid." He rolled the glass between his fingers. "I thought it was all behind me."

"If this information is correct, it's far from behind you. Edmond must be a relative. Father, brother, uncle…"

Beau snorted. "No doubt out for revenge."

Gabe filled his glass a second time, holding it to his lips, but not drinking. "Do you recall where Eldridge was from?"

Pinching the bridge of his nose, Beau shook his head. "Tennessee…Louisiana…" Staring at his empty glass, he tried to remember conversations he had with the man. "Cotton. He told me they raised cotton." Suddenly, his brows shot up. "Alabama."

Gabe tipped the glass back, swallowing the contents. Setting it down, a thin smile formed on his lips. "I believe Allan Pinkerton just got himself a new client."

# Chapter Fifteen

"Sorry I'm late." Caro's warm breath formed a white cloud as she stopped next to the wagon Cash parked outside Allie's dress shop. Handing him two pies, she tightened her coat around her.

"You aren't late." Cash pulled out his pocket watch. "By my calculations, you're early." He winked at her, then continued loading blankets and food into the wagon. "Allie is almost ready. Why don't you go inside and wait there? No sense standing in the cold."

"I believe I will." She dashed inside, closing the door behind her, spotting Allie at the counter. "You aren't working, are you?"

"Heavens no." Tucking some fabric into a satchel, she closed it, then slipped into her coat. "Rachel wanted me to bring some material for shirts. Baby Patrick is growing so fast she can't keep enough of them. Of course, he's not a baby any longer."

"No, not at all. And now he'll have a baby brother or sister." She'd been happy when she heard the news Rachel and Ginny were both expecting. Caro was happy for them, but today, for no apparent reason, a wave of sadness spread through her.

"I'm ready." Allie filled her arms, then walked to the door, pulling it open. "Oh good. Beau is here."

Caro had been following Allie outside, coming to a halt at hearing his name. "Beau?"

Allie looked at her. "He's coming with us. The conversation is so much more entertaining when Cash and Beau are together."

"I'm sure," Caro mumbled, moving slowly toward the wagon.

If Allie noticed the sarcasm in her voice, she didn't react. "Good morning, Beau. I'm so glad you're coming with us."

Beau turned away from Cash, offering Allie a warm smile. "Good morn…" The greeting died on his lips when he saw Caro.

"Caro is coming with us. Isn't that wonderful?" Allie ignored the obvious tension between the two, glancing at Cash. "Is everything ready?"

"It is." He helped his wife onto the wagon, then turned toward Caro. "May I?"

"I'll help her up." Beau's deep voice caught Caro off guard, causing her to swivel, almost plowing into him as he stepped behind her. "Easy." Placing his hands on her shoulders, he steadied her, then dropped his hold and leaned forward, whispering in her ear. "Appears we're going to be riding together. Might as well do our best to be civil."

Gritting her teeth, she sent him a too sweet smile. "It's wonderful to see you again. I'm so looking forward to today."

He chuckled at the obvious insincerity, then nodded toward the wagon. "Let's get you settled."

Allie had been right. As uncomfortable as Caro was sitting next to Beau, the trip had been entertaining. The two normally subdued men opened up when around each other, regaling the women with stories of their escapades as bounty hunters, leaving out any upsetting details. Caro found herself wishing she could start over with Beau without the mistakes she'd made or the hurt she'd caused. The more he and Cash joked, the more her regret grew.

Supper had been a boisterous affair. Several of the ranch hands joined the crowd, along with several friends from town. Moments before Rachel and Ginny set the food on the table, Gabe and Lena arrived. Mack and Caleb had persuaded him to accept the Pelletier's invitation, leaving the town in their capable hands. The rowdy cowhands arrested for being drunk and disorderly had paid a fine and been released, the bartender deciding not to press charges. No one knew where they were now, except they'd hightailed it out of Splendor as soon as they stepped out of the jail.

After supper, most everyone stayed, mingling and taking the time to catch up. The constant work, whether by farmer, ranchers, or those in town, made it difficult to take time away to relax and simply enjoy the company of others. Caro even had a chance to speak with Matthew and Nolen Volker, the two young men who'd ridden to her place looking for work. They now worked for Dax and Luke and were happy to be here, but made it clear they'd be willing to move to her place if she needed them.

The return trip to town was much more subdued than the ride out. She and Beau had kept distance between themselves during supper, then spoke little as they sat side by side in the wagon on the way home. She felt as if they were polite acquaintances rather than two people who once loved each other.

Entering town, Cash stopped the wagon in front of Allie's shop. They lived in an apartment upstairs with plans to build a home in the future. Cash already owned the land, although neither seemed in a hurry to leave the convenience of living in town.

Beau helped Caro down. "I'll walk you back to the hotel."

She shook her head. "That's not necess—"

She hadn't finished when shouts had them all turning. Caleb came running up, stopping beside them.

"Sorry to bust in on your time off, but I was about ready to ride out to find Gabe."

"What is it, Caleb?" Beau took a step away from Caro, wishing he had a few more minutes with her. Even though they'd spoken little, being near her brought him a sense of peace he found around no one else.

"Sheriff Sterling sent an urgent message for Gabe. The Dawson gang robbed the bank in Big Pine as they were closing last night. Cleaned it out and took off."

"Anyone killed?" Cash asked.

Caleb shook his head. "He didn't say. Sterling warns us to be on guard."

Cash turned to Allie. "Until we know what's happening, I want you to get inside and stay there."

"But, Cash—"

"Don't argue with me on this. We'll meet with Gabe and decide how to deal with the Dawsons if they ride into town. I need to know you're safe until we figure it out." Kissing her, he turned back to Caleb. "Gabe is on his way back. Beau and I will meet you at the jail."

Beau felt a hand on his arm and turned to face Caro. "What is it, Beau?"

He looked at Cash. "I'll be there in a few minutes. I'm going to walk Caro back to the hotel." Slipping her arm through his, he escorted her across the street and up the steps to the entrance of the St. James. Opening the door, he felt the immediate rush of heat from the large hearth in the foyer. Walking toward it, he withdrew her arm from his.

"Thank you, but there was no need for you to bring me back, Beau. You're needed at the jail."

Keeping his arms at his sides, he stared down at her for several long moments, his face a mask. "I didn't have a chance to thank you for finding out about Edmond Eldridge."

Her eyes widened. "But I—"

He held up a hand, stopping her. "Don't even begin to deny you weren't the one who contacted Pinkerton. We both know you're a terrible liar."

She bit her bottom lip, hiding a grin. "All right. I hope it was helpful."

His eyes softened. "More than you know."

She drew in a breath. "Well, then..."

"There's something else I want to say, although I know I have no right."

Caro cocked her head to one side, her brows drawing together. "What is it?"

"You heard what Caleb said. The Dawson gang is a serious threat. Louis and Clem are the men who shot Bull and Noah. We expect them to try to hit the bank here." He glanced around the hotel lobby, lowering his voice. "I'm asking you to stay in town and inside the hotel for a few days."

His concern touched her, but she had responsibilities. "Beau, I have a house to finish and two men who work for me. I can't leave them out there to wonder where I am."

"I'll either send someone to let them know what's going on or ride out myself. I just want to know you're safe." He glanced away, not wanting her to see the true depth of his unease.

"I suppose one more day in town will be all right, but I can't promise anything beyond that. I'll ask Noah if Toby can ride out and talk to Merritt and Gus."

Beau let out a breath, surprised at the relief he felt. "Good." He continued to watch her, wanting to lean down and capture her lips, knowing he couldn't. "I'd better get to the jail." After one last look, he turned to leave.

"Beau?"

Glancing over his shoulder, he lifted a brow at the familiar jolt of his name on her lips. "Yes?"

"Thank you."

A snowstorm raged through town that night and the following day, prohibiting most travel in Splendor. Businesses stayed open for the hardiest customers, but for most, life within town had slowed to a crawl.

"The weather may work in our favor, Gabe." Beau closed the door to the jail, removing his hat and slapping it against his thigh.

The sheriff stood at the window, watching the storm worsen, the wind whipping the flakes in all directions. "I can't imagine the Dawsons braving the weather to ride this way. My guess is they've found a place to hide until it clears."

"How certain are you they'll ride this way?" Hanging his coat on a hook, Beau walked to the stove and poured a cup of coffee.

Turning from the window, Gabe paced to his desk, pushing aside the wanted posters he'd been studying. "I'd say it's a safe bet they will end up in Splendor. We have profitable businesses and ranches, and only one bank. The weather will slow them down some, but they'll show up. I'm certain of it."

"Do Noah and Bull know?"

"I spoke with them at Thanksgiving supper. Since Louis and Clem were the ones who shot them, they deserve to know they might be returning. We could use their skills, although I hate putting them in danger."

"Do you think you could keep them out of it?"

Gabe blew out a weary breath. "Only if we can capture the outlaws before Bull or Noah know what's happening." Sitting down, he rested his arms on the desk. "I heard back from Pinkerton this morning. He agreed to take me on as a client and get more information on Edmond Eldridge. It could be days or weeks before I hear back from him."

"It's a start, and I appreciate it." Beau thought of Caro and how she'd been the one to contact Allan Pinkerton, setting all this in motion.

He'd spoken to Noah earlier, learning Caro had stayed in town. Even with the weather, Toby hadn't hesitated to ride out, letting Merritt and Gus know she wouldn't be coming out today. He'd ridden back, surprising Beau with the news they were digging a root cellar during the snowstorm. If that's what Caro wanted, so be it.

"As far as the Dawsons, all we can do is keep vigilant and protect the bank."

Beau's attention switched back to Gabe. "What do you want us to do?"

"Two deputies inside the bank from the time it opens until Clausen locks it up."

"And at night?"

Gabe rubbed his brow. "One man inside at night. Clausen had a lot of work done after the robbery attempt a few years ago. The front and back doors have locks and bars. If they get inside, he installed two sets of bars between the tellers and the safe as a precaution. It would take nitroglycerine to open the safe Clausen had ordered from back east. Nitro isn't easy to get, and it's dangerous to transport and use."

Beau chuckled. "You're saying they'll attack during the day."

Gabe nodded. "If they know anything about the Splendor bank, they'll rob it when it's open. If they plan to surprise us, they'll strike soon."

"How's that, Merritt?" Gus stood back, his back stiff and body shaking with the chill. They'd worked all day on the root cellar, ignoring the cold.

Merritt climbed up the ladder, looking back down into the hole. "Should be plenty big enough. We'll install a door tomorrow."

"It'll be nice to work inside again." Gus rubbed his hands together, blowing on them. "Are we done for the day?"

Merritt grabbed the pick and shovel. "Let's get a fire going in the barn. We'll eat and bunk down early."

Gus nodded. "I'll get the wood."

The distant sound of pounding hooves came from the direction of the trail. Merritt set the tools down, facing the two men as they reined their horses to a stop a few feet away, both glancing around. Without preamble, one of the men stared down at Merritt.

"We're looking for the Davis ranch."

Gus stood next to his brother, crossing his arms, his gaze narrowing on the men who appeared to be just a few years younger than them. "You talking about Beau Davis, the deputy?"

"That's him. Is this his place?"

Merritt stepped forward. "Nope. It's the Iverson property. Don't think we've met before. You boys have names?"

The two men looked at each other. "I'm John Smith. This is my brother, Joe."

"John and Joe Smith, huh?" Merritt couldn't hide his skepticism. "Where you from?"

"Here and there. Born in Alabama." John shifted in the saddle, his eyes darting between Merritt and Gus.

"I'm Merritt Teal, and this is my brother, Gus."

John nodded at them. "Is the Davis place close?"

Something about the look of the Smith brothers bothered Gus. They looked as if they hadn't eaten in days. "Go back to the trail and ride west. It's a couple miles down, but he's not there. He owns the land, but hasn't built the house. He lives in town."

John mumbled a curse. The sky had started to darken, snow beginning to fall again. "Guess we got some wrong information. We heard he was looking for workers."

"Mrs. Iverson is more likely to have work than Davis. We don't know when she'll be back."

John nodded, tired eyes meeting his brother's. "Guess we'd better get going then."

"You boys got a place to go?" Merritt wasn't sure why he asked. Something about them reminded him of another young man from his past.

"No, sir. We don't."

"We don't have much to offer, but there's food and a dry place to bed down."

John sighed at the same time Joe straightened in the saddle. "We'd be obliged."

Merritt motioned toward the barn. "Come on then. We were just getting ready to start a fire."

After the first sound sleep she'd had in weeks, Caro woke the following morning. Stretching, she pushed off the covers, hurrying over to the window and opening the curtains. Seeing a clear sky, she dashed to the wardrobe, grabbing work clothes. She wouldn't stay cooped up in the hotel another day. And she had no intention of telling Beau.

Slipping into a heavy coat, she went downstairs to the dining room, hoping for a quick breakfast and a packed lunch with enough food for herself, Merritt, and Gus. It would be a long day, and Caro already knew she wouldn't return until dark.

Twenty minutes later, she walked toward the livery. Today she'd take the wagon, pick up additional materials at the lumber mill, then leave before Beau had a chance to see her.

"Caro. I didn't expect to see you today." Noah came out of the blacksmith shop, wiping his hands on a well-worn rag. "Are you going to ride out to your house?"

"It's such a beautiful day, I couldn't stay inside another minute. May I use the wagon?"

He nodded, heading back into the livery. A few minutes passed before he drove the wagon out the gate. "Your wagon should be ready before Christmas."

"That's wonderful news, Noah. Then you'll have use of your wagon again, although I may need to leave mine here until I move into the house."

Noah chuckled. "I have two wagons here and one at the house for Abby. Using one of mine is no problem. And you can keep yours here as long as needed. Abby and I bought the lot behind the livery. As soon as I have time, I'll expand." Standing next to the wagon, he helped her up.

Caro took the lines, biting her lower lip. "Perhaps you could wait a bit to say anything to Beau about me leaving. I need to get supplies and food from Stan Petermann, then get materials at the lumber mill. Shouldn't take too long." She hurried to clarify. "I don't want you to lie. I'm just asking you not to seek him out to let him know I left."

Noah placed his hands on his hips, shaking his head. "I'm supposed to meet Gabe at the jail this morning. If Beau is there, I make no promises."

She nodded. "I understand."

"Caro?"

She glanced down at him.

"An hour is all I can wait before I head to the jail."

A broad smile broke across her face. "Thanks, Noah." Slapping the lines, she wasted no time turning the wagon toward the general store.

Finishing her errands an hour later, she left for her place. The sun was out, but patches of the trail remained frozen. A mile out of town, she released a relieved breath. Caro would be at her place in another thirty minutes. She couldn't wait to see what Merritt and Gus had accomplished. They'd told her they planned to work all day on Thanksgiving. She knew there'd be quite a bit to see.

Making the turn off the main trail to her house, Caro halted the wagon at the sound of gunfire. She reached below the seat, knowing Noah would have placed a loaded rifle and shotgun there for her use. One for use against any human threats, the other for animals. So far, she hadn't used either one.

A cold, clammy sensation flashed through her when another shot rang out. Settling the shotgun across her lap, she slapped the lines, moving forward at a slow pace. Rounding the last bend in the trail, she stopped, her heart pounding at the sight of a man she didn't recognize pointing a gun at Gus. Another man stood a few feet away, hands at his sides. Merritt was nowhere in sight.

Lifting the shotgun, her whole body shook as she pointed it toward the man with the gun. Sucking in a breath, she exhaled, then pulled the trigger.

# Chapter Sixteen

Panic and disappointment flooded Caro when the shot hit the ground in front of the man, sending up a spray of dirty snow. Before she could aim again, Gus came running up to her.

"What the hell are you doing? You could have killed someone."

"I was trying to hit the man in front of you." Her voice shook with indignation and anger.

His jaw dropped. Gus set his hands on his hips, glaring at her. "What in tarnation for?"

She blinked a couple times, glancing at the other men, noticing the one holding the gun smiling. He didn't appear to be a menace. "Well, it looked like he had his gun pointed at you, and I thought..."

Gus burst out laughing. She'd never heard him laugh. For that matter, she'd never heard Merritt laugh, either. Composing himself, he grinned.

"John was showing me how he aims it. He's been practicing while he and his brother waited for you to return from town."

"Oh..." She set the shotgun on the seat and picked up the lines, embarrassment heating her face.

"Bring the wagon up to the house and I'll introduce you."

Gus walked alongside the wagon as Caro moved forward, stopping near the barn. Helping her down, he turned to the others.

"Mrs. Iverson, this is John Smith and his brother, Joe. They're looking for work."

Caro greeted each, noticing how young they appeared and how thin they were, as if they hadn't eaten in days. She directed her question to John. "Are you from around here?"

"No, ma'am. We're from Alabama."

"And what brings you out this way? Family?" Her gaze shifted between the brothers, studying their features.

"We don't have any family, ma'am. Been picking up any work we could." John glanced at Joe. "We'd heard the Montana Territory was growing, and hoped maybe we could figure a way to claim some land."

Nodding, she studied them once more. "How old are you, Mr. Smith?"

John straightened, lifting his chin. "I'm nineteen, ma'am, and Joe is seventeen."

She blew out a breath, her mind reviewing all the work still needing to be done. They were young, even younger than she first thought. "What kind of work can you do?"

John's face brightened. "Whatever you need, ma'am. We've earned our keep farming, working cattle, building barns and houses, pretty much whatever you can think of. We don't need much. A place to sleep, a couple meals a day..." His voice trailed off as if he didn't dare ask for more.

"You'll have to sleep in the barn until there's time to build a bunkhouse. I bring out food from town twice a week. You do your own cooking over a campfire. I can pay a small wage, and you'll take orders from me. What do you say?"

A smile appeared on John's face. "It all sounds real good, ma'am."

"When can you start?"

John looked at Joe, who couldn't hide his relief. "Right now, ma'am."

"You can start by unloading the wagon, then fix yourselves something to eat." She turned toward Gus. "I'd like to see what you've done the last two days."

Mack kicked his horse, picking up speed as he raced back to town. When the weather cleared late the night before, Gabe asked him to ride toward Big Pine, taking a position off the main trail, hoping to spot the Dawsons. Neither believed they'd be that lucky. They'd been wrong.

An hour after the sun rose, he'd hidden near a group of large boulders, keeping watch on the trail. Three hours later, his wait ended. A group of six riders followed the trail to Splendor. Pulling out the wanted posters Gabe gave him, he used his field glasses to compare the sketches to the men on horseback. Even from this distance, he could pick out Louis and Clem riding at the front of the group.

He'd given them time to ride past, then jumped on his horse, taking a seldom-used trail back to Splendor. Pushing his horse hard, he'd barely stopped in front of the jail before dismounting and dashing inside. Gabe stood near the stove, pouring coffee, while Noah sat at the desk.

"They're on their way, Gabe."

"You're sure it's the Dawsons?" He set his cup down.

"Yes, sir. There are six of them. I'm guessing they're about two hours outside of town."

Gabe moved his gaze to Noah. They'd been having a conversation about Noah's son, Gabriel, and joking about both of them being married. After Mack's announcement, Noah's face hardened, a noticeable twitch in his jaw.

"Noah, I want you to stay out of this. Go home. Stay with Abby and Gabriel."

Standing, Noah crossed his arms, squaring off against his closest friend. "That's not going to happen. I'm getting my rifle. Tell me where you want me to set up."

Cursing, Gabe settled his hands on his hips, glaring at his childhood friend. "I know you have a score to settle, but you have a family who needs you. I can't risk you getting hurt. Hell, you're still working through the injuries from your *last* encounter with the Dawsons."

"That was an ambush. If it had been an encounter, you know those men would be dead."

A sharpshooter in the Union Army, Noah could hit a target dead-on from hundreds of feet away. And he could repeat the action over and over.

Mack cleared his throat. "We could use someone like Noah against the Dawsons, Gabe."

Noah glanced at Mack before returning his hard glare to Gabe. "Bull and I are your choices. With all due respect, I'm the better of the two." Bull hadn't been a sharpshooter during his time fighting for the North, but he was an excellent shot, a man they could count on.

Mumbling an oath, Gabe swallowed the ball of dread forming in his stomach. "You're going to set up somewhere even if I tell you to leave, aren't you?"

"I am."

Gabe shook his head, letting out a deep breath. "I want you on the south balcony at the top floor of the St. James. Tell whoever is at the front desk I said to give you the room key."

Noah nodded, moving toward the door, then stopped at Gabe's next words.

"Don't get yourself shot. I refuse to deliver bad news to Abby. Do you understand?"

A small grin lifted the corners of Noah's mouth. "Understood, Colonel."

"Are you clear on where you'll be posted?" Gabe pulled his gaze from the sketch he'd made to search each of their faces. He'd gathered his deputies at the jail not long after Noah left.

Caleb nodded. "It's clear to me."

The others agreed, Beau pointing to a spot on the drawing. "Noah will be here. What about Bull? You know he won't be kept out of it."

"I still need to speak with him, but I want him on the top floor of the Dixie. I'm going to ask Dirk Masters to take a window on the second floor of the Wild Rose."

"Dirk?" Cash asked, a brow rising.

"He's spoken to me a couple times about helping out if needed. According to Luke and Dax, their foreman is an excellent shot. I need the four of you in the bank or close by." Gabe straightened, his gaze darting between the men. "We have to consider all possibilities. With Noah, Bull, and Dirk posted overhead, the rest of us will have coverage should the Dawsons come in from different directions."

Mack rubbed his chin, taking another look at the sketch. "What about the shop owners and townsfolk? Do you plan to alert them?"

Gabe looked at Cash and Beau. "The businesses know you two the best. I want you to talk to them before they close today. Don't scare them. Just make sure they're aware of the danger and the need to be vigilant. If they hear gunfire, they're to lock their doors and keep everyone inside. As for the townsfolk, we'll do what we can to protect them. Unfortunately, we can't shut down Splendor, and without knowing when the Dawsons will strike, we aren't able to warn them."

Beau shook his head. "I don't know, Gabe. The Dawsons don't seem to care about shooting anyone who gets in their way."

"What do you suggest, Beau?"

"You think the Dawsons will strike within the next few days, right?"

"I don't see a reason for them to wait." Gabe lowered himself into his chair.

"And from what you've learned, we know at least one of their men will ride into Splendor beforehand to figure out what they're up against." Beau leaned a hip against the edge of the desk.

"I've heard from sheriffs in four towns where they've struck. The outlaws don't cover their faces. That's how arrogant they are," Gabe snorted. "Each time, someone in the bank recognized one of the Dawson men as coming in the day before, asking questions, then leaving."

Beau crossed his arms, his gaze moving between the men. "Then we put our efforts into identifying whoever Louis and Clem send in ahead of the robbery. If we can do that, we'll know they plan to strike the following day, which gives us a chance to warn the townsfolk."

Resting his chin on his hand, Gabe studied the sketch again. "Beau and Cash will take turns inside the bank, watching who comes and goes. Wear your guns, but not your badges. You're just customers doing your business. Mack and Caleb, I want you outside. One by the St. James, the other outside the Dixie. I'll let Clausen know. Watch for one or two men who ask questions, but don't open an account or do other bank business. Men none of us recognize. Men who don't fit."

Cash pointed to the two saloons on the sketch. "I'd expect them to go into the Dixie or Wild Rose, but not the general store. They're looking for whiskey, not a pair of boots."

Gabe nodded. "They might stop at the boardinghouse to eat. I'll let Suzanne and Nick know what we're thinking."

The room fell silent as each man thought through what must be done. After a few moments, Gabe spoke.

"We know what's coming. Let's make sure we're ready."

Dropping the lines, Caro's shoulders slumped in exhaustion. It had been a long, yet fulfilling day. The Smith brothers worked as hard as Merritt and Gus, stopping to rest only when Caro insisted.

If they continued at this pace, the changes suggested by Bull would be complete before Christmas, allowing her to move in sooner than she'd expected. It would also give the men time to build a bunkhouse large enough for the four of them.

"Caro. I wondered if you might have decided to stay at the house tonight." Noah walked toward her.

She grinned as he helped her down. "Not yet. I'd have to stay in the barn with four men, and I'm not ready to do that."

He cocked his head. "Four?"

Caro shrugged. "Two men rode in this morning, looking for work. Brothers from Alabama."

"You can't employ everyone who comes to your place, Caro."

Sighing, she took the blanket Noah handed her. "I know, but they're nineteen and seventeen. They looked as if they hadn't eaten in days. I couldn't turn them away."

Noah placed a friendly arm around her shoulders, shaking his head. Like Gabe, he and Caro had grown up around each other in New York. At one time, Noah had thought Gabe and Caro might marry. It never happened.

"Well, if you don't need the men in a few months, and they're still around, there should be plenty of work around Splendor. May I walk you back to the hotel?"

She leaned up, brushing a kiss across his cheek. "I can manage. Besides, you should be home with Abby and Gabriel."

He climbed onto the wagon, picked up the lines, then smiled down at her. "Yes. Everyone keeps telling me that."

Holding the blanket to her chest, she crossed the street toward Suzanne's boardinghouse. She'd been ready to push the door open when she spotted a familiar face through the window sharing a table with Suzanne and Nick. The last person she wanted to see was Beau, and knowing Suzanne, her friend would insist Caro join them.

Glancing down at her soiled clothing, she realized there were few choices at this time of day. If she returned to the hotel to bathe and change, the chances of falling asleep without eating were great.

Turning, she spotted the only other restaurant in Splendor. McCall's was owned by Betts Jones and her husband, Elmer. It sat at the opposite end of town between the law office and the general store, serving generous portions at reasonable prices. She'd become so accustomed to visiting Suzanne's, Caro rarely thought of McCall's.

Hoping they were still serving, she crossed the street, passing the Wild Rose, the jail, and several other businesses before entering McCall's. Not as large as Suzanne's, it did a brisk business. Tonight, most tables were occupied.

"Caro!"

Turning, she spotted Allie waving at her, Cash sitting next to her. He stood and walked over.

"Why don't you join us?"

She didn't have time to decline before Cash took her elbow, guiding her through the narrow spaces between tables. Pulling out a chair, he took her coat.

Allie smiled at her. "You look like you could use a good meal."

"And a hot bath."

Cash sat back down, reaching under the table to take Allie's hand. "We ordered the special."

"Sounds perfect." Caro settled back, glad for the company.

He held up a hand, indicating to Betts they wanted three meals. "Did you just return from your house?"

She nodded at Betts when the owner set a cup of coffee in front of her, then hurried away. "Yes. I hired two more men to help Merritt and Gus. They made a lot of progress today."

"Are they from here?" Allie asked, leaning back as Betts placed full plates in front of them.

Caro glanced down at the stew, her mouth watering, as Allie and Cash dug into their food. "Alabama."

Cash stopped his fork midway to his mouth. "Alabama?"

She nodded, placing a spoonful of stew in her mouth, not hearing the caution in his voice. "Oh, this is so good." Lifting her gaze, she saw Cash staring at her. "What?"

Cash set down his fork, lowering his voice. "Beau told me you contacted Pinkerton."

Caro's face reddened. "Yes."

"I'm glad you did. He said the people looking for him are named Eldridge. And they're from Alabama."

Her features stilled. She thought of John and Joe, how young they were, how hard they worked. "What are you thinking?"

He leaned back in his chair. "I'm not certain, other than it seems to be quite a coincidence that the Eldridges hired Pinkerton to confirm Beau's whereabouts, then not long afterward, your two men show up...and they're all from Alabama."

A ball of ice formed in Caro's stomach. She pictured John's face, then Joe's. When she'd met them earlier, the hope she'd seen in each broke her heart. She didn't need a doctor to tell her they were emaciated.

Shaking her head, she met Cash's concerned gaze. "No. I don't believe those two boys rode across country to harm Beau. They are nothing but skin and bones with dark circles under their sunken eyes." She glanced down at her full plate of stew, her appetite gone. "No matter what transpired between me and Beau, I'd never do anything to harm him."

Cash leaned forward, placing a hand on her arm. "I'd never suggest you would." He glanced at Allie, then returned his gaze to Caro. "I'm being cautious. No one knows why Eldridge paid Pinkerton to confirm Beau's location. The only plausible explanation was to seek revenge for the death of his brother. He's a wealthy plantation owner who isn't going to do the dirty work himself. He'd hire others to do it for him."

Caro clutched her hands together in her lap, still unable to picture the Smith brothers as killers. "They don't look like someone gave them money to exact vengeance."

"Can they handle a gun?"

She sucked in a breath, recalling how John had shown Gus his skill at shooting. Later in the afternoon, he and Joe had shown them how accurate they were with their six-guns. Caro wondered if she could be wrong about them.

"Would you mind if I ride out to your place and meet these brothers?"

Shaking off her doubt, she nodded at Cash. "If you have the time."

"I'll make time."

# Chapter Seventeen

Caro tossed and turned all night, unable to sleep. Each time she closed her eyes, the faces of John and Joe assaulted her, followed by an image of Beau.

Merritt had mentioned being suspicious of the two at first. He'd shaken his head, saying something about John Smith and Joe Smith. Then he and Gus had spent the day working with them, and any hesitancy about the boys seemed to disappear. Cash making a possible connection between Eldridge and the brothers wasn't so easy to dismiss.

Flinging off her covers more than once, she'd paced her hotel room, recalling the events of the day. What bothered her most was Merritt telling her the brothers had ridden out looking for the Davis place, hearing he might need workers. When he told them Beau wouldn't be building for months, he suggested they talk to her.

She knew Stan Petermann at the general store and Silas Jenks at the lumber mill would mention her place to anyone looking for work. They would also mention the Pelletiers and Bull, since he was drawing plans for the clinic and other structures people hoped to build in the spring. She wondered how they'd learned about Beau's ranch or his plans.

If Cash's suspicions were correct, and she had a high regard for his instincts, men bent on exacting vengeance against Beau might be working for her.

After letting her mind roam in circles until well past midnight, Caro finally allowed exhaustion to claim her a few hours before dawn.

Beau stood by the bank entrance, taking one more look up and down the street before going inside. He saw Gabe sitting on a chair outside the jail, sipping coffee, appearing to be lost in thought. Beau knew otherwise. The sheriff didn't miss anything, the same as the others posted around town, watching for any sign of the Dawsons.

The night before, Cash and Beau spoke with the store owners, giving them information about the gang, warning them to be vigilant. They'd been instructed to close up and keep everyone inside at the first sound of gunfire. Most had been through this before. People didn't live in a frontier town, far from the protection of a fort, without knowing the dangers. All owned guns, and they knew how to use them.

Beau's gaze moved to the Dixie. Mack stood outside, leaning against a wall. After being shot, his arm was almost back to full use. With a turn of his head, Beau spotted Caleb across the street at the St. James, sitting at a table by the window. Beau already knew Cash waited inside his wife's dress shop for his turn to play a bank customer. They'd play their roles every day until the Dawsons showed or were spotted in another town.

Once inside, he studied the few customers who'd been waiting for the bank to open. He knew each one, greeting them as he stepped up to one of the tellers. Reaching into his pocket, he took out a few dollars and added them to his growing savings account. He took his time, as did the teller, the man behind the counter aware of Beau's real reason for being in the bank.

The plan he and Cash concocted meant whichever of them was in the bank would stay there until someone they didn't recognize walked in. After a few minutes, the two deputies would change places, giving them both a chance to study the person. Beau and Cash would continue this all day until the bank closed.

After an hour, a young man stepped inside. Beau had seen him arrive on the stage a few days before. Dressed in clothes more suitable for a lawyer than an outlaw, Beau doubted he had any connection to the gang. Still, he took a good look before walking outside and into Allie's shop.

"One new face." He took off his hat.

"I saw him. Doubt he's our man." Cash stood, walking to the counter with his empty coffee cup. "You want some?"

Beau joined him, taking the full cup of coffee. "All seems quiet so far." He took a sip, then glanced over the rim at Cash. "Did you see Caro leave the hotel this morning?" He tried to make his question sound casual, knowing he probably failed.

"No, but I wasn't looking for her. Why?" Cash considered telling him about the Smith boys, deciding to hold off until they were done for the day. He was pretty certain Beau would want to be a part of what Cash had planned—riding out to Caro's place and talking to the Smiths.

Beau shrugged. "No reason. She's generally out early on a day as nice as this one. Likes to get an early start."

"She joined Allie and me at McCall's for supper last night after she returned from her place. She looked exhausted. Maybe she needed a day to rest." Tightening his gunbelt, Cash grabbed his hat. "It's my turn at the bank. At least I can make Allie's deposit while I'm there."

He walked to the door, pulling it open. "You don't mind staying here, do you? I'd like someone close to Allie if the Dawsons do pay a visit."

Beau sat down in the chair Cash had used near the front window. "Just consider me part of the family."

Noon came and went, Beau and Cash exchanging places several times, seeing no sign of anyone suspicious. During one of Beau's turns inside the bank, Cash spied Caro leaving the St. James, heading toward Noah's livery at the other end of town. He thought of the Smith brothers, deciding he'd ride out there as soon as the bank closed.

Seeing Beau leave the bank, Cash decided he needed to tell him of Caro's new men.

"Clausen shut down early today." Beau joined Cash inside the dress shop, grabbing the only other chair and pulling it over to the window. "I sure was hoping the Dawsons would send their man in today."

Cash leaned back in his chair. "Seems we'll need to wait another day." Standing, he picked up his hat. "I'm going to ride out to Caro's place."

Beau's head snapped toward his friend. "What for?"

"She hired a couple new men and has some concerns. I offered to talk with them." He paused a moment, adjusting his gunbelt.

Beau nodded, his gaze shifting as he processed the information. "It's not like Caro to doubt her decisions. What's her concern?"

"They're brothers...from Alabama."

Standing, Beau buttoned his coat, moving toward the door. "I'm going with you."

"I thought you might."

Caro surveyed the work accomplished so far, stunned at the progress. Taking the stairs, she moved from one room to another, ending up in what would become her bedroom. Making a slow turn, a smile spread across her face. She could picture her bed, wardrobe, and dressing table placed inside the spacious room, as well as the curtains Allie had made.

"Mrs. Iverson?"

Her stomach dropped when she turned to see Joe standing in the doorway, his long hair almost obscuring his eyes. She hadn't seen Joe or his brother when she arrived. Merritt told her they'd taken some food, planning to ride the property while they took a break. Caro found herself wondering if there was another reason for the ride. She hated the fact she held doubts about them.

"Yes, Joe?"

He shuffled his feet before glancing up. "Me and John found some wild horses when we rode your property. We wondered if you'd want us to try and bring them in, put them in the corral we're building."

She didn't know much about wild horses. Like most untamed animals, they were constantly on the move and hard to catch.

Caro stepped toward him, clasping her hands in front of her. "Do you and John know about horses?"

He nodded. "Yes, ma'am. We worked for a rancher before coming here. He taught us a whole lot."

"Why did you leave?"

Joe shrugged. "We didn't have much choice. There was a land war. Some men raided the ranch one night and shot the owner, insisting their boss now owned the property. The next day, we were told to get out." He fell silent for a few moments before continuing. "We hated leaving the widow, but she said to go. I think she was afraid they'd shoot the rest of us if we didn't leave."

Caro sucked in a breath. She'd heard of land wars, not understanding how a man could murder another, then claim his land. "Is that where you learned to shoot?"

A sly grin lifted the corners of his mouth. "No, ma'am. We learned from a man who took us in a few years before that. He was a gambler who needed help with a small plantation he'd won in a card game. Me and John was living in the alley behind the saloon and asked him if he had work. We stayed with him a couple years, 'til he lost the property gambling." Sighing, he pursed his lips. "Anyway, he gave us our guns and taught us to shoot. Said we were old enough to make enemies and had to protect ourselves."

Caro cleared her throat, her emotions in turmoil over his story. "How old were you?"

"I was thirteen and John was fifteen. We'd practice more if we had the money for bullets." He rubbed the back of his neck, beginning to look uncomfortable. "So...what do you want us to do about the horses?"

"I think trying to bring some back is a marvelous idea. If the corral is done in time tomorrow, go ahead and ride out, see if you can find them."

She didn't think Joe could smile any brighter. "Yes, ma'am. I'll go tell John."

"Joe? Where did you actually grow up? You mentioned being from Alabama."

His gaze darted around the room, then he bent his head, focusing on the floor. "Someone left us outside a minister's house in Birmingham. His wife found us in the morning and took us in. John was three, and I, well...I must've been about one. They named us, made us a part of their family." He sucked in a shaky breath. "They died in a carriage accident when I was ten. Since they never adopted us, we were told we had to leave. We were completely on our own."

Of all the stories Joe could have told her, she hadn't expected this. They'd been abandoned, raised by what sounded like a good couple, then kicked out when the couple died.

"No friends would take you in?"

"Not with the war going on. People had enough for themselves and not much more." He straightened, his eyes shining a little too bright. "But we did all right. We made it out here, didn't we?"

Her mouth curved into a kind smile, her eyes sympathetic. "Yes, Joe. The two of you *did* make it out here."

Nodding, he dashed downstairs and out the front door. When Caro heard him shouting for John, she moved to the window. Looking down, she saw the two brothers standing together, talking in excited voices, broad smiles on their faces. A few minutes later, they moved toward the corral and out of view.

Thinking over all Joe had said, she found it increasingly difficult to believe either of them had been sent to harm Beau. Since the end of the war, more and more people felt compelled to move west. Most were good people. Even with the coincidence of the boys once living in Alabama, she believed they fell into this group.

Taking one more look around the room, she headed down the stairs and outside. Merritt and Gus stood by the barn, appearing to be in a heated conversation, their voices rising before they saw her walking toward them. Gus made one more comment, poking Merritt in the chest, then left to join John and Joe in the corral.

"Is everything all right, Merritt?"

His gaze followed his brother, his jaw working. Shaking his head, Merritt cleared his throat. "A little disagreement within the family." He glanced at the sky. "Looks like we've got weather rolling in. Might be able to get a couple more hours of work in before we have to stop for the night." Sighing, he turned his attention to her. "We plan to finish the corral first. Afterward, we'll work inside. Should be finished by the end of the week."

Her eyes widened. "Does that mean I can have Allie bring the curtains out on Monday?"

"Yes, ma'am. You can move your belongings in any time after." He shifted toward the corral, his gaze narrowing to where Gus spoke with John.

Caro wanted to ask again about the argument Merritt had with Gus, deciding it was between the two of them. "Is the root cellar ready for me to bring in extra supplies?"

"It is. We installed steps and the door yesterday." He hooked his thumbs into his pants, glancing again at Gus. "Guess I'd best go help them."

She followed him, stopping at the finished part of the corral. Something wasn't right. Caro wouldn't interfere, deciding to keep watch on the men. Stepping onto the lowest rail, she rested her arms on the top, trying to hear what the men were saying. All four stood together, John and Joe saying little as Merritt and Gus continued their discussion. After a couple minutes, the Smith brothers walked away, continuing their work on the corral. Not long after, Gus and Merritt did the same.

Stepping to the ground, Caro decided to stoke the fire outside the barn. She needed a fresh pot of coffee, and figured the men did, too. The sky had darkened, and she doubted they'd go a full day without more snow.

Bending beside a pile of wood, she loaded her arms, straightening at the sound of horses approaching. Turning, her chest tightened at the sight of Beau riding toward her, Cash next to him. Taking a few steps, she dumped the wood next to the dwindling fire, brushed her hands together, then drew in a deep breath.

Caro expected to see Cash, not Beau. They hadn't spoken since their ride back to town Thanksgiving night when he'd learned about the Dawsons robbing the bank in Big Pine.

"Caro." Beau didn't move to dismount as Cash reined to a stop beside him.

"Hello, Caro. Thought I'd bring Beau along to talk to the Smith brothers. Hope you don't mind."

"No, of course not. It's just..." She thought of her discussion with Joe, how she'd felt when she learned how he and John had survived to make it to Montana.

Cash slid to the ground, followed by Beau. "What is it?"

Glancing over her shoulder at the four men working to finish the corral, she shook her head. "I've learned more about John and Joe. I just don't think they're a danger to anyone."

Beau stepped closer. "What have you learned?"

His closeness, the concern in his voice and compassion in his eyes had her face flushing as an unwanted rush of desire rolled through her. It had always been this way when Beau was close. Touching a hand to her forehead, Caro bit her lower lip to regain control. Lifting her gaze, she locked on his, telling him what she'd learned during the conversation with Joe.

"I simply don't believe they're a threat to you...or anyone."

Beau rested his hands on his hips, letting out a breath. "You may be right, Caro. Still, I think it's best for Cash and me to meet them."

Nodding, she glanced at the corral, seeing Joe and John laughing as they worked. "All right. Let's get this over with."

Leaving their horses, Beau and Cash followed her toward the men.

"John, Joe, this is Beau Davis. He owns the property west of here. I believe he was who you were trying to find before you spoke with Merritt and Gus. And this is Cash Coulter, a friend. They're both deputies in Splendor."

Taking off their hats, the boys took a couple tentative steps forward, not responding to the introduction.

"Beau, Cash, this is John Smith and his brother, Joe. They started working for me a few days ago."

They all nodded, falling into a tense silence. After a few moments, Beau focused his gaze on John. "Mrs. Iverson says you're from Alabama."

"Yes, sir."

Beau glanced between the two, directing his question to Joe this time. "You're a long way from home, son. Why Montana?"

The young man shrugged, shifting his weight from one foot to the other. "No particular reason. We followed the work, hoping to get on someplace permanent." He lifted his gaze to Beau's. "There's a lot of older, more experienced men out looking. We kept moving until we got here." Joe looked at Caro, offering an appreciative smile. "Mrs. Iverson was good enough to put us on."

Beau listened to his explanation, his gaze shifting between the two, noticing how thin they were. Caro had mentioned they hadn't eaten in days by the time she met them, how they devoured whatever she offered.

Cash stepped forward. "How'd you here about Mrs. Iverson needing workers?"

John nodded to the other two hired hands. "Merritt and Gus said she might need more help. When we stopped at the lumber mill in town, the owner said Mr. Davis might need help." He switched his gaze to Beau. "We stopped here on the way to your place and found out you weren't going to build until spring."

Beau shook his head. "Silas Jenks, huh?"

"Yes, sir. If he's the man who owns the lumber mill."

Beau crossed his arms, planting his feet shoulder width apart. "You boys were lucky to get work from Mrs. Iverson. She's a good woman. If you do your work and show respect, I'm certain she'll treat you fairly. You don't, you'll be answering to me." He narrowed his gaze. "Do I make myself clear?"

Both nodded, John answering. "Yes, sir, Mr. Davis. We understand."

"Good, then none of us have anything to worry about."

Caro cleared her throat, still reeling from Beau's obvious warning to John and Joe. "Well, if we're done here, why don't you and Joe get back to work."

John took one more look at Beau and Cash. "Yes, ma'am."

Caro turned away, taking measured steps toward the barn, knowing Beau and Cash followed. She took slow breaths in an attempt to calm the anger at Beau's warning. Stopping outside the barn, she whirled on him.

"You threatened them, Beau."

Staring down at her, he nodded. "Yes, I did."

"You had no right to do that. They're *my* men, not yours."

His gaze hardened, his voice rough. "They're *your* men, but they live in *my* town. I'm a deputy, sworn to keep people safe. I had every right to let those boys know where I stand. I'm sorry if you don't like it."

She crossed her arms. "Well, I don't. You came here to talk to the boys, not intimidate them." Glancing at the corral, she saw all four men working, not appearing to be bothered by Beau's comments. She wondered if her concern was justified or if her unease around Beau caused her shrewish behavior. Letting out a deep sigh, Caro returned her gaze to his. "What do you think of them?"

"Unless they're real good liars, I don't think they pose a threat to anybody. Still, I'd keep a tight rein on them."

Throughout his conversation with the boys, Beau had been aware of Merritt and Gus standing a few feet away. They'd listened, then retreated into their own private conversation. Something about the way they continued to shoot looks at Caro had Beau on edge. When Gus jostled Merritt, he'd almost broken off the discussion with John and Joe to find out what was going on. Instead, he continued to glance their way, but didn't interfere.

Cash stepped next to Caro. "I agree with Beau. They've been moving around, trying to earn enough money to eat. I think we're looking in the wrong direction. We'd be better off getting information on Eldridge."

Beau turned his attention back to Caro. "Gabe's working with Pinkerton on that. We should have something soon. It's getting dark. Caro, we'll ride with you back to town."

"I'm not ready to go." She was, but the last thing she needed was to spend more time around him.

He lifted a brow. "That so? And just when were you going to head back?"

"Well, I planned to finish a few things…"

"Wait until tomorrow. It's going to rain, or snow if the temperature keeps dropping. You need to get back."

Crossing her arms, she glared at him. "I'm a grown woman. You can't force me to ride back with you."

Cocking his head, he grinned. "Is that what this is about? You don't want to ride back with me?"

"No. Absolutely not."

He chuckled. "Uh-huh."

Too focused on each other, neither noticed Cash driving the wagon up next to them. He jumped to the ground. "Let's go, Caro. Allie will have supper waiting. You can eat with us."

"Hey. What about me?" Beau gripped Caro's elbow, guiding her to the wagon.

"What about you? You know you're always welcome."

Placing his hands on Caro's waist, he hoisted her onto the seat before she had a chance to protest.

Picking up the lines, she glared at both of them. "Don't *I* get a say in any of this?"

"No," they both answered, then swung up atop their horses, turning them toward Splendor.

# Chapter Eighteen

Caro seethed all the way back to town. She'd allowed Beau and Cash to push her into leaving without giving them much of an argument.

It didn't help they were right about the weather. Rain started not long after leaving her property, converting to snow before they arrived back in town. Her warm coat and gloves did little to stop her teeth from chattering or hands from shaking.

"Are you all right, Caro?" Beau rode beside her, his hat pulled low, bandana drawn up to cover most of his face.

She nodded, drawing her arms close to her sides to preserve body heat.

"If you want, I can tie Smoke to the back of the wagon and drive."

Glancing at him, she shook her head. They weren't far from town and she had no intention of stopping. Even though the warmth of Beau's body sitting next to her sounded appealing, all she wanted was to get the wagon back to Noah and order a warm bath.

"Let me know if you change your mind." He moved Smoke forward a few yards, glancing over his shoulder often to make certain Caro kept up.

Mindful of his watchful gaze, she shifted on the hard wooden seat, doing her best to ignore his presence. She forced her mind to think of anything other than the man who rode a few feet away—the wild horses Joe talked about, the curtains Allie had made, the furniture she'd ordered from back east. Nothing helped.

Shaking her head and blinking her eyes, Caro did her best to brush the dampness from her face. The gathering snow obscured the trail, making driving the wagon more difficult. She kept her focus straight ahead, knowing Cash rode at the back, keeping his head down to ward off the chill of the growing wind.

Seeing the last bend in the trail before reaching Splendor, Caro let out a relieved sigh. Less than a minute later, the glow of lantern lights and fires blazing through uncovered windows spread a strange warmth through her. Pulling the wagon to a stop in front of the livery, she turned to climb down, hesitating at Beau's outstretched arms.

"Come on, Caro. It's cold."

Catching her lower lip between her teeth, she leaned down, placing her hands on Beau's shoulders. An instant later, she stood on the ground, his hands still secure on her waist, his face so close, his warm breath caressed her skin. Lifting her head, she stilled at the intense, smoldering look in his eyes. Her heart pounded as her throat constricted, making it hard to think or breathe.

Caro couldn't look away from the undisguised desire she saw on his face. For a moment, she thought—prayed—he'd kiss her, knowing it would be a mistake. He no longer loved her, although she'd lost none of her love for him. Drawing in a slow breath, she started to close her eyes when she felt him loosen his grip and step away. Her chest squeezed at the sense of loss.

"I'll walk with you to Cash and Allie's."

She didn't have time to respond before Beau took her hand, tucking it through his arm. "But the wagon..."

"Cash already told Noah you're back. He'll take care of it." He felt her shiver. "It won't be long before you'll be standing by a fire, warming up. And don't even think about arguing. As Cash said, Allie will have supper ready, and she always makes enough for more than two people."

As he tucked her closer to his side, all Caro's objections were swept aside. It might make her seem weak, but if this was how she could be close to Beau, she'd accept it without argument.

Cash walked ahead of them, opening the door to his wife's shop, gesturing toward the stairs. Walking to the back, Caro sighed, already feeling warmer. Slipping her arm from Beau's, she followed the unmistakable aroma of cooked meat as she reached the top landing, lifting her hand to knock.

"Don't bother, Caro. Just go on inside." She did as Cash suggested, an instant wave of heat surrounding her.

The apartment wasn't large. One big room with living areas separated by furniture or curtains. A wood stove divided the living room from their bedroom and provided most of the heat. A second stove for cooking sat tucked into a back corner, a large pot resting on top.

"Caro, come in." Allie set down a spoon, wiping her hands down her apron as she walked toward her. "Let me take your coat and hang it by the fire." She set it on a hook, then turned to see Cash. Wrapping her arms around his neck, she gave her husband a welcoming kiss. "I thought you might have been caught in the sudden storm." She stepped away, taking his coat and Beau's, hanging them next to Caro's.

Cash placed a hat on a shelf above the coats, making room by the stove for Caro and Beau. "We left just in time. If we'd stayed much longer, we might have been stuck for the night."

Beau chuckled. "That would've meant sharing the barn with four other men. Not a real problem, except..." He glanced at Caro.

"Except for me," she interjected. "I *do* like my privacy."

"Well, I'm sure you're all hungry. Sit down and I'll fill the plates."

Taking a seat, Caro watched Allie move around the cramped kitchen, impressed with her efficiency. The kitchen in Caro's own house would be at least three times as large once the men finished their work.

Doing her best to ignore her body's reaction to the feel of Beau's knee touching hers under the table, she concentrated on the full plates of food Allie set in front of each of them.

"This looks wonderful, Allie." Caro hadn't realized how famished she was until she inhaled.

"It's just venison stew. Nothing fancy. I'm sure yours is every bit as good."

Beau snorted, glancing at Caro, ignoring Allie's surprised stare.

Caro's face reddened a little, sending Beau an exasperated glance as she scooped up a forkful. "I've never cooked much, as Beau knows." Placing the food in her mouth, she chewed slowly, letting out a groan of appreciation. "This is very good."

Smiling, Allie forked a piece of meat. "It's easy. If you like, I'll show you how to make it."

Taking a bite of the lightest biscuit she'd ever eaten, Caro nodded. "Would you include a lesson on your biscuits?"

"Of course."

Beau picked up another biscuit, held it up, and smiled. "Caro, if Allie teaches you to make biscuits like this, I might reverse my decision to not have supper at your place." His smile faded at the confused looks from Cash and Allie.

Caro shifted in her chair, the unease she felt earlier returning. "I invited Beau to come for supper after I've moved into the house. He politely declined."

Cash could see a muscle tick in Beau's jaw. He hadn't considered how volatile their relationship might be when he invited both for supper. Setting down his fork, Cash chuckled. "Forget about Beau. Allie and I will be happy to ride out anytime."

"That's a wonderful idea, Cash." Allie shot Caro an encouraging look. "What better place to show you how to make biscuits than in your own kitchen."

"Consider it an invitation. You and Cash will be the first friends I entertain." Caro pointedly ignored Beau. "Cash, you can be the judge of how well I do."

"As long as I don't have to compare them to Allie's, I'd be happy to do it. I may need to eat several to be certain of my opinion, though."

Beau ate in silence, listening as the others continued to talk about Caro's house, her desire to learn to cook, and the new curtains Allie made. She spoke of the furniture ordered, the wild horses John and Joe hoped to catch, and plans for a new bunkhouse. With each word, Beau's firm belief she didn't plan to stay in Splendor unraveled a little more. She didn't sound like a woman who planned to leave anytime soon. She also didn't look like a woman who favored living in a fancy home in San Francisco, preferring operas to community suppers, afternoon soirées to church fundraisers.

"Beau?"

Lifting his head at Cash's voice, his somber features didn't change. "Apologies. My mind was somewhere else."

Cash studied him a moment. "Caro asked when you planned to start building your house."

Beau shifted his gaze to Caro, a familiar flicker of regret gripping him. "It depends on the weather. March if possible. April at the latest. Why?"

"I was saying that Matt and Nolen Volker are experienced carpenters. They're at the Pelletier ranch now, but mentioned they'd be interested in making a change. I thought you might consider using them."

"Bull already mentioned them to me." He didn't tell her he'd spoken with them at Thanksgiving supper, deciding he'd use them if Dax and Luke didn't mind. For tonight, he felt the need to keep his thoughts to himself, even the few that didn't include Caro.

He'd thought of little except her in the days following their time making love in her hotel room. It had been a poor decision, one he regretted more than she knew. Not because of how he felt. Beau accepted how much he still loved her. His regret came from the hurt in her eyes when he hadn't been able to offer more. In truth, he knew the reasons he'd been unable to ease her doubts, give her the hope she needed. And in his mind, they were justified.

Beau knew he should probably explain himself to Caro, but not the fear encircling him each time he thought of her leaving a second time. He had no intention of sharing his overwhelming weakness for her.

He needed to know she chose Splendor because it called to her as much as it did him. She had to build her own life first, show she had the grit to stay in such a harsh land whether he was a part of her life or not. If she did, they'd have a

263

solid chance of making a life together. For this to work, they needed time—a risk in itself.

The longer he held off stating his feelings, the bigger the chance someone else could take his place and capture her heart. A woman as fine as Caro would attract the attention of every eligible man for miles. A widow of means, on her own, running a property the size of hers would be a target too great for most men to ignore.

Beau's eyes burned and his nostrils flared at the thought of another man stepping in to take what was his. The calculated risk had turned into a game of time Beau wasn't certain he wanted to play.

"Let me help you with those, Allie." Caro stood, picking up plates, pulling him back to those around the table.

"Nonsense. You've put in a long day, and from the sound of it, have another long one ahead of you tomorrow."

Beau frowned at the comment, wondering what he'd missed. Standing, he grabbed his coat and Caro's. "If you're ready, I'll walk you back."

"There's no reason to push yourself this hard, Caro." Beau stood inside the St. James, Caro's arm still tucked through his. It took less than two minutes to cross the almost empty street from Allie's store to the hotel. The only words spoken had been his question about how much work she still had to do.

Her violet eyes sparked, turning the color of the dark amethyst necklace his grandmother used to wear. A necklace his sister, Genevieve, now owned, although it would never mean more than any other trinket to her everlasting eight-year-old mind.

"Of course there are reasons. If the men continue as hard as they've been working, I'll be able to move into the house next week. As nice as the St. James is, I'm ready to be back in a house."

"I understand your desire to get into your own place. My question is why you have to be there every day when you have four men doing the work. Surely you can hire more if you need to."

The flare of anger in her eyes told him his opinion had been a mistake. Pulling her arm from his, she settled her hands on her hips. "I assume you're referring to my vast wealth. How I can hire whomever I want without lifting a finger?"

"Caro..."

She drew in a breath, exhaling slowly. "This isn't about money, Beau. I enjoy being out there, watching the men complete their work, seeing the house come back to life. I know you don't think I have many useful skills, but I'm still able to help."

"I never said—"

"You may not have said it in so many words, but I know you've thought it."

He winced, knowing she'd pegged him right. "Fine. I won't deny I've thought perhaps you'd be more suited for other activities."

She narrowed her gaze, her face beginning to flush. "Such as?"

Beau sighed. This wasn't how he wanted to end the evening. It seemed every time they were together, it ended in an argument or misunderstanding. Taking a step closer, he held out his hands, palms up.

"Caro, I don't want to fight with you. It's been a long day and we're both tired. Can we call a truce?"

Letting out a shaky breath, she nodded. "You're right." Biting her lower lip, she gazed up at him. "I should get upstairs."

"Probably." He made no move to leave.

"Well...I want to thank you for riding all the way out to talk with John and Joe. Your opinion of them does matter to me." She fidgeted with the buttons on her coat, shifting her weight from one foot to the other.

His features softened. "I'm glad Cash asked me to join him." He hesitated a moment. "You know, you can ask me for help anytime." Beau still didn't budge from where he stood. Raising his hand, he tucked an errant strand of hair behind Caro's ear, feeling a shudder ripple through her. He wanted to draw her to him, wrap his arms around her, kiss her senseless. The decision was taken from him when Caro stepped away.

"I should go to my room. You're welcome to stop by my place whenever you're in the area."

Nodding, he pushed away the overwhelming urge to tell her how much he still loved her. He had decisions to make, which would only get more confusing if he acted on his urges.

"Good night, Caro."

A sweet smile crossed her lips. "Good night, Beau."

"My instincts tell me they're part of the Dawson gang." Beau had followed two men outside after they'd entered the bank not long before closing, asked a few questions, then left. He and Cash watched them through the window of Allie's shop.

He'd never seen either one. Their clothing and manner indicated long hours in the saddle, a difficult existence, and callous, possibly brutal temperament. Beau had seen the type many times during and after the war. Men who may have been honorable and kind at one time became people without conscience or remorse.

Cash nodded. "I felt a prickle of unease when I saw them dismount and go inside." He'd been waiting in Allie's shop for his turn to play customer. After three days of watching, both men felt they'd finally found their targets. "I'm thinking of following them." Cash stood, meaning to turn away when he felt Beau's hand on his arm.

"No. It's best we don't do anything that will spook the Dawsons. Let's find Gabe and the others. Someone will need to get word to Dirk at Redemption's Edge."

Cash still wanted to follow them, find out where the gang had been hiding, but agreed Beau's idea was the best choice. "I've already seen Bull and Noah in town. It's certain Gabe will want us to be ready at first light."

# Chapter Nineteen

"It'll be easy, Louis. We'll be in and out of the bank before the sheriff knows we're in town." Clem Dawson sat on a log by their fire, working a ball of chewing tobacco in his mouth.

His brother stared into the flames. "I don't know. Seems they'd be looking for us to show up after we robbed the bank in Big Pine."

"Maybe, maybe not." Clem turned his head, spitting into the nearby bushes. "The boys seemed real enthusiastic when they rode back to camp. Said they saw the sheriff outside the jail paying little attention to what was going on."

"We know he has a couple deputies. Where were they?"

Clem shrugged. "Who knows? Three men aren't going to stop us. Even if they know about Big Pine, they don't know if or when we plan to rob the bank. I say we go in tomorrow morning, surprise them, then ride south, out of the territory."

Sitting on a log across from Clem, Louis leaned forward to pick up the dented coffeepot, filling his cup. "Don't know that I'd risk it. We did real good at the bank in Big Pine. Plenty of money to last a while. I say we ride on, come back when they think we've cleared out of the territory."

Clem stood, pacing away, running a hand through his hair. Rounding on his brother, he spat into the bushes once more. "It don't make sense to just leave when the bank in Splendor is a few miles away and unguarded."

Louis leaned back, resting the cup on his leg. "What about the men we shot the last time we were there?"

"What about them? As far as we know, they're both dead. If they're not, what danger could they be to us?"

Louis shook his head. He knew when his brother got something in his mind, he gnawed on it and didn't let go. Clem would fight him until Louis gave in or they came to blows.

Leaning to his side, he grabbed more wood, tossing it on the fire. His gut told him they needed to lay low, take their money and leave the area. They had plenty to get them through the winter. Seeing the hard set of Clem's jaw, the straightening of his spine, Louis realized arguing would delay the inevitable.

Standing, Louis tossed out the remaining coffee. "Get the boys together. We ride to Splendor in the morning."

"Is everyone in place?" Gabe checked his six-shooter one more time, did the same with his rifle, then glanced up at Beau.

"Noah is on the balcony of the St. James, Bull is at the Dixie, and Dirk is positioned on the second floor of the Wild Rose. Cash, Caleb, and Mack are watching the north and south entrances to town. I'll be taking my place at the bank."

Gabe pulled out his pocket watch, flipping it open. "Fifteen minutes before the bank opens."

Beau moved to the door, resting his hand on the knob. "Nick is also keeping watch inside the Dixie. Clay refused to sit back and watch. He's staying inside the clinic, but his gun is ready."

Gabe should've known his business partner, Nick Barnett, and one of the town doctors, Clay McCord, wouldn't wait this out. "Is Rosemary at the clinic today?" He hoped Clay had the sense to keep her out of town until they dealt with the Dawsons.

"She is. Clay warned her, but she refused to stay at the ranch. With Rachel pregnant, Dax refused to let her leave for town."

Gabe let out a frustrated breath. "Nothing I can do about any of them now. Best get in place."

"You know, there's still a chance they'll leave Splendor alone."

Gabe shifted his stance, his gaze narrowing. "Do you believe that?"

Beau shook his head. "No, I don't."

Caro woke on a reluctant groan, pulling the covers up under her chin. After a few languid moments, she stretched, allowing her eyes to open a crack. Blinking several times, she gasped at the light streaming into her room.

Tossing off the covers, she hurried to the window, almost stumbling on the clothes she'd failed to put away the night before. The noise from the already crowded street could be heard through the glass. The sun's rays bouncing off the buildings told Caro she'd overslept.

Chastising herself, she picked up the dress from the day before and dashed to the wardrobe to select the rest of what she'd need. Her stomach rumbled. Placing a hand on it, she thought of skipping breakfast, knowing she couldn't afford to go without food if she were to accomplish anything at the house.

After washing her face, she combed her long hair, twisting it into a tight bun. As happened each morning, she knew Noah would have the wagon waiting. All she had to do before leaving was down a quick breakfast and purchase a few supplies at the general store. Taking one more glance in the mirror, Caro slipped on her coat and stepped into the hall.

Beau's spine straightened, his muscles tensing when one of the two men he and Cash had spotted the previous day walked into the bank. Moving toward the front window, Beau pulled a paper from his pocket, pretending to read it as he watched the man move his gaze from one person to the next. When he spotted Beau, he lingered a moment before continuing to the others.

Beau shifted enough to glance out the window. The second man he'd seen the day before sat on his horse, his head turning from side to side as he scanned the crowded street. Beau knew Cash would recognize each man, and would've already signaled the others. The fact he couldn't see either of the Dawson brothers bothered him more than a little.

He started to turn his attention to the man in the bank when his eye caught movement down the street. Five men on horseback rounded the corner by the church, staying in close formation as they approached the bank. Three reined to a stop. The other two cut to the right in a move that would have them circling behind Allie's shop and the bank. Beau's hand instinctively went to his gun, resting it on the handle.

Before Beau could turn away from the window, another movement caught his attention. His gut clenched at the sight of a woman with blonde hair, brown hat, and worn coat leaving the St. James. Panic rolled through him when Caro stood on the boardwalk, her gaze fixed on the men dismounting in front of the bank. He needed to warn her, caution her to get back inside and out of the path of danger.

Luck wasn't on his side. What happened next fell beyond his control as three of the men in front rushed inside, guns drawn, closing the door, leaving one man outside to keep watch. The man he'd been watching inside the bank drew his gun, pointing it at Beau's chest.

"Everyone stay calm."

Beau recognized the one talking as Louis Dawson. Next to him stood his brother, Clem. One man still sat on his horse, two others waiting behind the bank. He didn't worry too much about them. As a precaution, Gabe had ordered the back door and windows be barricaded.

By now, Noah would have his Spencer repeating rifle trained on the front door, ready to shoot the outlaws as they came out. With his skill, he could have at least three on the ground before anybody could react.

Bull had borrowed the Sharp's rifle Noah used in the war. He might not be as good a shot, but he could still be counted on to hit his mark. That left Gabe, Cash, and the others. The Dawsons and their men wouldn't make it out of Splendor alive.

Horace Clausen stepped forward, his hands up. "Tell me what you want and I'll get it. No one needs to get hurt."

Louis walked toward him, motioning with his gun. "The money behind the counter and in your safe. And you'd better not try something foolish. The men won't hesitate to shoot."

"Believe me, we don't want trouble." Clausen moved behind the counter, opening drawers, pulling out money. "The rest is in the safe."

Louis glanced over his shoulder. "Clem. Gather this money."

Beau's job was to make certain no one in the bank became a victim. His gaze moved between the outlaws, keeping track of their locations. Clausen and his employees had played their parts well. Besides himself, there were no other patrons in the bank. So far, all had gone according to plan...except for Caro. He wanted to glance outside, make certain she'd moved down the street and out of harm's way, but he couldn't.

Caro rested a hand on the stair railing outside the St. James, hesitating to continue on to Noah's livery. Something wasn't right. She couldn't explain why, but the group of men who rode into town didn't fit. They spoke to someone already out front, then dismounted, looked around, and went into the bank.

Taking one hesitant step down, she stopped again, her hand wrapping around the handrail in a tight grip. Glancing down the street, she saw Mack, Caleb, and Gabe all focusing on the bank. Shifting, she spotted Cash leaning against the doorframe of Allie's shop. Without a doubt, she knew something was about to happen.

Her chest squeezed. Gabe and all his deputies were accounted for—except one. She hadn't seen Beau. Thinking back on the previous evening, she tried to recall if he mentioned riding out of town today. He hadn't.

The longer she waited without seeing Beau, the harder it became to move away. Her body didn't want to respond, her feet refusing to move. Shifting her gaze toward the jail, she saw Dirk Masters walk out of the Wild Rose, a rifle in hand, his gaze focused on the bank. She'd seen the Redemption's Edge foreman in town many times, but never with such an intense look on his

276

face. This was a man on the hunt, his determined steps taking him toward the bank. Stopping at the general store, he slipped inside, his attention now on the man waiting with the horses in front of the bank.

Unable to draw a solid breath, Caro took another step toward the street as panic began to rule her movements. A vague notion of someone speaking her name pierced her senses, but didn't stop her. Glancing toward Gabe, she saw him wave a warning in her direction. Shaking her head, she watched her childhood friend's face turn from worry to anger. Her head told her to heed his signal. Her heart had other ideas.

If she lived to be a hundred, Caro would never be able to completely recall what happened next or the way she reacted.

When one of the tellers coughed, drawing the attention of the outlaws, Beau took the opportunity to glance outside, his heart squeezing when he saw Caro walk across the street toward the bank.

"Enough." Louis Dawson stood a few feet from the teller, his gun aimed at the older man's chest. In the next instant, he raised it toward the ceiling, pulling the trigger. The deafening crack of gunfire reverberated through the hushed room.

Clem's panicked gaze shot to his brother. "Damn it, Louis. Anyone outside could've heard that. We gotta get out of here."

Louis didn't answer Clem as he glanced at his other men. "Outside. Now."

The four outlaws kept their guns aimed at those inside the bank as they backed toward the door. Louis stepped outside first, followed by the other two men, then Clem. Without holstering their guns, each turned toward their horses, stopping at the sight of several armed men surrounding them.

"Drop your guns."

Louis heard the deep growl, spotting the badge on the man issuing the order. Shaking his head, he turned toward Gabe. "You can't kill us all. We'll get a few of you."

"Don't be stupid, Dawson. There are close to a dozen men with guns on you."

"He's right, Louis. We'll never make it out of here alive."

Louis glanced over his shoulder at Clem, shaking his head. "I ain't living my life in prison. We fight our way out of here." Lifting his gun, he aimed it at a woman several feet away, her face drawn in fear. "She'll be the first one to die."

Without looking, Gabe murmured a curse, knowing Louis had spotted Caro. "You kill her and you'll hang."

Not answering, Louis pulled the trigger, then dropped from a single bullet to his head, the action setting off an explosion of gunfire. Screams were drowned out by the piercing sounds of bullets and cries of those hit. The acrid aroma of gunpowder overpowered the crisp, clean smell of the morning air. The crowded street erupted in chaos. Horses bolted in panic, throwing off their riders. Those on wagons found it hard to control their animals as the fight continued. After what seemed hours, when only a few minutes had passed, the gunfire ceased, replaced by wails and moans of the injured.

"Caro!" Beau burst from the bank, his gun still smoking. He didn't glance down at the bodies lying at his feet. His complete attention was focused on the body lying in a crumpled heap in the middle of the street.

Dropping beside her, Beau rolled her over, his breath hitching at the blood on her forehead.

"Is she..." Gabe's words died on his lips as he watched Caro's eyelids flutter, not opening, a low moan escaping her lips. The flesh wound wasn't deep, but could still be serious. Letting out a harsh breath of relief, he patted Beau on the shoulder. "Doc needs to take care of her."

Slipping his arms under her body, Beau lifted Caro. "I have her." Taking determined strides toward the clinic, he didn't see Caleb and Cash bending over a fallen Dirk Masters.

# Chapter Twenty

"Give me some room." Doctor Clay McCord shooed everyone out except his assistant, Rosemary. "You, too, Beau."

Crossing his arms, he planted his feet shoulder width apart, daring Clay to force him out. "I'm staying."

Having no desire to waste time arguing, Clay nodded. "As long as you stay out of our way."

"I'm finished, Doctor." Rosemary took a step back after cleaning Caro's wound, allowing Clay to examine her forehead.

Dropping his arms to his sides, Beau took a slight step forward, halting when Clay glanced up, his eyes narrowing in warning. Although moaning every so often, Caro still hadn't regained consciousness. With each passing minute, Beau became more concerned, believing the wound might be more serious than he'd first thought.

Straightening, Clay spoke without looking up at Beau. "It doesn't appear to be serious. A bullet grazed Caro's forehead, causing her to lose consciousness. I'll need to suture it. Do you want to wait in the front?"

Beau shook his head. "No."

Clay worked quickly to close the wound, swiping an arm across his forehead when he finished.

A soft moan had all three staring at Caro. Another moan preceded her eyelids fluttering before opening to thin slits. Blinking a few times, she tried to lift a hand to her head.

"Hold on, Caro." Clay grasped her hand, lowering it to the table. "You need to take it slow."

"What...happened?" The fear in her strained voice tore at Beau's heart. He stepped forward, taking her hand in his and squeezing.

"You were shot, sweetheart."

Caro blinked again. "Beau?"

"I'm here, Caro."

She tightened her hold on his hand. "You're all right."

He swallowed the lump in his throat, nodding.

"I thought..." She closed her eyes, her voice trailing off.

"You thought what, sweetheart?"

When she didn't respond, Clay stepped forward. "She needs to rest, Beau."

A sharp pounding on the door preceded Cash pushing it open. "Doc. We've got Dirk Masters and he's in a bad way."

Rosemary gasped, placing a hand over her mouth, her eyes wide.

"Bring him in here. Beau, help me move Caro to the other room."

Without hesitating, Beau scooped her into his arms, moving swiftly past the men carrying Dirk into the room. Laying her on the bed in the other exam room, he brushed hair from her face, wincing at the sutures on her forehead. Leaning down, he kissed her cheek, then slowly straightened.

"Clay asked me to bring you this." Rosemary stood in the doorway holding out a blanket. "I need to help with Dirk." She dashed away, but not before Beau saw the extreme worry on her face.

Stepping out of the small room and into the front area, he heard raised voices, watching as Gabe, Cash, and Caleb left the room where they'd carried Dirk.

"How is he?"

Cash walked up to Beau. "Not good. A bullet to his chest. But not before he downed the two riders who came out from behind the bank. Honestly, I don't know how he got them both."

Beau scrubbed a hand down his face. "I didn't even wait to find out what happened."

Cash snorted. "Caro and Dirk were our only casualties. Noah killed Louis Dawson and another of the outlaws. Bull got Clem. We aren't quite sure who shot the others, but we won't need to worry about any other members of the Dawson gang. They're all dead."

Beau nodded, mumbling what sounded like *Thank God*.

Gabe walked up beside them as Caleb stepped outside. "How's Caro?"

"A bullet grazed her forehead. Doc sutured her up."

Moving past Beau, Gabe pushed open the door to the second room, glancing at a sleeping Caro. "Did she ever wake up?"

"For a couple minutes. Doc says she needs rest, but should come through all right." Shoving his hands in his pockets, he studied the floor a moment before returning his gaze to Gabe. "When Doc lets her go, I'm taking her to my place."

Gabe closed the door to where Caro slept. "Only if it's what she wants."

Beau took a step closer to his boss, his gaze hard. "I'd never force her to do anything."

Holding up both hands, Gabe backed away. "As long as we have an understanding."

"We do. Don't worry. She'll be glad to have someone watch over her while she heals."

"Absolutely not, Beau. I cannot stay in your house." Caro sat on the edge of the bed in the small examination room, her face red, arms crossed. She'd woken twice during the night, rousing Beau, who slept in a hard wooden chair against the wall. By the time the sun filtered in around the edges of the door, she was wide awake. "What would people think?"

He grinned, which infuriated her even more. "Everyone knows you were shot, sweetheart. They also know someone has to take care of you until Doc says you're all right to be alone."

"That someone does not have to be you."

Crossing his arms, Beau leaned against the doorframe, undeterred by her protests. "Then who?"

Closing her eyes, her mind scanned those who might be able to watch her for a few days. "Rosemary?"

Beau's face clouded, his smile fading.

"What?" Caro's brows knitted together, her gaze searching his.

He pushed away from the door, pacing the small room. "She's been up all night with Dirk Masters. They don't know if he's going to make it."

"He was shot?" Caro's hand went to her mouth.

"The son of a gun shot two of the outlaws before one of them hit him in the chest. He bled pretty bad. Doc had a hard time—almost lost him more than once." Beau had been up more than once to see how Dirk was doing. Both times, Rosemary sat next to the bed, holding his hand in hers, clutching a Bible in her lap.

Dirk and Bull had been the ones to find Rosemary, her brother, Ben, and two other orphans when they rustled cattle from the Pelletiers. Gabe, Dax, and Luke had put the fear of God in each of them before coming to an agreement about working off what they'd stolen by helping at the ranch. During her time staying at Redemption's Edge, Rosemary and Dirk had earned a reputation for reacting to each other the same as water and kerosene. There'd been times Rachel had thought they might come to blows.

Although several years younger than Dirk, Rosemary never gave an inch, testing him every time he gave an order until he'd been ready to take her over his knee. The one thing saving everyone's sanity was Rosemary's request to learn nursing from Rachel's uncle, Doc Worthington, and his associate, Clay.

With Worthington visiting back east, Clay and Rosemary worked together, giving rise to speculation about them being sweet on each other. Watching her tonight as she kept a close vigil over Dirk, he wondered if what they felt for each other was animosity or something much different.

"Poor Dirk."

Beau stopped pacing, his gaze locking on Caro. "We have to believe he'll make it. According to Rosemary, he's too darn ornery to die."

"Let's hope she's right."

Picking up the blanket, Beau wrapped it around her shoulders. "Let's get you home before too many people are in the street."

"No, Beau. I simply *cannot* stay with you."

"It's for the best."

"I can't. Why can't you understand?"

"There's nothing to understand. You've been hurt." A grin turned up the corners of his mouth. "You need someone to keep watch on you a few days, Caro, and I'm the man for the job."

She would've found his insistence endearing if the real reason for her discomfort wasn't so painful. He'd made it abundantly clear he didn't want her in his life as more than a friend. The realization of what she'd lost was still too raw for more than a neighborly nod when they passed on the street. In time, she hoped she could give him the friendship he wanted, but that day had yet to come. For now, Caro needed to be as far away from Beau as possible, not sharing a house with him tending to her.

Lowering her gaze, she focused on the floor, her voice a mere whisper. "I can't be around you, Beau. Please, try to understand."

Stepping closer, he lifted her chin with a finger, his face somber. "I haven't given up on us, Caro. I hope you haven't, either."

Her eyes widened. "But—"

Touching her lips with his finger, he silenced her. "Let me take care of you. We'll figure it out as we go along." Brushing a quick kiss across her lips, he didn't give her time to protest before slipping his arms around her, lifting her to his chest. For the first time in what seemed like forever, his world began to feel right.

"He hasn't woken up yet, Doctor."

Clay looked at Rosemary, noting the dark circles and red-rimmed eyes. Not for the first time, he wondered if her feelings for Dirk were deeper than most believed. "Let me have a look."

Checking Dirk's bandages, he let out a relieved sigh at finding no signs of infection. "The bleeding is under control. His pulse and heart rate are steady. Given time, and the lack of infection, Mr. Masters just might make it." He turned, gripping Rosemary's arm and squeezing. "I see you have your Bible."

Shrugging, she let her gaze wander down Dirk's chest, now wrapped in a thick bandage. "I thought it might help."

"Medicine isn't perfect, Rosemary. I'm certain Dirk will appreciate whatever help we can give him."

"Hello? Doctor McCord, are you in there?"

"I'll be back in a moment, Rosemary." Walking to the door of the exam room, he pushed it open, a grin spreading across his face. "Good morning, Miss Barnett. I hope you aren't ill." From the first time Clay met Nick Barnett's daughter, Olivia, she had a strange effect on him. With her dark brown hair and green eyes, she turned heads wherever she went. Although friendly, she never seemed to let her guard down, always keeping her distance.

"No, I'm fine. It's my father and Mrs. Briar."

Clay's face grew serious. "Are Nick and Suzanne all right?"

"Oh, they're fine. It's just, well...they've decided not to wait any longer to get married. They plan to have a ceremony this weekend and hope you'll be able to attend. I know it isn't fashionable to post invitations this way, but..." She shrugged, a slight tinge of red coloring her cheeks. Like everything else about her, Clay found it appealing.

"Of course I'll attend. Rosemary Thayer is in the back." He glanced over his shoulder.

"Oh, she's also invited. Nick has sent word to the Pelletiers and a few other ranchers, as well as their other friends in town." She bit her lower lip, her gaze darting around the room. "Well, I suppose I should be going."

Although he knew he shouldn't, Clay searched for a reason for her to stay longer. At twenty-eight, he couldn't hope to garner the attention of a nineteen-year-old beauty such as Olivia. Still...

"Perhaps one evening after the wedding, you'll allow me to escort you to supper."

Her brows lifted, mouth curving into an infectious smile. "Why, that would be lovely, Doctor McCord."

A warmth and anticipation he hadn't felt in a long time moved through him. "Wonderful. We'll speak at the wedding and confirm a day."

She nodded, the flush on her cheeks deepening. "I really should go. I look forward to seeing you this weekend."

Clay watched her leave, a little of the sadness he'd experienced in his life going with her.

Beau leaned against the door frame of his bedroom, watching Caro sleep. It had been two days since he'd spirited her out of the clinic and into the small house behind the jail. Two days of sleeping in his bedroll on the floor next to where she slept.

More than once, he had to suppress the urge to stretch out on the bed, wrap her in his arms, and draw her against his chest. Listening to her soft breathing, the slight noises she made as she slept had almost been his undoing.

He'd given a lot of thought to Caro and their stormy relationship. Except it hadn't been stormy until her return from San Francisco. Before she left, they'd shared so many memorable times. They'd been careful while in public, keeping their relationship and assignations private. A few of their closest friends knew, others guessing at their connection after she left. He'd never realized the extent to which a man could love a woman. Not until she no longer held a place in his life.

Her return had thrown him into a bout of denial, blinding him to his true feelings, pushing an even greater wedge between them. He'd been sure she'd leave again, unable to find happiness in the small frontier town where he'd made his home. Now, he wasn't so sure.

By this time next year, he'd be in his own place, and he didn't want to live there alone. He wanted Caro to join him.

"I can't stay here forever, Beau. At some point, I'll have to go back to the hotel."

Caro's words jolted him from his private musings. Pushing away from the door, he walked toward the bed. "I didn't know you were awake."

She pushed up, sitting with her back against the headboard, the covers drawn up under her chin. "I've been watching you for a few minutes. You were so deep in thought, I didn't want to disturb you."

Sitting on the edge of the bed, he took her hand in his. "You could never disturb me, Caro."

She wished she could say the same about him. "I doubt that's true. I seem to have disturbed you a great deal since returning from California."

He chuckled, then sobered, remembering his first glimpse of her at the Pelletier's party after she'd arrived back in Splendor. She'd returned from San Francisco the day before, arriving at the ranch unannounced, surprising everyone.

"I never expected you to return."

Her lips drew into a thin line. Squeezing his hand, she let out a shaky breath. "Looking back, I should have sent you a message asking if you still wanted me. It would've saved both of us more hurt."

"And if my reply was I'd met someone else, would you have still returned?"

Closing her eyes, she drew in a slow breath. "I don't know." Then she shook her head. "Probably not." No matter how much she wanted a life in Splendor, it would've been too painful to watch him build a life with someone else.

A weary smile tilted up the corners of his mouth. "Well, you're here now and it doesn't appear you're going anywhere."

Opening her eyes, her back stiffened. "I'm definitely *not* going anywhere. In fact, my house will be ready to move into within a few days. By Christmas, I'll be settled. In fact, I plan to have a housewarming party. You'll be invited, of course...although I doubt you'll be inclined to attend."

Beau winced, knowing he'd been the one to state he had no intention of visiting once she moved in. Cupping her face in his hands, he locked his gaze with hers. "If you want me there, I'll come."

Caro studied him, her heart pounding. She wanted nothing more than for him to lean in and kiss her the way he used to. The same as she wanted for the last two days. Instead, he'd been a total gentleman—caring for her, cooking meals, checking her wound. She no longer wanted to be pampered. She wanted Beau to love her again, make love to her the way he used to, with a passion that left her breathless and wanting more.

As if in answer to her prayers, Caro's breath caught as he leaned in, brushing his lips over hers. It was gentle, tentative, as if he were asking permission. Caro didn't let him wait long. Wrapping her arms around his neck, she deepened the kiss, hearing a deep groan of approval from Beau.

Breaking the kiss, he drew her down, stretching out beside her, whispering in her ear. "I want you, Caro."

She searched his face, seeing the raw emotion in his eyes. "For how long?"

Stroking a thumb across her lower lip, he spoke what was in his heart. "As long as you'll have me."

# Chapter Twenty-One

Beau sat in a chair in his front room, tears welling in his eyes as he glanced again at the letter he'd received from his father that afternoon. They'd received the latest payment for the care of his sister, Genevieve. Written in the broad, flourishing sweep of his father's hand, the message informed him they wouldn't be needing further monies as Genevieve had passed away in her sleep a few nights before. The letter continued, but Beau's mind stilled on the news of her death.

By the time the letter reached him, she'd been gone for weeks, the services well in the past. His heart squeezed, knowing he'd never hear the final words said over her grave, the tribute to a vivacious girl whose future had been cut short by a brother who'd allowed himself to become distracted. No one blamed him. There'd been no recriminations, no hushed words of blame said behind his back. Everyone had absolved the twelve-year-old Beauregard Davis, except the boy himself. Now sweet Genevieve was gone, and so was a part of his life he'd never be able to reclaim.

"Beau?" Caro walked in the front door, dropping to her knees in front of him. "What's wrong?"

His throat swelled with emotion, aching at the reality of his father's news. Scrubbing a hand down his face, he handed Caro the letter. The night before, they'd talked of many things, including regrets. She'd been the only person he'd shared all the details about Genevieve with, the guilt he carried with him, the financial support he provided. Caro's carefully uttered words soothed him, insisting he was doing all he could, contending he shouldn't blame himself for an accident out of his control. He'd held her afterward, resting his chin on the top of her head, doing his best to accept what she'd said.

Finishing the last line, shaking her head, Caro handed the letter back to him. "I'm so sorry. After last night, hearing what happened, I'd hoped to meet Genevieve someday." As she wrapped her arms around him, all Beau could think about was how he'd lost a sister who'd owned a piece of his heart and how close he'd come to losing another woman who meant so much to him.

"One more day, Caro. That's all I'm asking." Beau slid his legs into his pants the following morning, pulling them up to rest on the curve of his hips, turning toward her. "I'll ride out this morning, talk to your men, then come back with a list of any additional supplies. Tomorrow, we'll go out together and deliver them." Seeing Caro's gaze focus on his bare chest, then move lower, his brows lifted, a smile playing across his lips as he chuckled. "You're insatiable."

Immediately looking away, her face flushed. "I have no idea what you're referring to, Mr. Davis."

He leaned down, dropping a kiss on her lips. "Oh, I think you do."

With a feigned gasp of disbelief, she threw off the covers, intending to dress and go with him. Standing, she lifted a hand to touch the wound on her forehead, feeling woozy. Steadying herself against the bed, she sat back down.

Beau watched, making no move to her side of the bed. "Now will you stay?"

She scowled, her lips twisting in exasperation. "Fine, but I'm going out tomorrow whether you approve or not."

"I'll ask Doc McCord to stop by later today. As long as he says you're fine..." He shrugged, ignoring her irritated expression. Moving around the bed, he sat beside her, wrapping an arm around her shoulders. "You gave me a bad scare. All I'm asking is for Clay to check on you once more." Brushing a kiss across her lips, he stood. "I need to let Gabe know I'll be gone for a few hours. Do you need anything before I leave?"

The way he tended to treat her as a child infuriated Caro, while making her feel loved and cared for at the same time. He'd made it clear his concern came from a combination of love and fear. As he'd said last night, holding her in his arms, a fraction of an inch change in the wound's location and he'd be standing by her grave instead of making love to her. Rather than being resentful at his controlling attitude, she tried to keep those thoughts in her mind.

"No, I'll be fine. Please let the men know I'll be out tomorrow." She settled against the headboard, pulled the covers up, and crossed her arms, daring him to argue with her.

He nodded, his expression bland. "I'll give them your best." Before she could respond, he grabbed his hat and left, not hearing her annoyed sigh.

"You sure you don't mind me leaving town for a few hours?" Beau stood next to Gabe, who sat outside the jail, taking a rare break.

"Go ahead. With the Dawson gang taken care of, I suspect it will be pretty quiet around here for a while." Gabe leaned back in the chair, crossing his arms. Even with his coat, the cold winter wind pierced through his clothes. "I suppose you'll be moving in with Caro."

Beau startled. They'd agreed to give their relationship another try. He felt certain it would end in marriage, but after her response the last time he asked her, he didn't want to think too far ahead.

"She hasn't invited me and I haven't asked. Besides, I'll have my own place by this time next year."

Gabe nodded, a grin tipping up the corners of his mouth. "It sure will be convenient to ride between Caro's house and your new place."

Beau snorted, not responding. If they married, he hoped she'd move into his house. Right now, he didn't want to speculate or bring it up to Caro. "I'd better get going. I need to pick up more food for Caro's men before I head out."

Once his errand was done and he'd secured the food in his saddlebags, Beau grabbed Smoke's reins, mounting in one smooth movement. Glancing up at a sky dotted with a few white clouds, he felt a chill as the wind picked up. Christmas would soon be upon them, and if the last couple years were any indication, the town could expect to spend it in a couple feet of snow.

Leaving town, he thought of how he and Caro had seemed to settle the rift between them. He'd come to believe she'd be staying in Splendor with or without him in her life. The thought of her with another man wasn't acceptable, not even thinkable. They loved each other. Now they had to find a way to make it last without letting old wounds get in the way.

Whistling, he turned his thoughts to the house he planned to build. The plans were drawn, Bull already committing to help him. He felt confident there'd be others needing work. With the money left in the account from his grandfather, he'd be able to create a comfortable place for him and Caro where they could raise a family.

A brief surge of guilt washed over him at the reason he no longer had to horde the funds. He'd vowed to use little of it as long as Genevieve lived. Accepting the truth was bittersweet. He thought of his sister, knowing if she'd lived, she and Caro would've been fast friends. His parents would love her as much as he did. Once his house was built, he promised himself to find time to take her back east. It had been too long since he'd been home.

Reining left at the split in the trail, Beau looked once more at the sky. Clouds were moving in, shifting into a pattern indicating snow. He'd meet with the men, deliver the food, find out what else they needed, then head back to town. *To Caro*, he thought as her house came into sight.

"Any change, Rosemary?" Clay leaned over Dirk, checking the bandages again, looking for any sign of infection.

She shook her head, her eyes showing the dejection she'd been fighting for hours. "Nothing. He's moaned a few times, but never opened his eyes. It's been several days. What if he never wakes up?"

He expected to see tears well up in her eyes, as they had the day Dirk had been shot. Although her face seemed haggard and there were dark circles under her eyes, Rosemary's expression remained stoic, ready for whatever he might say. Clay placed a hand on her shoulder, his voice calm.

"We won't worry about that yet. His breathing is normal, heartbeat strong, and there's no sign of infection. I have every reason to believe he'll wake up soon."

"There was so much damage. Do you think he'll be able to return to work at the ranch?"

"Dirk has a robust constitution. A lesser man wouldn't have made it this far. If I were a betting man, which I am on occasion, I'd say he'll be back to work within weeks." He took a better look at Rosemary, studying the color of her skin and her frail appearance. "When was the last time you ate something?"

She shook her head, her gaze locked on Dirk. "I'm not sure. Maybe yesterday."

"That's not acceptable, Rosemary. You can't help our patients if you don't keep yourself fed and healthy." Digging into his pocket, he pulled out some money, holding it out to her. "I'll stay here while you go to Suzanne's to eat."

Glancing up at him, she bit her lower lip. "Would you mind getting something for me? I don't want to be away if he wakes up."

He sighed, but nodded. "If it will make you feel better. I won't be gone long."

Rosemary watched as Clay left the clinic, then turned back to Dirk. His features were calm, almost boyish as he slept. The lines of worry usually etched on his strong face were smooth, as if he hadn't a single care.

She thought back on the day he and Bull had found her, her brother, and the other two orphans rustling a few head of cattle. He'd been furious, treating her as a common criminal. He'd even threatened to turn her over his knee if she didn't do as he and Bull said.

Even after the Pelletiers and the sheriff had come to an agreement on having the orphans work off the debt, Dirk hadn't let up on her. He treated the other three boys as any other ranch hand. His attitude was markedly different with her—more demanding, critical, and impatient. They'd argued over everything, until she'd come to expect a confrontation each time they saw each other. She'd hated him, wanting nothing more than to leave the ranch and get away from such a boorish soul.

Once she moved into a small room at Suzanne's boardinghouse to learn about nursing from Doc Worthington and Clay, it hadn't taken long for her to miss their lively encounters. She'd wake up thinking she had to prepare herself for another skirmish with Dirk. Then she'd look around her room and deflate a little, knowing it could be days or weeks before she'd see the insufferable man again. Rosemary had yet to figure out the reason for her reaction.

"Water..."

She jumped at the raspy voice. Standing, she hovered over him, staring at his closed eyes. "Dirk? Can you hear me?"

His face scrunched into a frown, his eyes opening to slits. "What are you..." He coughed, shaking his head when Rosemary attempted to lift it. "Water."

Pouring a glass, she held it up. "You'll have to let me help you." This time, she slipped a hand behind his head, refusing to let him shake her off, then pressed the glass to his lips. "Drink this."

Taking a few tentative sips, he choked a little, then took some more. Clearing his throat, his glazed eyes fixed on her. "What are you doing here?" His voice was as gruff and unforgiving as she remembered.

Setting down the glass, she glared down at him. "Helping you stay alive."

His eyes widened. "Stay alive?" Trying to sit up, he groaned in pain, then fell back. "Where am I?" The gritty voice sounded as if he'd swallowed a cup of sand. Picking up the glass, Rosemary helped him take more water.

"You're at the clinic. You were shot by one of the outlaws."

"That's plum crazy. I don't remember any..." He squeezed his eyes shut, then opened them quickly, letting out a ragged breath. "The Dawsons."

"According to Gabe, you killed two of them before another one shot you in the chest. You've been here for several days."

"Days..." He ground the word out before trying to sit up again. "I have to get back..." He winced in pain.

"You aren't going anywhere." Rosemary placed her hands on Dirk's shoulders, gently pushing him back down.

"Leave me be, girl."

"Neither of us is that lucky, and I'm *not* a girl. I'm afraid you're stuck with me. Doc McCord left me to take care of you, and you're going to behave."

Dirk turned his head, trying to focus on her with glazed eyes. He didn't have to look too hard to know she was right. Rosemary wasn't a girl. A fact he'd been doing his best to ignore since the day he'd caught her rustling.

"Sounds as if our patient has decided to join us." Clay walked into the room, his arms laden with food for him and Rosemary. "It's good to see you awake, Dirk. How do you feel?" He set down the items in his arms.

Dirk grimaced. "How do you think?"

"Dirk." Rosemary's face darkened at the disrespect in his voice.

Clay chuckled. "It's all right, Rosemary. I'd feel the same if it were me."

"How bad is it?" Dirk's voice had calmed, his features expressing an amount of worry Rosemary hadn't noticed before Clay returned.

Clay didn't believe in watering down the truth. "Bad. We didn't think you'd make it, but you fooled us. Since it appears you've been trying to sit up, let me take a look. I don't want the bandages to loosen."

Rosemary stepped away, giving Clay ample room to inspect the wound. She'd done her best to hide the enormous relief she felt when she heard his raspy voice. It didn't take him long to transform from an unresponsive patient to his normal, cantankerous self. The change gave her an enormous sense of comfort, but she couldn't explain why.

"All looks good. You'll need to stay here a few more days, of course, but I do believe you'll live long enough to see your grandchildren."

Dirk choked, his face grimacing in pain. "I don't plan to marry again or have children, Doc." He winced at the slip he'd made, hoping neither Clay nor Rosemary caught it.

"I didn't know you were married."

Closing his eyes, Dirk let out a breath. "She's dead."

Clay's voice softened. "I'm sorry."

"It's been a while now." Opening his eyes, Dirk refused to look at Rosemary, not wanting to see her reaction. "Why can't I go back to the ranch? Rachel Pelletier knows what to do better than the girl you've got here."

Clay ignored Rosemary's quick intake of breath. "Rachel is pregnant and doesn't need another chore added to what she already does. Besides, this *young woman* has come a long way in a few months. She's quite qualified to help me take care of you."

"Couldn't prove it by me."

Rosemary almost missed Dirk's mumbled response, her face turning to stone at the insult.

"Well, Dirk, I'm afraid Rosemary and I are all you've got. Now, you're going to stay in here one or two more days. If you're still doing all right, we'll move you to the other room where there's a more comfortable bed." He turned to Rosemary, nodding toward the food. "Why don't you take that into the house and eat? When you're done, come back here and I'll take my turn."

Rosemary couldn't move fast enough to get away. Scooping up the wrapped plates, she disappeared outside.

Clay turned back to Dirk, his eyes taking on a hard glint. "Rosemary is turning into a fine nurse. I know you two have a history of not getting along, but it's best for your recovery if you do. You may not know, but she refused to leave your side for days, hardly ate, and wouldn't allow me to relieve her. It's up to you, Dirk, but if it were me, I'd show her some respect."

Closing his eyes, Dirk nodded. "I'll do my best, Doc."

"I hope you will."

# Chapter Twenty-Two

Beau struggled to sit up, nauseous from the pain radiating in his head. The rope binding his wrists made it hard to move, while the extreme darkness made it difficult to see. Worse, he couldn't remember how he'd gotten here, who had attacked him, or if he'd been here for minutes, hours, or days.

Cursing roundly, Beau forced himself to fight through the pain and right himself against the wall behind him. Once settled, he felt the cold seep through his shirt. The sensation made him wonder where his coat had gone and why he was in a place with dirt walls.

Blinking a few times, he forced himself to concentrate. He remembered being with Caro at his place, riding toward her ranch, seeing her place in the distance. An image of the house was the last thing he recalled before his memory failed.

Voices from above had him straining to listen. He didn't know if the sounds came through a door to the space where he was held prisoner or through the ceiling above. Shifting, he tried to stand. His boots slipped on the damp dirt, causing him to topple over. Mumbling more curses, he righted himself and tried again. This time, using the dirt wall as leverage, he achieved success.

At over six feet tall, he touched low spots of the ceiling, causing bits of dirt to fall onto his head. At least they hadn't taken his hat. Again, he heard voices. Beau couldn't make out what was being said, but the exchange had risen in intensity, indicating a possible argument. As they spoke, he began to understand small pieces of the conversation. When he heard *Caro* and *Davis*, a cold chill ran through him.

Then the voices stopped and heavy footsteps moved across the floor above. Beau turned in circles, letting his eyes adjust to the darkness. After a few more minutes, a sliver of light appeared across the room, maybe six feet away. Thankful they hadn't bound his feet, Beau crossed the small space, halting when his boots hit a hard surface. *Stairs,* he thought. Looking up, he saw light coming through small slits in the wooden door. A door made of old wood he recognized. *Caro's house.* They were holding him in the root cellar completed a few weeks before.

His mind sorted through the possibilities. He wondered why anyone would take him prisoner, especially men hired by Caro. Merritt and Gus Teal had worked for Ty Murton, who recommended them. As far as he knew, they'd never given her any cause for alarm.

The Smith brothers, John and Joe, were a different story. Cash had been suspicious of them from the start, not comfortable with the story they spun. Beau had dismissed them as unfortunate casualties of the war and economy. The fact they'd been born in Alabama seemed more coincidence than threat. He'd never heard Caro utter a word of disappointment in their work. Instead, she'd praised them for their desire to build a better life, citing their idea to go after the wild horses in order to build a herd, which excited her.

Whether the Teal or Smith brothers took him captive didn't matter as much as the reason why. Ransom was one possibility. There could be a good deal of money made by holding him, counting on Caro to pay the sum demanded.

Even in his current situation and the pain in his head, he chuckled. A few days ago, he wouldn't have taken a bet that Caro would pay to save his ornery hide. Much had changed since the shooting.

After the war, he'd made enemies as a bounty hunter. Families and friends of the men he'd captured or killed often threatened revenge. He and Cash had been the object of their grief and hatred more than once. No one had ever made good on their threats, and Beau believed if someone wanted to track him down, it would have happened long ago.

That left the shooting of Lieutenant Perry Eldridge as a possible motive. His family paid Pinkerton to locate Beau, verify he lived in Splendor. There could be just one reason for their inquiry—they intended to kill the man responsible for their relative's death. He doubted the Eldridge family would do the deed themselves. People such as them would hire somebody, paying handsomely for the service.

He heard voices outside. A few minutes later, the sound of horses riding away thrust him into action. He glanced around the room and up the stairs to the door that would provide his freedom. Leaning forward, he balanced himself against the rails on either side as he took each step. His head pounded, screaming for some type of relief. Beau knew the only relief he'd get would come from escape.

Reaching the third step from the top, he braced himself with both legs, touching his head to the door. Gritting his teeth against the pain he knew would follow, he pushed up with all the strength he had left, cursing when the door didn't budge.

With his wrists tied behind him and the steep steps, he had no other options. Knowing it was a waste of time, he braced his legs on the steps once more, pushing his head against the door. As happened the first time, he gained nothing. Before Beau could step down, the door flew open, the butt of a gun coming down hard, generating an explosion of pain, knocking him to the ground and into blackness.

"Noah, I need to ride out to my place. Would you mind saddling my horse?" Caro steadied herself against the wall of the livery, her face strained with concern.

Noah wiped his blackened hands on a rag, stuffing it into a pocket as he studied her features. "Are you sure you feel up to riding? You don't look so well."

She, Gabe, and Noah had grown up together, been friends most of their lives. No matter how hard they tried, there was little they could get past each other.

"Beau rode out to my place this morning. He planned to return by mid-afternoon, but he hasn't." She swallowed the ball of concern welling in her throat. "I'm worried about him."

Slinging an arm around her shoulders, he turned Caro away from the livery. "You need to talk to Gabe. He'll take care of finding Beau."

She didn't protest as Noah escorted her the short distance to the jail. Pushing the door open, he let her pass in front of him, hearing her let out a relieved breath when she saw Gabe at his desk.

"Caro. What a nice surprise." Taking a closer look, Gabe frowned, gesturing toward a chair. "Sit down and let me know why you're here."

Shaking her head, she stayed standing. "It's Beau. He left for my place this morning and hasn't returned."

"I understand you're concerned, but it isn't that late. There's still a couple hours before the sun sets."

Biting her lower lip, she lowered herself into a nearby chair, hands clasped in her lap. "You think I'm overreacting."

He glanced at Noah before standing to walk around the desk. Leaning against the edge, he looked down at her. "I think you're worried, as I would be if Lena weren't back by the time I expected. Did Beau say when he planned to return?"

Letting out a sigh, she tried to relax. "He didn't give me a time. Just said he'd be gone a few hours. It's been over six."

Noah walked up to her chair and crouched down, taking her hand in his. "You know how Beau is. He probably stayed to help your men with something. The weather's clear, so we know he's not caught in a storm."

She looked at Noah, then Gabe. "Noah's right, isn't he?"

"I think so. I'd give him a couple more hours. If he still hasn't returned, I'll ride out and look for him."

"And I'll go with Gabe." Noah's face softened. "Why don't you let me walk you back to Beau's place? I'll stay in town until Gabe and I know if we need to start looking for him." He held out a hand, helping her to her feet.

"Thank you both. I'm sure you're right and he'll be riding back to town any time now." Linking her arm through Noah's, she let him escort her to Beau's home. "Thank you, Noah. I think the shooting has affected me more than it should."

"Don't apologize, Caro. Getting shot would upset anyone. It did me."

She knew Noah still struggled with using his left arm after being shot by the Dawson brothers months before. Thankfully, no one had to worry about those outlaws any longer.

Giving him a wry smile, she stepped inside the house. "You can't fool me, Noah Brandt. Getting shot made you angry, not upset. I believe the anger got you through the worst of it."

Nodding, he stepped back onto the street. "You may be right. Anger and Abby's unwavering support got me through it."

Closing the door, Caro leaned against it. She wanted to believe Noah and Gabe. They didn't seem at all worried about Beau, believing he'd gotten distracted with work at the house. Her instincts said otherwise, but she'd go with their counsel. At least for now.

Beau didn't believe the pain he'd experienced earlier could've gotten worse. He'd been wrong. Being kicked in the head by a horse couldn't be worse. Every muscle ached when he tried to shift positions, and now they'd bound his legs. The blow had come so fast, he hadn't had a chance to see his attacker. A vague recollection of tumbling down the stairs remained, but nothing else. Opening his eyes caused a flash of excruciating agony so intense it made his stomach roil.

"What now?"

"Do what we came here to do."

Beau tried to match the voices with faces, coming up empty. He needed to push through the pain and concentrate, figure out who these men were and why they held him in the dank root cellar under the house.

"We can't do it here."

"Agreed. The others will be back soon. We need to be gone before then."

Beau stilled as he recognized the voices. He would've bet good money against the chance it was these two men. He cleared his throat, forcing his eyes to open to slits.

"Why?"

Merritt's attention shifted from Gus to Beau. "You're awake. It'll be more fun finishing this with you knowing what's happening."

Confusion swamped Beau. He had no idea what he'd done to these men. "I don't understand..."

Gus stepped next to Merritt. "It's simple. We're honoring a promise to our mother. She demanded your death, and now it will happen."

"Your mother?"

Gus crouched down beside him. "Mrs. Swanson. You remember the name?"

He'd expected to hear the name Eldridge. His head throbbed so much, he couldn't stand to shake it. "Swanson? No. Should I?"

"See, Gus. There's been so many, he don't even remember the names of who he's killed. Guess it gets easier and easier."

"Shut your mouth, Merritt." Gus leaned forward, his hot breath brushing across Beau's face. "You *do* recognize the name Merle Swan, right?"

Hell yes, he remembered. A brutal killer who took pleasure in torturing women before he killed them. The outlaw broke into homes, took cash, jewelry, and the women. A few days later, their battered bodies were usually discovered not far from where he'd taken them, buried in shallow graves.

Beau and Cash had spent weeks tracking Swan down, then turned him over to the law. They never stayed once they received their bounty. This time, they made an exception, staying through the trial, watching the hangman slide the noose over Swan's head, then pull the handle. He'd never shown a shred of remorse, laughing at the townsfolk until he fell to his death. It had been the most disgusting sight Beau had ever witnessed.

"Who's Swan to you?"

"He was our older brother." Gus's voice held both anger and anticipation, which didn't bode well for Beau.

"It's been years. Why now?"

Gus snorted. "That's easy. By the time we found you, we were out of money. Murton hired us on for a spell, then Mrs. Iverson. When we figured out you were sweet on her, we knew our chance had come. It just came a little sooner than we expected."

Merritt shifted from one foot to the other, glancing up at the root cellar door and the dimming evening light. "We got to get him out of here, Gus. We can kill him on the trail and leave his body for the animals."

"Guess it's time for you to meet your maker, Davis." Gus grabbed Beau's arms, yanking him up. Drawing a knife, he cut through the rope around his ankles. "Don't try to get away. We'll both have our guns on you. Unlike Merritt, I don't have a problem leaving you here for Mrs. Iverson to find."

Yawning, Caro stretched her arms and legs before sitting up in bed. She'd meant to take a short rest. Instead, she'd fallen into a deep sleep.

Tossing off the covers, she dashed to the clock in the front room, her heart pounding when she saw the time. After seven, and from what she could tell, Beau hadn't returned. Rushing back to the bedroom, she dressed, slipped into her shoes, grabbed a heavy coat, gloves, and hat, and hurried to the livery, thankful to see the glow of a lantern. As she drew closer, surprise enveloped her at the sight of men and horses. She rushed up to Gabe.

"What's going on?" She gazed up at him, her eyes wide with fear.

Settling hands on her shoulders, he stared down at her. "Beau hasn't returned. Noah went by the house, but didn't want to wake you. We're riding out to find him."

"Wait. I'm going with you." She started to turn, but he kept a firm grip on her shoulders.

"No, Caro. I won't have you in the middle of what we might find."

"You can't force me to stay here, Gabe. Please, don't make me follow you."

Gabe glared at her, irritated. "You see the men behind me?"

She glanced over his shoulder, seeing Noah, Cash, Caleb, and Mack already mounted. "Yes."

He kept his voice calm. "All five of us are trained for what we might find. Can you say the same?"

Caro shook her head. "You know I can't."

"What do you think Beau will say if we find him and you're with us?"

"Probably the same as you would say if it were you missing and Lena wanted to ride out."

"That's right." A self-satisfied grin appeared on Gabe's face before his features stilled at her next words.

"But...I know Lena, and I'm certain she'd tell you the same as me. She wouldn't be left behind, and neither will I. It's up to you. Either let me ride with you, or I'll follow. It's your choice."

Sucking in a deep breath, he searched for calm. He wanted to pick Caro up, put her in a cell, and lock the door. If anything happened to her, he'd never forgive himself, and neither would Beau. Gritting his teeth, he glanced over his shoulder.

"Noah, please saddle Caro's horse."

"But—" Noah's protest died on his lips.

"Just do it." His features taut, he gave Caro a stern stare. "You *will* stay with Noah and me. You'll do whatever either of us says. No argument, or I'll lock you in the jail right now. Do you understand?"

Instead of nodding, she threw her arms around his neck. "Yes, I understand. Thank you."

He held her a moment, then disengaged her arms from his neck, setting her aside. "Wait to thank me until we've found Beau. Starting now, I don't want to hear another word from you."

Pursing her lips, trying to hide a grin, she nodded. Anticipation and determination filled her as the fear subsided. Looking at the faces of the men, she saw strength and a common purpose. Without a doubt, she knew they'd find Beau, and she'd be right beside them.

"Something isn't right." John Smith closed the gate on the outer pasture, locking in the wild horses they'd herded from miles away. It had been worth the long hours searching and the hard ride back.

Joe moved up beside him. "What do you mean?"

"Look there. See the light glowing from inside the root cellar?"

Joe blinked a few times, trying to focus. It had to be half a mile to the house. "I guess, though it's hard to tell from this distance."

"I'm telling you. There's a light in the root cellar. Someone's down in that empty hole. Why?" John grabbed the reins to his horse and swung into the saddle.

Joe shrugged. "Maybe Gus and Merritt are storing materials down there."

"Could be. Let's find out." As they got closer, John got a sick feeling in his stomach. A horse he didn't recognize stood saddled at the side of the barn. Merritt and Gus's horses stood alongside it, saddled and ready to ride. "Dismount and stay quiet. I don't like what I see."

Joe did what John asked, following his brother's lead when he drew his gun. As they got closer, loud voices rose from the root cellar, then the sound of a struggle and a loud groan before Gus came through the door, pulling another man up by the arms, Merritt carrying the man's legs. The man's hands and ankles were bound, and he appeared to be out cold.

"He's a heavy sonofabitch, ain't he, Gus? We shouldn't have knocked him out." When Merritt reached the top, he dropped Beau's legs, sucking in a deep breath as Gus released Beau's arms.

"What in tarnation are they doing, John? He looks like one of the deputies who rode out here."

The older brother shook his head. "He is." John noticed neither Merritt nor Gus held their guns. If he and Joe were going to make a move, it had to be now. "Whatever they're doing isn't right. You with me?"

"Ain't I always?" Joe ground out.

John walked into the open, Joe next to him, their guns pointed at Merritt and Gus. "What are you boys doing?"

The two men swiveled quickly, reaching for their own guns.

"Don't try it. You've seen how fast Joe and I are. You'll be dead before your fingers touch your guns." John moved closer, his gaze moving between the brothers and Beau. "Leave the deputy right there and move over to my right. Don't do anything foolish."

Gus nodded, his eyes narrowing as he watched John and Joe. He didn't believe either had ever killed a man, doubting they'd start now. If he could get to his gun, at least one would fall before the other knew what had happened. Shifting so his gun was out of their sight, he made a quick move to grab the handle.

"Don't do it, Gus." John's warning came too late.

Joe's bullet whizzed past him, hitting Gus in the shoulder. John aimed at Merritt, halting when the man threw his arms up and backed away. John ran forward, placing a booted foot on Gus's chest.

"Don't move." He turned toward Merritt, watching as Joe held his aim steady on the man. "Drop your gunbelt. Real slow. You don't want Joe to think you have some foolish idea you're going to shoot us."

"Hell no. I'm not that stupid." His hands shook as he unbuckled the belt, letting it and the gun drop to the ground.

"Kick it toward Joe."

Merritt did as John asked, his gaze moving to his brother. "Gus. You all right?" The only response was a groan.

"He's alive, which is more than you planned for the deputy." John pressed his boot hard into the wound in Gus's shoulder, a bleak expression on his face at the loud scream.

"Hell, you didn't have to do that." Merritt took a step toward Gus, then stopped when John raised his gun.

"Maybe not, but it's always rankled me to see two men go after another. Sit down with your back to the house and put your hands behind your back."

Merritt dropped to the ground, hurrying to put his arms behind him.

"Good decision." John moved over to Beau, crouching next to him. "Deputy, do you hear me?" Getting no response, he untied his hands before shaking his shoulder lightly. "Deputy, you alive?"

Beau's deep groan preceded his hand moving to his head. "What the..."

"Stay still. Looks like Merritt and Gus worked you over pretty good." John turned at the sound of approaching horses, raising his gun, then lowering it when he saw Caro with several other men. "Looks like some help has arrived, Deputy."

Almost falling from her horse to get to Beau, Caro stifled a cry at the battered body on the ground. Seeing the slow rise and fall of his chest, she knelt beside him, lifting his head, resting it in her lap.

"Beau?"

Fighting the incessant pain in his head, he forced himself to open his eyes. "Caro..." His eyes drifted shut.

"Let's take a look at him." Cash dropped down next to Caro while Gabe, Caleb, and Mack took care of Merritt and Gus, then spoke to the Smith boys. Running his hands over Beau's legs and arms, then looking for bullet wounds, he let out a relieved breath. "They hit him pretty hard, but I don't find any broken bones. The blood is from the beating, not bullets. He's likely to have a mighty strong pain in his head for a spell." He glanced over at Caro, seeing tears spilling down her cheeks. Putting an arm around her, he squeezed. "Hey. It's going to be all right. Beau's too ornery for God to want him yet."

"How is he?" Gabe knelt on the other side of Beau, wincing at the sight of his bruises and swelling.

"I'm fine," Beau ground out, tired of hearing them talk about him as if he weren't there. Forcing his eyes open, he looked at each of them. "Thanks. I doubt I would've made it through the night."

"It's John and Joe you need to thank." Gabe nodded toward the two standing next to Caleb and Mack. "Those boys recognized you, saw what was happening, and decided to help you out."

"I'll be." Cash breathed the words out. He'd been against Caro putting the young men to work. Beau had sided with her.

"I'd better ride back to town and get the wagon. Beau's in no condition to ride." Gabe stood, starting to turn away.

"I can ride. Get me on Smoke and we'll head back to town."

Leaning forward, Caro stroked a strand of hair off his forehead. "Beau, it's best not to ride yet."

He blinked a couple times, each movement an effort of pure will. "Sweetheart, if we're going to marry, you need to start listening to me."

Her jaw dropped, eyes going wide. "Marry? Who says..." She let the rest die on her lips when she looked down to see his eyes closed, his face slack.

Cash stood, clasping Gabe on the back. "Guess we're going to have another wedding pretty soon."

Nodding, Gabe smiled. "Appears you just might be right."

# Epilogue

*Two weeks later...*

"I'm glad Nick and Suzanne put the wedding off a few weeks." Gabe put an arm around Lena's shoulders, drawing her close, then looked at Beau and Caro standing on the other side of the church reception hall, holding hands. They'd almost lost both of them over the course of the last couple months.

"Nick will listen to reason once in a while. It helped that Suzanne wanted to wait until Beau and Dirk were both recovered. Any idea where Nick is taking her for their honeymoon?"

"He's not saying, but I don't think they'll be going anywhere until after the snow clears. Besides, Christmas is next week and Suzanne is cooking some of the food for the celebration at Redemption's Edge." Gabe nodded at Beau and Caro as they made their way toward them. He'd received a telegram from Pinkerton a day after Beau's ordeal. After learning more about the shooting from an officer who'd been part of Beau's inquiry, Eldridge had come to terms with his brother's death. The family decided to move on with their lives, removing the threat looming over Beau and Caro's future.

"Beautiful wedding. And Suzanne looks stunning." Caro placed a kiss on Lena's cheek, then one on Gabe's.

"The party is pretty good, too." Beau held up a glass of punch, most likely embellished with something extra.

"Have you two set a date for *your* wedding?" Lena asked.

"The spring," Caro answered.

"After Christmas," Beau said at the same time. They looked at each other, both sets of eyes flashing in amusement. "Guess it will be as soon as I can talk Caro into it."

"There's still work to do at the house. John and Joe are hard workers, but I'm going to need a couple more, and Beau will need help building his house." Caro looked across the room. "I spoke to Dax and Luke. They said it's all right with them if I ask Matt and Nolen Volker to work for me for a while."

"I see Dutch McFarlin is back in town." Beau nodded at Luke talking with Dutch across the room. "Last I heard, Pinkerton had a job for him in California."

Gabe set his empty glass on a nearby table. "He got as far as Utah before Pinkerton sent him a telegram saying the man they were after was killed in a gunfight. Dutch asked his boss for some time off. Looks like he decided to spend it here."

"He's a good man. At the rate Splendor is growing, you may need to add another deputy."

Gabe lifted a brow. "I'm thinking about it, Beau."

"Look at those two, Lena." Caro lifted her glass toward Olivia Barnett and Clay McCord. "Do you think the doctor may have an interest in Nick's daughter?"

Lena laughed, raising her glass to her lips and taking a sip. "I think several men have an interest in her and Nora Evans."

Gabe's brows shot up. "My sister?"

Lena looked at her husband. "Why not? She's beautiful, smart, and quite eligible. Have you seen the way Mack and Caleb watch her?"

Gabe shook his head, his jaw tight as he glanced at Beau. "Do you think either of them have an interest in courting her?"

Beau opened his mouth to reply, then closed it at the sound of an argument several feet away. Looking behind him, he saw Dirk and Rosemary glaring at each other, his arms crossed, her hands balled into fists on her hips. Rachel and Ginny Pelletier stood next to them, amused expressions on their faces.

"You are *not* to order me around, Dirk Masters. You aren't my boss any longer." Rosemary's face colored more with each word.

"Someone has to keep an eye on you." Dirk glared at her, his frustration rising. "You are *not* riding to Big Pine alone. I'm going with you."

"I'm perfectly capable of riding over there for supplies. Besides, Dax said one of the men from the ranch would be available to ride with me." A smug expression crossed her face when she saw Dirk's jaw slacken. Her victory was short-lived.

He recovered quickly, leaning toward her, crowding Rosemary's space. "And that ranch hand is me."

"It most certainly *is not*. In fact, I'm going to go talk to Dax now." She turned, stomping across the room toward Dax.

Dirk shook his head. He'd been recovering well from the gunshot wound to his chest. Some days, though, he wished he was still stove-up in bed. "That blasted girl is going to be the death of me."

"*Woman*, Dirk." Rachel smiled, noticing Ginny put a hand over her mouth to stop from laughing. "But I guess you'll have to figure that out for yourself."

Thank you for taking the time to read Deep River. If you enjoyed it, please consider telling your friends or posting a short review. Word of mouth is an author's best friend and much appreciated.

Please join my reader's group to be notified of my New Releases at:
http://www.shirleendavies.com/contact-me.html

I care about quality, so if you find something in error, please contact me via email at
shirleen@shirleendavies.com

# About the Author

**Shirleen Davies** writes romance—historical, contemporary, and romantic suspense. She grew up in Southern California, attended Oregon State University, and has degrees from San Diego State University and the University of Maryland. During the day she provides consulting services to small and mid-sized businesses. But her real passion is writing emotionally charged stories of flawed people who find redemption through love and acceptance. She now lives with her husband in a beautiful town in northern Arizona.

I love to hear from my readers.

Send me an email: shirleen@shirleendavies.com
Visit my Website: www.shirleendavies.com
Sign up to be notified of New Releases:
www.shirleendavies.com
Check out all of my Books:
http://www.shirleendavies.com/books.html
Comment on my Blog:
http://www.shirleendavies.com/blog.html
Follow me on Amazon:
http://www.amazon.com/author/shirleendavies
Follow my on BookBub:
https://www.bookbub.com/authors/shirleen-davies

Other ways to connect with me:

Facebook Author Page:
http://www.facebook.com/shirleendaviesauthor
Twitter: www.twitter.com/shirleendavies
Pinterest: http://pinterest.com/shirleendavies

# Books by Shirleen Davies

## *Historical Western Romance Series*
### MacLarens of Fire Mountain

Tougher than the Rest, Book One
Faster than the Rest, Book Two
Harder than the Rest, Book Three
Stronger than the Rest, Book Four
Deadlier than the Rest, Book Five
Wilder than the Rest, Book Six

### Redemption Mountain

Redemption's Edge, Book One
Wildfire Creek, Book Two
Sunrise Ridge, Book Three
Dixie Moon, Book Four
Survivor Pass, Book Five
Promise Trail, Book Six
Deep River, Book Seven

### MacLarens of Boundary Mountain

Colin's Quest, Book One,
Brodie's Gamble, Book Two
Quinn's Honor, Book Three

# *Contemporary Romance Series*

## MacLarens of Fire Mountain

Second Summer, Book One
Hard Landing, Book Two
One More Day, Book Three
All Your Nights, Book Four
Always Love You, Book Five
Hearts Don't Lie, Book Six
No Getting Over You, Book Seven
'Til the Sun Comes Up, Book Eight

## Peregrine Bay

Reclaiming Love, Book One
Our Kind of Love, Book Two

# Tougher than the Rest – Book One
## MacLarens of Fire Mountain Historical Western Romance Series

*"A passionate, fast-paced story set in the untamed western frontier by an exciting new voice in historical romance."*

Niall MacLaren is the oldest of four brothers, and the undisputed leader of the family. A widower, and single father, his focus is on building the MacLaren ranch into the largest and most successful in northern Arizona. He is serious about two things—his responsibility to the family and his future marriage to the wealthy, well-connected widow who will secure his place in the territory's destiny.

Katherine is determined to live the life she's dreamed about. With a job waiting for her in the growing town of Los Angeles, California, the young teacher from Philadelphia begins a journey across the United States with only a couple of trunks and her spinster companion. Life is perfect for this adventurous, beautiful young woman, until an accident throws her into the arms of the one man who can destroy it all.

Fighting his growing attraction and strong desire for the beautiful stranger, Niall is more determined than ever to push emotions aside to focus on his goals of wealth and political gain. But looking into the clear, blue eyes of the woman who could ruin everything, Niall discovers he will have to harden his heart and be tougher than he's ever been in his life…Tougher than the Rest.

## Faster than the Rest – Book Two
### MacLarens of Fire Mountain Historical Western Romance Series

*"Headstrong, brash, confident, and complex, the MacLarens of Fire Mountain will captivate you with strong characters set in the wild and rugged western frontier."*

Handsome, ruthless, young U.S. Marshal Jamie MacLaren had lost everything—his parents, his family connections, and his childhood sweetheart—but now he's back in Fire Mountain and ready for another chance. Just as he successfully reconnects with his family and starts to rebuild his life, he gets the unexpected and unwanted assignment of rescuing the woman who broke his heart.

Beautiful, wealthy Victoria Wicklin chose money and power over love, but is now fighting for her life—or is she? Who has she become in the seven years since she left Fire Mountain to take up her life in San Francisco? Is she really as innocent as she says?

Marshal MacLaren struggles to learn the truth and do his job, but the past and present lead him in different directions as his heart and brain wage battle. Is Victoria a victim or a villain? Is life offering him another chance, or just another heartbreak?

As Jamie and Victoria struggle to uncover past secrets and come to grips with their shared passion, another danger arises. A life-altering danger that is out of their control and threatens to destroy any chance for a shared future.

# Harder than the Rest – Book Three
## MacLarens of Fire Mountain Historical Western Romance Series

*"They are men you want on your side. Hard, confident, and loyal, the MacLarens of Fire Mountain will seize your attention from the first page."*

Will MacLaren is a hardened, plain-speaking bounty hunter. His life centers on finding men guilty of horrendous crimes and making sure justice is done. There is no place in his world for the carefree attitude he carried years before when a tragic event destroyed his dreams.

Amanda is the daughter of a successful Colorado rancher. Determined and proud, she works hard to prove she is as capable as any man and worthy to be her father's heir. When a stranger arrives, her independent nature collides with the strong pull toward the handsome ranch hand. But is he what he seems and could his secrets endanger her as well as her family?

The last thing Will needs is to feel passion for another woman. But Amanda elicits feelings he thought were long buried. Can Will's desire for her change him? Or will the vengeance he seeks against the one man he wants to destroy—a dangerous opponent without a conscious—continue to control his life?

## Stronger than the Rest – Book Four
**MacLarens of Fire Mountain Historical Western Romance Series**

*"Smart, tough, and capable, the MacLarens protect their own no matter the odds. Set against America's rugged frontier, the stories of the men from Fire Mountain are complex, fast-paced, and a*

*must read for anyone who enjoys non-stop action and romance."*

Drew MacLaren is focused and strong. He has achieved all of his goals except one—to return to the MacLaren ranch and build the best horse breeding program in the west. His successful career as an attorney is about to give way to his ranching roots when a bullet changes everything.

Tess Taylor is the quiet, serious daughter of a Colorado ranch family with dreams of her own. Her shy nature keeps her from developing friendships outside of her close-knit family until Drew enters her life. Their relationship grows. Then a bullet, meant for another, leaves him paralyzed and determined to distance himself from the one woman he's come to love.

Convinced he is no longer the man Tess needs, Drew focuses on regaining the use of his legs and recapturing a life he thought lost. But danger of another kind threatens those he cares about—including Tess—forcing him to rethink his future.

Can Drew overcome the barriers that stand between him, the safety of his friends and family, and a life with the woman he loves? To do it all, he has to be strong. Stronger than the Rest.

# Deadlier than the Rest – Book Five
## MacLarens of Fire Mountain Historical Western Romance Series

*"A passionate, heartwarming story of the iconic MacLarens of Fire Mountain. This captivating historical western romance grabs your attention from the start with an engrossing story encompassing two romances set against the rugged backdrop of the burgeoning western frontier."*

Connor MacLaren's search has already stolen eight years of his life. Now he is close to finding what he seeks—Meggie, his missing sister. His quest leads him to the growing city of Salt Lake and an encounter with the most captivating woman he has ever met.

Grace is the third wife of a Mormon farmer, forced into a life far different from what she'd have chosen. Her independent spirit longs for choices governed only by her own heart and mind. To achieve her dreams, she must hide behind secrets and half-truths, even as her heart pulls her towards the ruggedly handsome Connor.

Known as cool and uncompromising, Connor MacLaren lives by a few, firm rules that have served him well and kept him alive. However, danger stalks Connor, even to the front range of the beautiful Wasatch Mountains, threatening those he cares about and impacting his ability to find his sister.

Can Connor protect himself from those who seek his death? Will his eight-year search lead him to his sister while unlocking the secrets he knows are held tight within Grace, the woman who has captured his heart?

Read this heartening story of duty, honor, passion, and love in book five of the MacLarens of Fire Mountain series.

## Wilder than the Rest – Book Six
### MacLarens of Fire Mountain Historical Western Romance Series

*"A captivating historical western romance set in the burgeoning and treacherous city of San Francisco. Go along for the ride in this gripping story that seizes your attention from the very first page."*

*"If you're a reader who wants to discover an entire family of characters you can fall in love with, this is the series for you." – Authors to Watch*

Pierce is a rough man, but happy in his new life as a Special Agent. Tasked with defending the rights of the federal government, Pierce is a cunning gunslinger always ready to tackle the next job. That is, until he finds out that his new job involves Mollie Jamison.

Mollie can be a lot to handle. Headstrong and independent, Mollie has chosen a life of danger and intrigue guaranteed to prove her liquor-loving father wrong. She will make something of herself, and no one, not even arrogant Pierce MacLaren, will stand in her way.

A secret mission brings them together, but will their attraction to each other prove deadly in their hunt for justice? The payoff for success is high, much higher than any assignment either has taken before. But will the damage to their hearts and souls be too much to bear? Can Pierce and Mollie find a way to overcome their misgivings and work together as one?

# Second Summer – Book One
## MacLarens of Fire Mountain
## Contemporary Romance Series

*"In this passionate Contemporary Romance, author Shirleen Davies introduces her readers to the modern day MacLarens starting with Heath MacLaren, the head of the family."*

The Chairman of both the MacLaren Cattle Co. and MacLaren Land Development, Heath MacLaren is a success professionally—his personal life is another matter.

*Following a divorce after a long, loveless marriage, Heath spends his time with women who are beautiful and passionate, yet unable to provide what he longs for . . .*

Heath has never experienced love even though he witnesses it every day between his younger brother, Jace, and wife, Caroline. He wants what they have, yet spends his time with women too young to understand what drives him and too focused on themselves to be true companions.

*It's been two years since Annie's husband died, leaving her to build a new life. He was her soul mate and confidante. She has no desire to find a replacement, yet longs for male friendship.*

Annie's closest friend in Fire Mountain, Caroline MacLaren, is determined to see Annie come out of her shell after almost two years of mourning. A chance meeting with Heath turns into an offer to be a part of the MacLaren Foundation Board and an opportunity for a life outside her home sanctuary which has also become her prison. The platonic friendship that builds between Annie and Heath points to a future where each may rely on the other without the bonds a romance would entail.

*However, without consciously seeking it, each yearns for more . . .*

The MacLaren Development Company is booming with Heath at the helm. His meetings at a partner company with the young, beautiful marketing director, who makes no secret of her desire for him, are a temptation. But is she the type of woman he truly wants?

Annie's acceptance of the deep, yet passionless, friendship with Heath sustains her, lulling her to believe it is all she needs. At least until Heath drops a bombshell, forcing Annie to realize that what she took for friendship is actually a deep, lasting love. One she doesn't want to lose.

*Each must decide to settle—or fight for it all.*

## Hard Landing – Book Two
### MacLarens of Fire Mountain
### Contemporary Romance Series

Trey MacLaren is a confident, poised Navy pilot. He's focused, loyal, ethical, and a natural leader. He is also on his way to what he hopes will be a lasting relationship and marriage with fellow pilot, Jesse Evans.

*Jesse has always been driven. Her graduation from the Naval Academy and acceptance into the pilot training program are all she thought she wanted—until she discovered love with Trey MacLaren*

Trey and Jesse's lives are filled with fast flying, friends, and the demands of their military careers. Lives each has settled into with a passion. At least until the day Trey receives a letter that could change his and Jesse's lives forever.

*It's been over two years since Trey has seen the woman in Pensacola. Her unexpected letter stuns him and pushes Jesse into a tailspin from which she might not pull back.*

Each must make a choice. Will the choice Trey makes cause him to lose Jesse forever? Will she follow her heart or her head as she fights for a chance to save the love she's found? Will their independent decisions collide, forcing them to give up on a life together?

## One More Day – Book Three
### MacLarens of Fire Mountain Contemporary Romance Series

Cameron "Cam" Sinclair is smart, driven, and dedicated, with an easygoing temperament that belies his strong will and the personal ambitions he holds close. Besides his family, his job as head of IT at the MacLaren Cattle Company and his position as a Search and Rescue volunteer are all he needs to make him happy. At least that's what he thinks until he meets, and is instantly drawn to, fellow SAR volunteer, Lainey Devlin.

*Lainey is compassionate, independent, and ready to break away from her manipulative and controlling fiancé. Just as her decision is made, she's called into a major search and rescue effort, where once again, her path crosses with the intriguing, and much too handsome, Cam*

*Sinclair. But Lainey's plans are set. An opportunity to buy a flourishing preschool in northern Arizona is her chance to make a fresh start, and nothing, not even her fierce attraction to Cam Sinclair, will impede her plans.*

As Lainey begins to settle into her new life, an unexpected danger arises —threats from an unknown assailant—someone who doesn't believe she belongs in Fire Mountain. The more Lainey begins to love her new home, the greater the danger becomes. Can she accept the help and protection Cam offers while ignoring her consuming desire for him?

*Even if Lainey accepts her attraction to Cam, will he ever be able to come to terms with his own driving ambition and allow himself to consider a different life than the one he's always pictured? A life with the one woman who offers more than he'd ever hoped to find?*

## All Your Nights – Book Four
### MacLarens of Fire Mountain
### Contemporary Romance Series

*"Romance, adventure, cowboys, suspense—everything you want in a contemporary western romance novel."*

Kade Taylor likes living on the edge. As an undercover agent for the DEA and a former Special Ops team member, his current assignment seems tame—keep tabs on a bookish Ph.D. candidate the agency believes is connected to a ruthless drug cartel.

Brooke Sinclair is weeks away from obtaining her goal of a doctoral degree. She spends time finalizing her presentation and relaxing with another student who seems to want nothing more than her friendship. That's fine with Brooke. Her last serious relationship ended in a broken engagement.

Her future is set, safe and peaceful, just as she's always planned—until Agent Taylor informs her she's under suspicion for illegal drug activities.

Kade and his DEA team obtain evidence which exonerates Brooke while placing her in danger from those who sought to use her. As Kade races to take down the drug cartel while protecting Brooke, he must also find common ground with the former suspect—a woman he desires with increasing intensity.

At odds with her better judgment, Brooke finds the more time she spends with Kade, the more she's attracted to the complex, multi-faceted agent. But Kade holds secrets he knows Brooke will never understand or accept.

Can Kade keep Brooke safe while coming to terms with his past, or will he stay silent, ruining any future with the woman his heart can't let go?

## Always Love You— Book Five
### MacLarens of Fire Mountain
### Contemporary Romance Series

*"Romance, adventure, motorcycles, cowboys, suspense—everything you want in a contemporary western romance novel."*

Eric Sinclair loves his bachelor status. His work at MacLaren Enterprises leaves him with plenty of time to ride his horse as well as his Harley...and date beautiful women without a thought to commitment.

Amber Anderson is the new person at MacLaren Enterprises. Her passion for marketing landed her what she believes to be the perfect job—until she steps into her first meeting to find the man she left, but still loves, sitting at the management table—his disdain for her clear.

Eric won't allow the past to taint his professional behavior, nor will he repeat his mistakes with

Amber, even though love for her pulses through him as strong as ever.

As they strive to mold a working relationship, unexpected danger confronts those close to them, pitting the MacLarens and Sinclairs against an evil who stalks one member but threatens them all.

Eric can't get the memories of their passionate past out of his mind, while Amber wrestles with feelings she thought long buried. Will they be able to put the past behind them to reclaim the love lost years before?

## Hearts Don't Lie— Book Six
### MacLarens of Fire Mountain Contemporary Romance Series

Mitch MacLaren has reasons for avoiding relationships, and in his opinion, they're pretty darn good. As the new president of RTC Bucking Bulls, difficult challenges occur daily. He certainly doesn't need another one in the form of a fiery, blue-eyed, redhead.

Dana Ballard's new job forces her to work with the one MacLaren who can't seem to get over himself and lighten up. Their verbal sparring is second nature and entertaining until the night of

Mitch's departure when he surprises her with a dare she doesn't refuse.

With his assignment in Fire Mountain over, Mitch is free to return to Montana and run the business his father helped start. The glitch in his enthusiasm has to do with one irreversible mistake—the dare Dana didn't ignore. Now, for reasons that confound him, he just can't let it go.

Working together is a circumstance neither wants, but both must accept. As their attraction grows, so do the accidents and strange illnesses of the animals RTC depends on to stay in business. Mitch's total focus should be on finding the reasons and people behind the incidents. Instead, he finds himself torn between his unwanted desire for Dana and the business which is his life.

In his mind, a simple proposition can solve one problem. Will Dana make the smart move and walk away? Or take the gamble and expose her heart?

# No Getting Over You— Book Seven
## MacLarens of Fire Mountain
## Contemporary Romance Series

Cassie MacLaren has come a long way since being dumped by her long-time boyfriend, a man she believed to be her future. Successful in her job at MacLaren Enterprises, dreaming of one day leading one of the divisions, she's moved on to start a new relationship, having little time to dwell on past mistakes.

Matt Garner loves his job as rodeo representative for Double Ace Bucking Stock. Busy days and constant travel leave no time for anything more than the occasional short-term relationship— which is just the way he likes it. He's come to accept the regret of leaving the woman he loved for the pro rodeo circuit.

The future is set for both, until a chance meeting ignites long buried emotions neither is willing to face.

Forced to work together, their attraction grows, even as multiple arson fires threaten Cassie's new home of Cold Creek, Colorado. Although Cassie believes the danger from the fires is remote, she knows the danger Matt poses to her heart is real.

While fighting his renewed feelings for Cassie, Matt focuses on a new and unexpected opportunity offered by MacLaren Enterprises— an opportunity that will put him on a direct collision course with Cassie.

Will pride and self-preservation control their future? Or will one be strong enough to make the first move, risking everything, including their heart?

## 'Til the Sun Comes Up— Book Eight
### MacLarens of Fire Mountain
### Contemporary Romance Series

Skye MacLaren's life revolves around her family and the fierce bucking bull stock they provide to rodeos. She's competitive and competent, having no room in her life for a relationship—including one with a world champion rider and business competitor.

Gage Templeton's rodeo past and executive position with a national bucking stock supplier assures him of exciting work and nights with any woman he chooses. He'll let no one get close— until his company partners with a competitor, forcing him to work with the one woman who could turn his resolve upside down.

Knowing a relationship is the last thing either needs, both charge ahead, certain they can keep their explosive feelings for each other in check—and away from curious family and friends. Continuing their secret encounters becomes even harder when outside forces threaten both their businesses and the people they care about.

As Gage works to discover the threat meant to cripple his company, Skye's doubts increase. She wants more from the most magnetic man she's ever known, but protecting her heart must come first.

Desire, distrust, fear, and the pain of the past cloud their minds, even as they work together to identify the danger. Can two strong, determined people conquer the perils to their lives as well as their hearts?

## Redemption's Edge – Book One
### Redemption Mountain – Historical Western Romance Series

*"A heartwarming, passionate story of loss, forgiveness, and redemption set in the untamed frontier during the tumultuous years following the Civil War. Ms. Davies' engaging and complex characters draw you in from the start, creating an exciting introduction to this new historical western romance series."*

***"Redemption's Edge is a strong and engaging introduction to her new historical western romance series."***

Dax Pelletier is ready for a new life, far away from the one he left behind in Savannah following the South's devastating defeat in the Civil War. The ex-Confederate general wants nothing more to do with commanding men and confronting the tough truths of leadership.

Rachel Davenport possesses skills unlike those of her Boston socialite peers—skills honed as a nurse in field hospitals during the Civil War. Eschewing her northeastern suitors and changed by the carnage she's seen, Rachel decides to accept her uncle's invitation to assist him at his clinic in the dangerous and wild frontier of Montana.

Now a Texas Ranger, a promise to a friend takes Dax and his brother, Luke, to the untamed territory of Montana. He'll fulfill his oath and return to Austin, at least that's what he believes.

The small town of Splendor is what Rachel needs after life in a large city. In a few short months, she's grown to love the people as well as the majestic beauty of the untamed frontier. She's settled into a life unlike any she has ever thought possible.

Thinking his battle days are over, he now faces dangers of a different kind—one by those from his past who seek vengeance, and another from Rachel, the woman who's captured his heart.

## Wildfire Creek – Book Two
### Redemption Mountain – Historical Western Romance Series

*"A passionate story of rebuilding lives, working to find a place in the wild frontier, and building new lives in the years following the American Civil War. A rugged, heartwarming story of choices and love in the continuing saga of Redemption Mountain."*

**Luke Pelletier** is settling into his new life as a rancher and occasional Pinkerton Agent, leaving his past as an ex-Confederate major and Texas Ranger far behind. He wants nothing more than to work the ranch, charm the ladies, and live a life of carefree bachelorhood.

**Ginny Sorensen** has accepted her responsibility as the sole provider for herself and her younger sister. The desire to continue their journey to Oregon is crushed when the need for food and shelter keeps them in the growing frontier town of Splendor, Montana, forcing

Ginny to accept work as a server in the local saloon.

Luke has never met a woman as lovely and unspoiled as Ginny. He longs to know her, yet fears his wild ways and unsettled nature aren't what she deserves. She's a girl you marry, but that is nowhere in Luke's plans.

Complicating their tenuous friendship, a twist in circumstances forces Ginny closer to the man she most wants to avoid—the man who can destroy her dreams, and who's captured her heart.

Believing his bachelor status firm, Luke moves from danger to adventure, never dreaming each step he takes brings him closer to his true destiny and a life much different from what he imagines.

## Sunrise Ridge – Book Three
### Redemption Mountain – Historical Western Romance Series

*"The author has a talent for bringing the historical west to life, realistically and vividly, and doesn't shy away from some of the harder aspects of frontier life, even though it's fiction. Recommended to readers who like sweeping western historical romances that are grounded*

***with memorable, likeable characters and a strong sense of place."***

Noah Brandt is a successful blacksmith and businessman in Splendor, Montana, with few ties to his past as an ex-Union Army major and sharpshooter. Quiet and hardworking, his biggest challenge is controlling his strong desire for a woman he believes is beyond his reach.

Abigail Tolbert is tired of being under her father's thumb while at the same time, being pushed away by the one man she desires. Determined to build a new life outside the control of her wealthy father, she finds work and sets out to shape a life on her own terms.

Noah has made too many mistakes with Abby to have any hope of getting her back. Even with the changes in her life, including the distance she's built with her father, he can't keep himself from believing he'll never be good enough to claim her.

Unexpected dangers, including a twist of fate for Abby, change both their lives, making the tentative steps they've taken to build a relationship a distant hope. As Noah battles his past as well as the threats to Abby, she fights for a future with the only man she will ever love.

# Dixie Moon – Book Four
## Redemption Mountain – Historical Western Romance Series

Gabe Evans is a man of his word with strong convictions and steadfast loyalty. As the sheriff of Splendor, Montana, the ex-Union Colonel and oldest of four boys from an affluent family, Gabe understands the meaning of responsibility. The last thing he wants is another commitment—especially of the female variety.

*Until he meets Lena Campanel...*

Lena's past is one she intends to keep buried. Overcoming a childhood of setbacks and obstacles, she and her friend, Nick, have succeeded in creating a life of financial success and devout loyalty to one another.

When an unexpected death leaves Gabe the sole heir of a considerable estate, partnering with Nick and Lena is a lucrative decision...forcing Gabe and Lena to work together. As their desire grows, Lena refuses to let down her guard, vowing to keep her past hidden—even from a perfect man like Gabe.

*But secrets never stay buried...*

When revealed, Gabe realizes Lena's secrets are deeper than he ever imagined. For a man of his character, deception and lies of omission aren't negotiable. Will he be able to forgive the deceit? Or is the damage too great to ever repair?

## Survivor Pass — Book Five
### Redemption Mountain — Historical Western Romance Series

*He thought he'd found a quiet life...*

Cash Coulter settled into a life far removed from his days of fighting for the South and crossing the country as a bounty hunter. Now a deputy sheriff, Cash wants nothing more than to buy some land, raise cattle, and build a simple life in the frontier town of Splendor, Montana. But his whole world shifts when his gaze lands on the most captivating woman he's ever seen. And the feeling appears to be mutual.

*But nothing is as it seems...*

Alison McGrath moved from her home in Kentucky to the rugged mountains of Montana for one reason—to find the man responsible for murdering her brother. Despite using a false identity to avoid any tie to her brother's name, the citizens of Splendor have no intention of sharing their knowledge about the bank robbery which killed her only sibling. Alison knows her circle of lies can't end well, and her growing for Cash threatens to weaken the revenge which drives her.

*And the troubles are mounting...*

There is danger surrounding them both—men who seek vengeance as a way to silence the past...by any means necessary.

## Promise Trail – Book Six
### Redemption Mountain – Historical Western Romance Series

Bull Mason has built a life far away from his service in the Union Army and the ravages of the Civil War. He's achieved his dreams—loyal friends, work he enjoys, a home of his own, and a promise from the woman he loves to become his wife.

Lydia Rinehart can't believe how much her life has changed. Escaping captivity from a Crow village, she finds refuge and a home at the sprawling Redemption's Edge ranch...and love in the arms of Bull Mason, the ranch foreman. For the first time since her parents' death, she feels cherished and safe.

*In an instant their dreams are crushed...*

Bull is resolute in his determination to track down and rescue Lydia's brother, kidnapped during the celebration of their friend's wedding. He's made a promise—one he intends to keep. Picking the best men, they are ready to ride, until he's given an ultimatum.

*Choices can seldom be undone...*

As their journey continues, the trackers become the prey, finding their freedom and lives threatened.

*And promises broken can rarely be reclaimed...*

Can Bull and Lydia trust each other again and find their way to back to the dreams they once shared?

## Deep River – Book Seven
### Redemption Mountain – Historical Western Romance Series

Beauregard Davis, ex-Confederate Captain and bounty hunter, has put his past behind him to focus on his future. He's a lawman with a purpose and a dream—do his job to the best of his abilities, and build a life with the woman he loves. Beau believes his life couldn't be better...until the day she boards a stagecoach, leaving him behind.

Caroline Iverson has a dream she won't deny. Traveling west, she expects to experience adventure. Instead, Caro finds a good man and unanticipated love. She never imagines the difficult decision to leave him behind would come back to haunt her.

After months of burying his pain in alcohol, Beau emerges stronger, determined to concentrate on a future without Caro. Doing his best to forget the past, he focuses his energy on work and preparing to build a home.

He never expected her to return, looking to recapture the love the two once shared.

Adding to Beau's concerns, two threats hang over him—outlaws have targeted his town, and he's being tracked by unidentified foes.

Keeping the town, Caro, and himself safe are his main priorities. He'll do whatever it takes to protect them. Guarding his heart is another matter.

How does a man ignore an all-consuming love without exposing himself to a threat worse than the physical dangers he already faces?

# Reclaiming Love – Book One
## Peregrine Bay – Contemporary Romance Series

Adam Monroe has seen his share of setbacks. Now he's back in Peregrine Bay, looking for a new life and second chance.

Julia Kerrigan's life rebounded after the sudden betrayal of the one man she ever loved. As president of a success real estate company, she's built a new life and future, pushing the painful past behind her.

Adam's reason for accepting the job as the town's new Police Chief can be explained in one word—Julia. He wants her back and will do whatever is necessary to achieve his goal, even knowing his biggest hurdle is the woman he still loves.

As they begin to reconnect, a terrible scandal breaks loose with Julia and Adam at the center.

Will the threat to their lives and reputations destroy their fledgling romance? Can Adam identify and eliminate the danger to Julia before he's had a chance to reclaim her love?

# Our Kind of Love – Book Two
## Peregrine Bay – Contemporary Romance Series

Selena Kerrigan is content with a life filled with work and family, never feeling the need to take a chance on a relationship—until she steps into a social world inhabited by a man with dark hair and penetrating blue eyes. Eyes that are fixed on her.

Lincoln Caldwell is a man satisfied with his life. Transitioning from an enviable career as a Navy SEAL to becoming a successful entrepreneur, his days focus on growing his security firm, spending his nights with whomever he chooses. Committing to one woman isn't on the horizon—until a captivating woman with caramel eyes sends his personal life into a tailspin.

Believing her identity remains a secret, Selena returns to work, ready to forget about running away from the bed she never should have gone near. She's prepared to put the colossal error, as well as the man she'll never see again, behind her.

*Too bad the object of her lapse in judgment doesn't feel the same.*

Linc is good at tracking his targets, and Selena is now at the top of his list. It's amazing how a pair of sandals and only a first name can say so much.

As he pursues the woman he can't rid from his mind, a series of cyber-attacks hit his business, threatening its hard-won success. Worse, and unbeknownst to most, Linc harbors a secret—one with the potential to alter his life, along with those he's close to, in ways he could never imagine.

*Our Kind of Love,* Book Two in the Peregrine Bay Contemporary Romance series, is a full-length novel with an HEA and no cliffhanger.

## Colin's Quest – Book One
### MacLarens of Boundary Mountain – Historical Western Romance Series

*For An Undying Love...*

When Colin MacLaren headed west on a wagon train, he hoped to find adventure and perhaps a little danger in untamed California. He never expected to meet the girl he would love forever. He also never expected her to be the daughter of his family's age-old enemy, but Sarah was a MacGregor and the anger he anticipated soon became a reality. Her father would not be swayed, vehemently refusing to allow marriage to a MacLaren.

*Time Has No Effect...*

Forced apart for five years, Sarah never forgot Colin—nor did she give up on his promise to come for her. Carrying the brooch he gave her as proof of their secret betrothal, she scans the trail from California, waiting for Colin to claim her. Unfortunately, her father has other plans.

*And Enemies Hold No Power.*

Nothing can stop Colin from locating Sarah. Not outlaws, runaways, or miles of difficult trails. However, reuniting is only the beginning. Together they must find the courage to fight the men who would keep them apart—and conquer the challenge of uniting two independent hearts.

## Brodie's Gamble – Book Two
### MacLarens of Boundary Mountain – Historical Western Romance Series

Brodie MacLaren has a dream. He yearns to wear the star—bring the guilty to justice and protect those who are innocent. In his mind, guilty means guilty, even when it includes a beautiful woman who sets his body on edge.

Maggie King lives a nightmare, wanting nothing more than to survive each day and recapture the life stolen from her. Each day she wakes and prays for escape. Taking the one chance she may ever have, Maggie lashes out, unprepared for the rising panic as the man people believe to be her husband lies motionless at her feet.

*Deciding innocence and guilt isn't his job.*

Brodie's orderly, black and white world spins as her story of kidnapping and abuse unfold. The fact nothing adds up as well as his growing attraction to Maggie cause doubts the stoic lawman can't afford to embrace.

*Can a lifetime of believing in absolute right and wrong change in a heartbeat?*

Maggie has traded one form of captivity for another. Thoughts of escape consume her, even as feelings for the handsome, unyielding lawman grow.

As events unfold, Brodie must fight more than his attraction. Someone is after Maggie—a real threat who is out to silence her.

He's challenged on all fronts—until he takes a gamble that could change his life or destroy his heart.

# Quinn's Honor – Book Three
## MacLarens of Boundary Mountain – Historical Western Romance Series

Quinn MacLaren has one true love...Circle M, the family ranch. He makes it a habit of working hard and playing harder, spending time with experienced women who know he wants nothing more than their company. He buries the love he feels for one woman deep inside, knowing he'll never be the man she needs.

Emma Pearce is a true ranch woman, working long hours to help keep the family ranch thriving. Feisty, funny, and reliable, she's the girl all the single young men want—after they've sewn their wild oats. Few know Emma has her heart set on one man. A man who may never grow up enough to walk away from his wild ways and settle down.

When tragedy strikes, Quinn's right where he doesn't want to be—as temporary foreman of the Pearce ranch. Stepping in to fill Big Jim Pearce's shoes isn't easy. Neither is keeping his feelings for Emma hidden and his hands to himself. Honor-bound to do what is right, Quinn meets the challenge, losing Emma's friendship in the process.

Adding to Quinn's worries, something sinister is working its way through the thriving town of Conviction. Unforeseen forces are at work. Debt builds, families lose their ranches, and newcomers threaten to divide not only the land, but the people—including the Pearce family.

As events unfold, Quinn faces the difficult challenge of keeping his feelings for Emma hidden and his honor intact. Doing what he believes is right couldn't feel more wrong.

After all, what's a man without honor?

Find all of my books at:
http://www.shirleendavies.com/books.html

Avalanche Ranch Press, LLC
PO Box 12618
Prescott, AZ 86304

47174954R00215

Made in the USA
San Bernardino, CA
23 March 2017